EVERY MOVE YOU MAKE

Carla Cassidy

Also by Carla Cassidy

EVERY MOVE YOU MAKE

Carla Cassidy

A SIGNET ECLIPSE BOOK

SIGNET ECLIPSE
Published by New American Library, a division of
Penguin Group (USA) Inc., 375 Hudson Street,
New York, New York 10014, USA
Penguin Group (Canada), 90 Eglinton Avenue East, Suite 700, Toronto,
Ontario M4P 2Y3, Canada (a division of Pearson Penguin Canada Inc.)
Penguin Books Ltd., 80 Strand, London WC2R 0RL, England
Penguin Ireland, 25 St. Stephen's Green, Dublin 2,
Ireland (a division of Penguin Books Ltd.)
Penguin Group (Australia), 250 Camberwell Road, Camberwell, Victoria 3124,
Australia (a division of Pearson Australia Group Pty. Ltd.)
Penguin Books India Pvt. Ltd., 11 Community Centre, Panchsheel Park,
New Delhi - 110 017, India
Penguin Group (NZ), 67 Apollo Drive, Rosedale, North Shore 0632,
New Zealand (a division of Pearson New Zealand Ltd.)
Penguin Books (South Africa) (Pty.) Ltd., 24 Sturdee Avenue,
Rosebank, Johannesburg 2196, South Africa

Penguin Books Ltd., Registered Offices:
80 Strand, London WC2R 0RL, England

First published by Signet Eclipse, an imprint of New American Library,
a division of Penguin Group (USA) Inc.

ISBN 978-0-7394-9327-4

Chapter 1

"**P**lease join me in welcoming Annalise Blakely to the studio, the woman known in Kansas City as the Dollmaker." Cynthia Steward, the noon newscaster for channel 41, smiled at Annalise as the camera panned to her face.

Annalise fought the sheer terror that being on live television made her feel, and hoped her responding smile didn't show her nerves. "Thank you for having me, Cynthia."

"I understand that today is the thirtieth birthday of Blakely Dolls," Cynthia said, her blue eyes wide with feigned interest, as if Annalise were about to impart the secrets of the universe.

Annalise hated interviews, hated publicity, but knew they were a necessary evil in keeping her mother's dream alive. "Yes, it was thirty years ago today that my mother sold the very first Blakely doll." Annalise gestured toward the doll in the stand next to her. "My mother named her Annalise, and as you can see, she boasted real hair and incredibly detailed clothing."

"From all the reports I've read the little cottage

industry your mother began has grown into a thriving business," Cynthia said.

Annalise nodded and tried to ignore the massive camera with its red light aimed at her. "I have more than twenty employees working for me, and we produce about a thousand dolls a year. We sell not only to children but also to adults who appreciate the workmanship that goes into each of our creations."

The spiel fell effortlessly from her lips. She'd certainly heard her mother say the same thing over the years. "We come out with two new dolls a year, one in the early summer and one in the late fall," she continued. "In fact, I brought our newest edition to unveil here today."

The camera panned to the doll next to the Annalise doll. "This is Birthday Bonnie," Annalise said. A swell of pride shot through her as she looked at her latest creation.

The doll was dressed in lime and pink capris and a pink blouse that had embroidered balloons on the front. Her brown hair was in pigtails and her porcelain face held an expression of happy surprise.

"There will be five hundred Birthday Bonnies, each numbered and personally signed by me."

"It's been a pleasure having you here," Cynthia said. "And for those of you who are interested in getting your very own Blakely doll, you can find them at the Dollhouse in the Riverfront area, or at www.blakelydollhouse.com."

As the weatherman took over, Annalise got up, eager to leave the studio and the stress of the brief interview. Her best friend, Danika, awaited her.

"That was great," Danika said as they left the studio and walked out into the unusually hot June sunshine. "I don't know why you hate doing it so much. You're a natural in front of the camera."

"Yeah, well, I feel like my stomach is twisted into a million knots." Annalise stuck the two doll cases into the back of Danika's car, then climbed into the passenger seat.

"I have just the answer for twisted-gut syndrome," Danika said as she started the car. "Drinks at Eddie's."

"It's noon. I need to get back to the store," Annalise protested. "I only arranged for Samantha to be there until one."

"I rearranged with Samantha," Danika said smoothly. "She'll be there until five, when the shop closes. You and I are going to Eddie's for a late lunch and enough drinks to untwist the tummy, and I don't want to hear any arguments."

Duty battled with the idea of pleasure, and the anticipation of pleasure finally won. She couldn't remember the last time she'd taken time out to have lunch and drinks with anyone. Business and work seemed to consume every waking hour.

She settled back in the seat and breathed a deep sigh as she realized that for the moment she was in charge of nothing and Danika was in control. It was definitely a rare experience.

"Are you going to have the fall campaign ready to show to me tomorrow?" she asked.

"Yes, and that's the last bit of business you're conducting today," Danika replied.

Danika was not only Annalise's best friend, but she also owned her own advertising and public relations firm, and Blakely Dolls was one of her biggest clients.

"I'm anxious to see the new campaign," Annalise said.

Danika shot her a disgusted look. "You just can't do it, can you? You can't go two minutes without thinking about the business. That's why you aren't married."

"You aren't married either," Annalise protested.

Danika shot her a sly grin. "Yeah, but at least I sleep around. You don't even do that."

"I thought your goal was to untwist my gut. If this is going to be one of your infamous lectures, then I can only tell you my gut is twisting tighter with every breath you take," Annalise said.

"Okay, okay. No lectures," Danika said with a laugh. "Besides, I never give lectures to birthday girls."

Annalise winced. "Don't remind me."

"It could be worse. You could be turning forty instead of thirty. Besides, you need to take the time to enjoy life. You're young, you're gorgeous, and you're successful. Okay, sales are down a bit, but all doll sales are down. Too many computer games and gimmicks competing for the attention of little girls."

Danika raced through a yellow light at an intersection, then continued speaking. "It's time to make Annalise talk. Talking dolls are more popular than dolls who don't talk. Maybe you need to do a special-edition talking Annalise."

"She hasn't talked for thirty years. I'd suspect that means she has nothing to say," Annalise said drily. Apparently Danika didn't want to talk business unless it was to push her own agenda.

"Oh, she has lots to say," Danika exclaimed. "You know, like, 'Hi, my name is Annalise. Want to be my friend?'"

"I didn't realize Annalise was a relative of Donald Duck," Annalise said with a laugh.

"All right, so I'm not good at voices," Danika replied, then cast her a quick glance. "But I have an entire tape of little-girl voices whenever you decide to give the doll something to say." She pulled into a parking space in front of Eddie's, bumping the curb with her tire. "Just think about it." She cut the engine and flipped the mirror to check her lipstick and fluff her short, curly blond hair.

Annalise pretended not to notice the familiar cars parked in the area. Apparently this wasn't just a drink with a friend, but a gathering of friends and coworkers Danika had pulled together for a birthday bash.

She would have preferred that her birthday pass with as little fanfare as possible, but Danika never missed an opportunity to create a party.

As Annalise stepped from the bright, hot sunshine into the cool, dim interior of the neighborhood pub, a swell of voices yelled, "Happy birthday!"

He wet the end of his finger and touched it briefly to the curling iron, satisfied to hear the resulting sizzle. Good. It was ready.

He took a section of her long, lovely blond hair and carefully wrapped it around the hot iron. It would take him hours to do all of her hair, but perfection couldn't be rushed.

He knew exactly what her hair needed to look like when he was finished: long ringlets that would complement her oval face and porcelain complexion.

She was already dressed in the bridal gown, the jeweled buttons neatly fastened and layers of silk caressing her slender curves.

Carefully he untwisted the curling iron from her hair and sighed with happiness at the perfect spiral ringlet. He picked up the next section and repeated the process.

He'd had the little portable television on earlier to catch the noon news broadcast, but he now worked in silence. He liked the silence. His life had been filled with so much noise in the past. Ugly noise.

But he didn't want to think about that now, not when he was creating. When he was finally finished with her hair he stepped back to survey the results. Stunning. From the top of her head to her high-heeled white sequined shoes, every detail was perfect.

Sweet adrenaline rushed through his veins. "The coral blush is great. I was afraid it would be too much, but it was a perfect choice." He grabbed his digital camera. "A picture," he said. "We must have a picture." He was about to press the button when he realized what was missing.

He laughed at his own forgetfulness. "If we're going to take a picture, then you should hold the doll." He went to one of the glass cases that held the collection of dolls and opened the side door.

If you break one of my dolls, I'll break your neck. Do you hear me, boy? the voice screamed inside his head.

For a moment he froze, body trembling and heart

crashing. *Don't touch the dolls. Don't touch the dolls,* the voice screeched. So much noise. Ugly noise. *I'll hurt you, boy!*

"You can't hurt me now," he whispered aloud. "You're dead." He drew a deep breath and reached into the case, his fingers closing around the tiny waist of the silk-clad bride doll.

Her perfect little smile calmed him. Her bright blue eyes and golden ringlets were a perfect match for the woman who sat in his chair.

"Here we go," he said, and set the doll in her lap. He retrieved his camera and pointed it in her direction. "This picture will make a wonderful keepsake. Belinda the Bride and you." He clicked the button to take the first picture, then took another and another before finally setting the camera down.

He walked back over to her and removed the doll from her lap, then carefully placed it on the desk next to the mailing box.

He picked up the camera once again and looked at the pictures he'd just taken. He zoomed in, checking all the details. It was amazing how much she and the doll looked alike.

The dresses were nearly identical; the only difference was the buttons that ran down the front of the dress. He'd been unable to find buttons exactly like the miniature jewels on the doll gown, but the ones he'd chosen were close enough that to the naked eye they appeared to be a match.

Attention to detail—that was what made the difference. If you were going to make a woman look like a doll then you had to pay attention to the little details.

He punched the button to zoom closer and studied the bride's face. A wave of displeasure swept through him as he saw the red streaks and dots that discolored the whites of her eyes.

Petechial hemorrhages. He was going to have to figure out something different from strangulation. There was just no way to hide petechial hemorrhages.

It took him only minutes to print out one of the pictures, a glossy eight by ten. He carried it to the bulletin board and thumbtacked it into place.

"You had your dolls, Mother, and now I have the first of mine." Unfortunately he knew his wouldn't last long. He turned back to face the woman seated in the chair.

She was stunning. A perfect replica, but her doll-like perfection wouldn't last. All too soon she'd begin to decay. Her beautiful skin would discolor and her features would melt and she'd begin to stink.

He knew eventually he'd have to get rid of her, but not yet. For now he just wanted to sit and look at the first of his very own doll collection.

As he stared at his bride doll, he thought of the others he would create. There was Fairy Princess Penny, Carnival Clara, Hula Hannah, and more. Each one holding a particular memory for him, each one begging to be reproduced by him with his own brand of magic.

And of course, the queen of them all . . . the Annalise doll. She was the one that had begun it all, the first. And she would be the last of his creations, the one that would finally set him free.

* * *

Within minutes of arriving at the bar Annalise was seated at a table with Danika on one side and Sammy Winfield, her head seamster, on the other. Across from her was Ben Varrity, the man who worked magic with hair; Sarah Burns took care of the orders that came in; and Mike Kidwell was Blakely Dolls' lawyer.

The drinks flowed freely and the mood remained celebratory throughout the next couple hours. The people at the table were her family, the friends and coworkers who gave richness to her life.

They had watched her on the noon news show and teased her unmercifully about her performance. "You'd better be ready, because I'm booking you on every local television and radio channel over the next couple of weeks," Danika said, then laughed at Annalise's frown of displeasure. "Don't give me that look. Birthday Bonnie deserves all the publicity we can give her."

"Before you make another television appearance we need to trim up those lovely locks of yours," Ben said.

Annalise reached up and tugged a strand of her long, dark hair. "I'm thinking maybe it's time to do some layers."

"I'd rather have a Weed Eater layer my hair than have you touch it," Danika said to Ben.

Ben raised an eyebrow archly. "Honey, I thought that was what cut your hair."

"Children," Mike said, "it's Annalise's birthday. Can't you two act like adults for one day?"

Both of them grinned affectionately at each other. "I can if he can," Danika exclaimed.

"Well, I certainly can if she can," Ben replied.

Annalise laughed. Danika and Ben had a relationship much like that of six-year-old siblings. They bit and sniped at each other constantly, but beneath the verbal sparring was a genuine love for each other.

For the next hour Annalise allowed the conversation to swirl around her. She opened gifts, drank two gin and tonics and fought against the vague sense of unhappiness that had grown more pronounced in the past year.

By four o'clock she was ready to go home. She adored her friends and coworkers, but she'd heard Danika and Ben bitch at each other enough and she wanted to be alone.

"I'm going to catch a cab home," she said to Danika.

Mike half rose from his seat. "I'll take you home if Danika isn't ready to leave."

"Are you sure you don't mind?" Annalise asked.

He smiled and shook his head. "I've got tons of work waiting for me at home."

Annalise grabbed her purse and gift bags, said her good-byes to everyone, then together she and Mike walked out of the bar. "Did you have fun?" he asked once they were situated in his car.

"I did, although I have to confess I'm beat."

Mike's dark eyes cast her a quick glance before he pulled out of the parking space. "You should have more fun in your life."

Annalise didn't reply but instead gave a weary sigh and stared out the passenger window. Mike Kidwell was a young-looking forty-five. He was a handsome dark-haired man who inspired instant trust by his sincerity and the directness of his gaze.

He'd made it very clear in the three years since her mother's death that there was nothing he'd like more than to step into Annalise's life in a different way from just as the company lawyer.

But as much as she liked him there was no real chemistry with him, nothing that made her want to explore a more intimate relationship.

Besides, she had the business to worry about. Depressed sales, new items, publicity gigs—there wasn't time for personal relationships. Her mother had spent her entire life building the business; the last thing Annalise wanted was for it to fail beneath her leadership.

"I can feel your worry," Mike said, breaking the silence that had grown between them.

She flashed him a quick smile. "It seems to be a constant thing the last couple of months."

"You worry too much. All businesses go through flat periods, and it isn't as if you aren't still turning a healthy profit."

"I know. Maybe it's just the birthday blues or something weird like that." She frowned and chewed the inside of her bottom lip, then continued. "I have this feeling of holding my breath, that something is about to happen and I don't know if it's good or bad." She forced a small laugh. "Like I said, maybe just a little bit of birthday craziness."

"How about instead of taking you right home we swing by Amigos and get you one of their super-sized burritos."

"Thanks, Mike, but what I really want to do is get into my pajamas and spend a quiet night alone." She flashed him a look of apology. "Another time?"

"Another time," he agreed easily. Within minutes

he'd pulled up to the curb in front of the building she called home. She gathered her things, said good night, then got out of the car.

Mike waited as she unlocked her door and turned on the light before pulling away from the curb with a wave. The first floor of the three-story building was the Dollhouse, a retail store for Blakely dolls and accessories. She stepped inside and walked past the glass cases and counters to the back room.

Even with the light of day drifting through the windows, the workroom looked like the laboratory of a demented scientist. Doll body parts were everywhere, heads hanging from hooks from the ceiling, arms and legs scattered across a table and torsos in piles on every surface. The room held several sewing machines, a workstation for Ben to fix hair and a desk for her to sketch and brainstorm new items and dolls.

It was here, in this back room, that doll magic was created. And despite the worries, fears and hassles of the business end of things, there was still magic for Annalise when a new doll hit the market or when she brainstormed a great design for the next season's model.

She frowned as she spied a brown wrapped box on top of the desk. As she looked closer she realized it was addressed to her. It must have come in the mail while she was out today. She grabbed the box and carried it along with her other things to the staircase that led upstairs.

The second floor of the large building was used strictly for storage. Boxes and plastic tubs were stacked and labeled. Old furniture and equipment were scattered throughout. Annalise headed directly toward the stairs that led to the third floor.

There was a working elevator in the building, but she rarely used it. If truth were told she was more than a little bit claustrophobic, and she'd sooner climb up ten flights of stairs than step into the small enclosure.

She reached the third floor and entered a large landing, then unlocked the door that led to her loft apartment. When her mother had been alive they'd lived in an apartment down the street and this third floor had been empty.

After her mother's death Annalise had renovated this space to become a luxury loft apartment. It had been a gift she'd given to herself.

She stepped inside and her feet sank into the plush beige carpeting. Directly across from the entry a bank of windows allowed in the early evening sunlight.

The general impression of the loft was one of space and airiness. To her left was the kitchen area, complete with gray granite countertops and gleaming oak cabinets.

The living room area boasted an overstuffed gray-and-red sofa, glass-topped coffee and end tables and an entertainment center that not only held the usual electronic equipment but also her collection of miniature elephants.

Her father had bought her the first elephant for her sixth birthday, the year that he'd left her mother. Every year after that she'd received a new one on her birthday.

She glanced at the package she'd placed on the table. That was probably what it was, another birthday elephant from her father. It was so easy to buy a trinket rather than pick up the phone or come to visit her. So much less complicated simply to send a gift instead of facing the child he'd left behind.

About three times a year they would meet for lunch. They were dreadful meals between two related strangers attempting to find common ground. Her father had remarried five years after he'd left her mother, and he and his wife, whom Annalise had never met, had a thirteen-year-old son. The only thing she knew about Charlie was that he'd been an unexpected surprise.

Shaking her head she dismissed thoughts of her dad. The bedroom area of the loft was on the right, and she headed there, ready to get into her pajamas and curl up on the sofa.

Normally she worked long into the night, sketching new clothing for new dolls, trying to second-guess what little girls might consider hot in the coming months.

But tonight the last thing on her mind was work. She considered it a birthday present to herself to be a total lazy slob. She changed from her two-piece black power suit into a hot pink silk nightgown that struck her midthigh. She'd just washed the makeup off her face when the phone rang.

She grabbed the cordless and punched it on.

"I forgot to tell you the other part of your birthday present," Danika said. She sounded as if she'd indulged in several more drinks after Annalise had left the bar.

"I hope you are home and not driving," she said. "You sound like you're more than a little bit buzzed."

"I'm smashed, but don't worry, Mommy; I'm home. Ben drove me, and he's going to take me back to the bar tomorrow to get my car. Anyway, we were talking about your other birthday present. You know my cop friend, Tyler King?"

"You didn't." Annalise wished there were a way to reach through the phone line and strangle her friend.

"I gave him your number and told him you were a hot, horny broad who needed to get laid." She laughed as Annalise sputtered in outrage. "Okay, okay. I didn't tell him that. But I did tell him that you're a nice woman who needs a social life. He's a nice man who needs a social life. I think you two would be perfect for each other."

"The last perfect man you set me up with wound up in jail," Annalise reminded her friend drily.

"Who knew he was a corporate thief? Come on, Annalise, if Tyler calls, give him a chance. Besides, think of the irony—from a criminal to a cop." Danika laughed.

Annalise sighed. Although she'd never met Tyler King, Danika had been talking about him for the last couple months. Her friend had met the homicide cop at a party thrown by a neighbor, and although he wasn't her type for a love connection the two had become friendly.

"I'm not making any promises," Annalise finally replied.

"I had a feeling you might be difficult. I just wanted to let you know that I'd given him your number. Now I'm going to make a pot of coffee. I definitely had too many cosmos in honor of you."

"Make it a big bottle of water and go to bed. And thanks for the party."

They said their good-byes and Annalise hung up, her heart warmed by thoughts of Danika. They had been best friends since grade school, and it had been a friendship that had survived different colleges, a variety of life crises and time.

Her warm feelings cooled slightly as she thought of the fact that Danika had given her phone number to Tyler King. Danika was forever trying to play matchmaker, and most of the time Annalise managed to ignore her efforts. But she had been particularly persistent about Tyler King.

She left her bedroom and went back into the living room. She should make herself something for dinner, but she'd eaten enough pretzels and nuts at the bar to serve as a meal.

Her gaze fell on the package on the kitchen table. Might as well open it and see what kind of elephant her father had sent her this year. As she tore off the brown paper she frowned in surprise as she saw the familiar box. It was one of her own, a Blakely Dolls box.

Surely her father wouldn't have sent her one of her dolls. She wasn't even sure her dad owned one of the dolls. The rare times they spoke there were two topics they didn't discuss—her business and his marriage.

When she pulled the lid off the box her puzzlement grew. Nestled inside the tissue paper was a Belinda the Bride doll. A note was folded and tucked in beside her silk dress.

She pulled out the white sheet of paper and opened it.

I don't need this anymore. I have my own.

It was signed, *the Real Dollmaker*, and it definitely wasn't her father's handwriting. She picked up the brown wrapping paper and realized that not only was there no return address, but that there was also no postage stamp. Odd.

She picked up the note again and reread it and wondered how such simple words could cause a slight chill to sweep through her. There was certainly nothing ominous or threatening about the note.

Maybe it was the signature that created the edge of disquiet that whispered through her. The Real Dollmaker. It was as if a subtle challenge had been tossed out.

She forced a laugh to her lips and carried the box to the linen closet. "Looking for drama where there's none," she muttered to herself. And the last thing she wanted out of life at the moment was drama. She'd had enough of that when she'd been growing up.

All she wanted was for her mother's business to thrive beneath her leadership. She curled up on the sofa, punched on the television and tried to forget the doll and the strange note.

Chapter 2

Tyler King finished the last of his beer and motioned for the waitress to bring him another. Harry's Bar and Grill was a favorite watering hole for Kansas City cops. The place boasted the longest happy hour in the city.

But Tyler wasn't happy. More than anything else he was tired. At thirty-five years old he'd spent most of his career on the murder squad, which was made up of an elite group of homicide cops who worked the most heinous murders the city offered.

The last couple months had been relatively quiet ones, with just the usual drug-related, domestic-violence kinds of murders. But Tyler knew better than to be lulled by the quiet. The summer heat was moving in fast, and the murder rate always went up with the thermometer.

He'd read somewhere that one in every ten or so persons was a full-blown sociopath. He eyed the crowd in the bar with a touch of wry amusement. That meant at least five of the people around him were sociopaths, and they all had law enforcement badges.

"Here you are, darlin'." The waitress, Sally Jean, placed his fresh beer in front of him.

"Thanks, Sally."

"Where's that mouthy partner of yours? I thought the two of you were joined at the hip."

Tyler smiled at thoughts of his partner, Jennifer Tompkins. "She had a dinner date this evening."

One of Sally's blond eyebrows danced upward. "A date?"

"No, just dinner with friends."

"I thought maybe the two of you had something going on."

Tyler laughed. "Not on your life," he replied. "First of all I'd never date a partner, but more important, Jennifer has the capacity to make me more than a little bit crazy."

"She is a live wire," Sally replied, then hurried toward another table where a group of men were demanding drinks.

Jennifer was more than a live wire. At twenty-six years old she was the youngest and newest member of the department. Their partnership hadn't exactly been a match made in heaven. She'd started out abrasive and pushy, eager to make a name for herself.

But in the last couple of months she'd calmed down. Beneath Tyler's not-so-gentle tutelage she was learning the value of patience and the importance of being a team player. She was going to be a great cop one day, but she sure as hell wasn't somebody Tyler wanted to date.

He took a deep swallow of his beer and raised a hand in greeting to one of the other cops who had just come through the front door. Dating. He couldn't remember the last time he'd had a date.

Maybe this was the time to go out, to meet some-body and have a little fun. There were no real nasty cases pending; his hours were relatively normal ones. He thought of the phone number Danika had slipped him earlier that day.

Danika was his neighbor, and early that morning had stopped in to give him the phone number of her best friend. "Call her," she'd prompted. "Tyler, you either need to get a date or get a dog. You need something living and breathing to think about."

He took another swig of his beer. Maybe a dog wasn't such a bad idea. Feed a dog, let it outside a couple times a day and give it a scratch now and then and you got loyalty forever. No unrealistic ex-pectations, no whining about the long hours at work.

Dog or date? He dismissed the idea of either as he was joined at the table by a group of men, and the talk, as always, turned to murder.

The phone rang at seven thirty the next morning. Annalise was seated at her kitchen table, finishing the last of her coffee and a piece of toast. It was her father on the phone.

"Hi, honey," he said. "I'm sorry I didn't get a chance to call you yesterday and wish you a happy birthday."

"That's all right. I was pretty busy all day any-way," she replied. As always when she spoke with her father a small knot formed in her chest.

"I was wondering if you could get away for lunch today. We could meet across the park from your shop at that Italian place," he said.

She hesitated, ambivalent emotions sweeping through her.

"Come on, Annalise, surely you can get away for one hour," he urged.

"All right. Why don't we meet at Joey's at eleven?"

"Good, I'm looking forward to it."

After they hung up Annalise sat at the table and thought about her father. Danika insisted that it was the unsettled relationship with her father that made Annalise reluctant to form any meaningful relationship in her life.

Annalise suspected Danika watched too much *Dr. Phil*, but she had to admit her feelings were very mixed when it came to her dad. There was still a piece of her that was very much the little girl who was angry that when her father had left her mother, he'd left her as well.

She went from the kitchen table to the computer to check for orders that had come in from the Web site, not wanting to dwell on thoughts of her father any longer.

As she waited for the computer to boot up, she thought of the doll she'd received the day before. Strange that it had been a Belinda the Bride doll that had come back to her. That particular doll had been sold out over ten years ago. One of her employees had told her that the doll was now being sold on eBay for over eight hundred dollars. So why would somebody give her up? It was a mystery without an answer.

By eight thirty she had printed off the Internet orders and had them ready to hand to Sarah, who took care of shipping out the dolls to the appropriate addresses.

She left her apartment and went down the two flights of stairs to the store. Officially the store didn't open until ten, but there were always things to take care of before the doors opened.

By nine several of her employees had arrived and were at work in the back room. Dolls had to be assembled, hair had to be fixed and clothes had to be sewn. She was hoping the store would be busy that day. Generally when the announcement of a new doll went out many of the avid collectors showed up to buy one or place an order.

"Sorry I'm late," Ben said as he flew through the door at nine twenty. "Did you see on the news that there was a six car pileup on I-70 and traffic came to a screeching halt? But of course you didn't see it on the news. I forget that you're allergic to the news."

Annalise laughed. "Not allergic. I occasionally listen to the world news on the radio. I just don't want to know about all the tragedies that happen locally."

"And it's one of the eccentricities we love about you," he replied affectionately. As he disappeared into the workroom, the phone rang.

"The Dollhouse," she answered.

"May I speak to Annalise?" The male voice was deep and smooth.

"This is she."

"Hi, I'm Tyler King, a friend of Danika's, and she gave me your number."

"Hi, Tyler. Danika told me she was giving my number out to you." A bit of nervous tension twisted in her stomach. She had no idea what Tyler

King looked like, but the man had a voice she could listen to for hours.

"Danika is pretty persuasive, and she seems to think we should meet. I know it's short notice but I was wondering if you'd like to have dinner tonight."

Her first impulse was to decline. A blind date with Danika's neighbor seemed like a pretty unlikely match, but Danika would lose her mind if she heard that Annalise had turned him down. One meal, she thought; then she could tell Danika that it didn't work out between them.

"Tonight's fine. Dinner would be great," she agreed.

"Is there someplace in particular you'd like to go? Any favorite restaurant?"

"There's an Italian restaurant in the Riverfront area. It's called Joey's."

"I know the place."

"Why don't we meet there around six?" she said. "Would that work for you?"

"That will be fine. How will I know you?"

I'll be the one who looks like she'd rather be anyplace but there, she thought. "I'll be wearing yellow," she said, thinking of the new dress she'd recently bought at the nearby boutique.

"Then I'll see you at six."

Two meals at Joey's in one day. She had a feeling that after today she wouldn't want Italian food for a while. She wondered if Tyler had made the call to her for the same reason she'd accepted his invitation—because Danika could be a pain in the ass. At least by meeting him at Joey's, she could escape back home easily if things didn't go well.

She opened the store and all thoughts of lunch with her father and dinner with Tyler King fled her mind as she got to the business of making a living.

At quarter till eleven she put Samantha in charge and left the shop. The hot sun made her grateful she'd decided to wear a lightweight sundress.

The Riverfront area, although only a stone's throw away from downtown Kansas City, was a close-knit community in and of itself.

Saturday and Sunday mornings brought a huge influx of people to the area to shop at the open-air market. The market offered everything from fresh fruits and vegetables to jewelry and artwork.

Directly across the street from Annalise's shop was a park. On most nice days the benches and grassy areas were filled with shop workers and loft owners enjoying lunch, feeding the pigeons or simply enjoying a few minutes of fresh air. Today was no exception.

"Hey, Annalise." John Malcolm raised a hand in greeting. "Saw you on the television yesterday."

John was in his forties and lived in one of the apartments on the opposite side of the park. He worked as the building maintenance supervisor and often sat out here to eat his lunch.

"How are you doing, John?" She stopped by the bench where he sat.

"Just trying to stay sane." He flashed her a quick smile and pointed toward the four-story brick building he called home. "Owners don't want to spend any money, and the tenants want things they can't have. It's a constant battle with me right smack-dab in the middle." He pulled the other half of a tuna sandwich from a brown paper bag.

"How's the doll business? Looks like you've been busy this morning."

"Mostly repeat customers coming in for the new doll." She glanced at her watch. "I've got to run, John. I'm meeting somebody for lunch."

As she crossed the park she saw several neighbors and friends enjoying the warm weather. She waved to George Cole, who worked as an insurance salesman, and shouted a hello to Barbie Sandford, who owned a dress boutique where Annalise often shopped.

Approaching Joey's, she felt the small ball of tension return to the pit of her stomach as she thought of lunch with her father.

Joey Farino greeted her at the door, his broad face beaming a smile. Joey's mother had owned the restaurant for decades but had passed away a year ago and left it to her only son. Joey had taken over the restaurant and prided himself on good cuisine in a friendly atmosphere.

"There's my favorite dollmaker," he said, and kissed her on the cheek. "Your usual table?" he asked.

"That would be great, although there will be two of us today. I'm meeting my father for lunch."

"That's good. Family is always nice." He grabbed two menus and led her toward the back of the restaurant to a secluded table. About three times a week Annalise came in for lunch, and Joey always seated her at this particular table.

"Thanks, Joey," she said, and slid into the seat that faced the rest of the restaurant. From this vantage point she would be able to see her father when he came through the door.

At precisely eleven o'clock Frank Blakely walked into the restaurant. As usual he was dressed impeccably, today in a pair of navy slacks and a short-sleeved dress shirt. Not a single strand of his salt-and-pepper hair was out of place and he walked with the confidence of a successful man.

He *was* a successful man. After leaving her and her mother he'd gone to law school, gotten his degree and now owned a thriving law firm.

She loved him desperately and hated him at the same time. It was this dichotomy of emotions that made a relationship with him so difficult.

His handsome face broke into a smile as he saw her and hurried toward the table. "There's my girl," he said as he leaned down and kissed her on the cheek. He placed a gaily wrapped package on the edge of the table, then slid into the chair opposite her.

He picked up the menu but studied her instead. "You look tired, Annalise. I suppose you're working twelve-hour days."

"Gee, Dad, you sure know how to charm a girl," she replied drily.

He reached out and lightly touched the back of her hand. "You know I think you're beautiful, but I worry about you. You work too hard. You're young and pretty and you should be having more fun."

"I'm having fun," she protested. "In fact, I have a date this evening."

"Well, that's wonderful," he replied. "Is it somebody special?"

"It's our first date."

"Maybe it will be the start of something wonderful for you. I want you to be happy, Annalise."

Then why did you leave me? Why did you disappear from my life for so many years? That was what she wanted to ask, but didn't.

Instead the lunch passed as they all did, with superficial conversation and unspoken emotions and baggage from the past.

It was almost noon when she told her dad she needed to get back to the shop.

"You have to open your present before you go," he said.

"Let me guess—another elephant for my collection?"

He shook his head. "Not this birthday."

She tore the wrapping paper off the box and opened it. Nestled inside the tissue paper was a key. She looked at him curiously.

"It's a key to our cabin at the lake. We've got a two-week vacation planned for the end of August, and we'd love for you to join us there."

He couldn't have surprised her more if he'd stood up in the center of the table and emitted a primal scream. She stared at the key, and those ambivalent feelings roared through her once again.

"There's a map in there, too, to show you exactly where the cabin is located on the lake," he added.

"What does Sherri think about this?" she asked.

Her father smiled. "She thinks it's past time that she met the other woman in my life."

"I don't know if I'll be able to get away," Annalise said as she fumbled with her napkin.

"You've got two months to try to work it out. It would mean the world to me." His voice was low, filled with an underlying emotion that pierced through her armor and directly into the heart of her childhood pain.

"I'll see what I can do," she replied, and stood, wanting—needing—to escape. "Thanks for lunch."

"I'll call you."

Annalise gripped the birthday package to her chest as she left the restaurant. Her emotions were far too complex to sort out. All she knew for sure was that she was surprised by the gift of the key and the invitation. What she had to figure out was whether she intended to accept the invitation or if it was easier, less painful, to shove the key and the directions in a drawer and forget about them. Much like what she'd thought her father had done with her when he'd left them.

He watched her walking across the park to return to her shop. Annalise Blakely. The dollmaker. Her long, dark hair glittered with auburn highlights in the sunshine, and she moved with the confidence of a woman sure of her place in the world.

He knew where she worked. He knew where she lived. He knew all kinds of things about her. At least when the time came he wouldn't have to hunt for his Annalise doll.

Blood rushed through him, pounding in his head and making him half-breathless with excitement. He intended her to be his last . . . if he could control himself . . . if he could make himself wait until all the others were done.

Chapter 3

A dog would have been easier, Tyler thought as he buttoned the beige dress shirt. For a dog he wouldn't have had to shave. A dog wouldn't produce the nervous tension that knotted tight in the pit of his stomach. And it was ridiculous to be nervous at the prospect of a date.

He slapped some cologne on the underside of his jaw, then left the bathroom. Minutes later he was in his car, headed for Joey's Italian Restaurant.

It wasn't as if he'd never been on a date before. It was just that it had been a long time since he'd played the dating game.

His last meaningful relationship had been over two years ago. Stacy had moved out of his house after six months, screaming that he was as emotionally unavailable as the dead people with whom he dealt for his job.

Add that debacle to a marriage that had lasted eighteen months and it was no wonder he wasn't eager to jump into the fire of dating again.

His job was part of the problem. The divorce rate among homicide cops was unbelievably high. The crazy hours and the potential danger put stresses on a marriage. Coupled with those factors was the fact that Tyler had never met a good homicide cop who wasn't more than a little bit obsessive-compulsive, didn't suffer from control issues and wouldn't rather be hunting a killer than doing almost anything else on earth.

The one thing Tyler had learned during his brief marriage was that even though his wife, Vicki, had encouraged him to talk about his work, to share with her the details of his cases, it had been a mistake. The more he shared, the more she retreated from him.

As he drew closer to the Riverfront area, he steeled himself for the night to come. Knowing that Annalise and Danika were best friends, he could only assume that Annalise would have the same frenetic energy as her friend. He liked Danika, but a little bit of her went a long way. At least by going out tonight he would get Danika off his back. The woman was as tenacious as a tick on a dog's ear.

He sighed. A dog would have been so much easier.

He was familiar with the Riverfront area. At one time, before the developers had gotten serious about urban renewal, this part of town had been notorious for crime and had been a gathering place for the homeless of the city. The homeless were still a presence in the area, especially after dark, when the shops and restaurants closed and the pedestrian traffic waned.

He found a parking space not far from the restaurant. For several long moments he remained seated in the car. What in the hell was he doing?

He knew from past experience that he wasn't good for any woman, that the best kind of relationship he could have was a one-night stand with a woman who expected nothing more from him.

Getting out of the car he squared his shoulders and decided to get inside and get it over with. He was about fifteen minutes early for his reservation, and the restaurant was busy.

He checked in with the hostess, then took a seat in the bar area, where he could see the front door, and ordered himself a Scotch and soda.

He'd taken only a couple of sips of the drink when she walked through the front door. She wore a short pale yellow dress that both showed off her shapely legs and complemented her long, dark hair.

Fighting the impulse to immediately jump up and greet her, he instead took the opportunity to give her a good once-over. She wasn't beautiful, but she was uncommonly pretty, with wide, round blue eyes, an oval face and that sexy hair that cascaded down her shoulders.

She was slender, but not skinny, and carried herself with a self-confidence that was attractive. Once again the knot of tension in his stomach twisted. Even though she was pretty, that didn't mean that the evening was going to be any less awkward.

She gazed around, obviously seeking the single male who might be waiting for her. He stood to approach her, not wanting her to think he'd been sitting there checking her out. Even though that was exactly what he had been doing.

As he drew closer to her she smiled at the hostess, and her smile punched him in the gut. It lit up her features like a ray of warm sunshine piercing through gloomy skies, and for just a moment he wanted to wallow in that warmth.

"Annalise?"

She looked at him, and this close he could see the dark lashes that framed the blue of her eyes. "Tyler?"

He nodded. "Hi, it's nice to meet you." He held out his hand, and she slipped her slender one into his for a quick but firm shake. "I think our table is ready." He looked at the hostess for confirmation.

"Just follow me," she said with that brand of chirpy perkiness that seemed to be reserved for hostesses and grade-school teachers.

As he followed just behind the hostess and Annalise, he caught the scent of Annalise riding faintly in the air. Jasmine or some other exotic floral scent. Nice.

He frowned thoughtfully. Now the hard part began: making small talk with a virtual stranger.

"Your waiter will be with you shortly," the hostess said as she seated them, then left them alone.

"Have you ever eaten here before?" she asked as she spread her napkin across her lap.

"Once, a long time ago. If I remember right, the food was delicious."

"I eat here frequently and have yet to find something on the menu that isn't delicious," she replied.

The dreadful awkward silence descended as each of them picked up their menus and studied the fare. Tyler wasn't good at small talk. Most of the women he'd dated in the past had never met a silence they couldn't fill. They babbled about anything and everything, seeming to enjoy the sound of their own voices.

Annalise didn't seem to share that same trait. Unlike Danika, Annalise radiated a calm, quiet aura that was appealing, but at the moment he wished she shared some of Danika's chattiness to fill the charged silence.

"Do you have any recommendations?" he asked, desperate to say something.

She looked up from the menu, those amazing eyes of hers meeting his with a directness he admired. As a cop he was accustomed to people averting their gaze from his, as if to hide the lies they might hold in their hearts.

"My personal favorite is the veal. The sauce is to die for."

He closed his menu and flashed her a smile. "Then it's the veal for me." Before he had to worry about what the next topic of conversation might be, the waiter appeared to take their orders.

It was as the waiter left that the silence once again descended between them. Small talk, you idiot, an inner voice whispered. She leaned back in her chair, her gaze going around the restaurant as if seeking something or somebody to deliver her from him.

When had he lost the ability to know how to talk to a lovely lady? He couldn't even remember what Danika had told him Annalise did for a living. He was just about to ask when she directed her gaze back to him.

Annalise's stomach fluttered with nervous tension as she looked around the restaurant, trying not to stare at the man across the table from her.

God, he was a hunk. The moment she'd seen him a crazy fluttering had occurred in her stomach. Physically he was the kind of man who had always stoked her fantasies. Tall, with broad shoulders and lean hips, he had sharp-edged facial features that gave him a slightly dangerous look. His eyes were a dark gray bordering on black, and at the moment he looked as if he'd rather be anywhere but here.

So far the brief bit of conversation they had shared had been stilted, and an uncomfortable tension simmered between them just beneath the surface. Maybe things would have been easier if he hadn't been so attractive, if she didn't feel her heartbeat racing just a little too fast whenever she looked at him.

"It's been so long since I've been out on a date, I seem to have forgotten what to do," he said.

His words surprised her and managed to break some of the tension. "You're really in trouble if you're expecting me to take the lead. It's probably been as long since I've been on a date."

He flashed a smile that lit his dark eyes and softened his features. "Blind dates are the worst, aren't they?"

"They're dreadful," she agreed. "And the only thing that drove me to agreeing to this blind date is that I knew if I didn't, then Danika would drive me slowly insane."

He laughed, and at the sound of his low, sexy laughter a new burst of heat swirled in her stomach, and just that easily the awkwardness between them fell away.

By the time the waiter brought their orders they were discussing the misery of the dating scene for people no longer twenty-one or twenty-two years old.

"I read somewhere that most romances begin in

the workplace, but I've always thought that was a really bad idea," she said.

"I know Danika mentioned you own a company, but I don't think she told me exactly what it is you do."

"I make dolls."

He grabbed one of the pieces of warm bread from the basket in the center of the table. "Sounds interesting."

She laughed. "I've yet to meet a man who really finds dollmaking interesting. It was my mother's business until she died three years ago. Then I took it over."

"Is your father still living?"

She nodded and fought to keep any emotion out of her voice. "Yes. My parents divorced when I was six, and Dad is remarried and has a son. What about your parents?"

"Married to each other and alive and kicking. I'm their biggest disappointment in that I'm not married and haven't given them grandchildren."

"And why is that?" She couldn't imagine why he wasn't already married. He was certainly attractive enough, and after the ice had been broken between them he was proving to be likable as well.

He leaned back in his chair, his gaze thoughtful. "I was married briefly seven years ago. It didn't work out, and I've never felt the need to take the plunge into marriage again. What about you? Ever been married?"

"No. Came close once, but realized at the last minute that he wasn't right for me." She smiled.

He leaned forward, his eyes shining in a way that made her breath catch in her throat. Dark yet flirtatious, his gaze slid from her eyes to her lips and lingered there. "What? What are you smiling about?"

"Oh, nothing. I was just remembering the exact moment I realized Allen wasn't the man of my dreams."

"And when was that?"

He seemed genuinely interested, so she continued. "We were out having dinner together, and I got a call that a shipment of doll legs had come in and there was a defect. Each of the feet had six toes. I was upset, knowing that we needed to replace the legs and that it would take time to get the order filled correctly. Allen told me to stop freaking out, that it was just about dolls, and kids wouldn't notice the mistake anyway."

Tyler grinned. "Allen was obviously not a bright man."

She laughed, then sobered. "I certainly don't expect the man in my life to share my work, but I do expect him to respect what I do. And speaking of jobs, yours must be fascinating."

The light in his eyes instantly doused. "My work isn't the kind you want to talk about over the evening meal."

Forbidden territory. He obviously didn't want to discuss his police work. That was clear by the shutters that dropped down over his eyes, closing her out and keeping himself in.

"Then what do you do in your spare time?" she asked, hoping to keep one of those awkward silences from descending once again.

"I work out at a gym near my house. I like to read. I'm afraid my personal life is fairly boring."

Somehow she didn't believe him. An energy simmered inside him, one that made her believe nothing about him could be boring.

"What about you? What do you like to do in your spare time?" he asked.

"I'm the one who is pretty boring. It seems like all I do is work."

"That's not good." There was no question—the smile he directed at her was definitely flirtatious. "You know what they say about all work and no play."

As they lingered over dessert they talked about bad dates they'd had in the past, making each other laugh as they shared their experiences.

She liked him. Aside from the fact that just looking at him made her tingle in a delicious fashion, she liked that he was obviously intelligent, that he seemed content to allow their date to unfold without manipulating or forcing things. She also liked that he had a good sense of humor and that his laughter was low and sexy and infectious.

The waiter had just poured them each a second cup of coffee when Tyler's cell phone chirped. "Excuse me," he said, and pulled it from his pocket. "King," he barked into the phone.

His facial features immediately became hard and his eyes narrowed as he listened to the voice on the other end of the call. "Give me fifteen." He clicked off and looked at her apologetically. "I need to go. Unfortunately one of the drawbacks of my job is that I never know when I'll be needed."

"Please, don't apologize; I understand," she replied.

He got up from the table. "Will you be all right to get home?"

"Fine," she assured him.

"I'll take care of the check on my way out. I enjoyed this, Annalise. Can I call you?"

She smiled. "I'd like that."

He took two steps away from the table, then looked back at her. "And by the way, you look terrific in yellow."

A flush of pleasure swept over her as she watched him walk away. Would he call her? She hoped so. It had been a long time since she'd felt the kind of sexual awareness he'd stirred in her. It had been a long time since she'd met a man she'd like to get to know better.

When the waiter returned to the table she had the rest of her dessert boxed up with the remainder of her veal, then took the plastic leftovers bag and got up.

The veal would make a nice lunch the next day, and she had a feeling the last of the cheesecake would be gone before she went to bed.

She stepped out of the restaurant into the warm night air, her thoughts lingering on Tyler. She'd suffered through several interminable dates arranged by Danika, who believed that what Annalise needed more than anything in her life was somebody to love. This date with this man had been more than pleasant.

The grassy park was deserted as she started across. Despite the darkness of the night she wasn't afraid. She'd never been afraid in this area.

As she approached her place she spied a dark figure seated on the fire escape stairs that led up the side of the building. She instantly recognized the man who stood as she approached.

"Hi, Max," she said, knowing that her leftovers were never going to make it into her loft. She had no idea what Max's last name was, suspected that he didn't remember it himself. Max was one of the homeless who lived in the area. He was an alcoholic who called a packing crate home and showed up around the doll shop about once a week or so.

Annalise didn't know if he'd drunk himself into mental illness or if his illness had caused his alcoholism. She only knew he was a lost soul, one of many who drifted from their hidey-holes when darkness fell.

"Bad Dumpsters," he said, and as he drew closer to her he brought with him the smell of spoiled fruit, sour body odors and the underlying scent of cheap wine. He was clad, as usual, in everything he owned: a pair of jeans that were the color of dirt and, despite the heat of the night, a navy sweatshirt beneath a filthy tweed coat.

"Tonight is bad-Dumpsters night, Anna. Coins would be nice."

"You know I don't do coins, Max," she chided. Max showed up when he was out of money to buy his booze, and on those nights he always complained about the lack of food in the Dumpsters, hoping she'd cross his palm with some cash.

"Max is hungry," he exclaimed, one of his massive hands rubbing his stomach.

She held out the plastic bag of leftovers. He snatched it from her and gripped it to his chest as he scurried away and disappeared into the shadows of the night.

Last winter she'd called social services about Max, hoping they could find a place for him, some family member who might care for him, but they'd been unsuccessful. Max had spent one wintry night in a shelter, then had escaped back onto the streets he called home.

As Annalise unlocked the shop door she recognized that she and Max shared something in common. Despite the fact that she loved her loft, she'd never really felt as if it were home. Maybe it was because she didn't spend a lot of time in the loft, or perhaps because she had nobody special to share the space with her.

She forced a laugh and told herself she was being silly. As she went up the stairs to the third floor she wondered if Tyler would call. She hoped he did, because for the first time in years she realized that keeping her mother's dream alive might not be enough for her.

As Tyler raced away from the restaurant, his thoughts lingered on the woman he'd just left. He'd found her intelligent, with a terrific sense of humor, and just shy of totally gorgeous. He'd almost forgotten those kinds of women existed.

She'd definitely affected him on a purely physical level. There had been a moment when she'd been talking to him that he'd fantasized about unzipping her dress and drawing it down over her slender shoulders. As he'd watched her eat he'd wondered what she would taste like.

It had been a pleasant interlude, but the phone call had jerked him right back to real life, a life that offered little time for pleasures.

Thoughts of Annalise fell aside as he saw ahead the beginnings of a crime scene investigation. Two

patrol cars were parked along the side of the high-
way, their headlight beams focused on something in
the nearby ditch. Tyler knew that something was a
body.

He got out of his car and approached the scene,
flashing his badge to the young patrolman who was
about to stop his forward progress.

"What have we got?" he asked.

"Nine-one-one got an anonymous tip that there
was a body by the side of the road, so we came out
here to check it out. It's a body, all right."

Before Tyler could reply a familiar car pulled up,
and his partner, Jennifer Tompkins, jumped out.
"Hey, what's going on?" she called as she hurried
toward them.

"I just got here myself. Don't know the particulars yet," Tyler replied. He pulled gloves and a
flashlight from his backseat. He tossed Jennifer a
pair of gloves, then looked at the officer. "Has the
crime scene unit been called in? The coroner?"

"Should be arriving anytime," he replied.

Tyler looked at Jennifer. "Let's go check it out."

Using his flashlight to guide them, he carefully
left the side of the road and went down the embank-
ment to the ditch where the victim lay.

"Ah, jeez," Jennifer murmured. The emotional
edge in her voice struck a chord deep inside Tyler.

The victim had been beautiful once. Despite the
early stages of decomposition it was easy to see that
she'd been a pretty young woman. "Look around
the area; see if you can find a purse or something for
identification," Tyler said to Jennifer.

He crouched down near the body and allowed
his mind to make initial assessments. She hadn't

been carelessly dumped. The body was meticulously arranged, with legs together and arms neatly at her sides. Her pale blond hair was perfectly coiffed in long ringlets, not a single strand out of place.

No, she hadn't been tossed out. She'd been carried here and posed in an area where she was sure to be found quickly.

There was no blood, no dirt staining the pristine white of the wedding dress she wore; nor was there a ring on her finger to indicate a wedding had actually occurred. Her fingernails weren't broken, but rather looked as if she'd just had a fresh manicure.

"There's a cell phone over here," Jennifer exclaimed from nearby.

"Bag it and tag it," Tyler replied, his attention not wavering from the victim. He focused his flashlight on her neck, where dusky bruises were evident beneath the collar of the gown. He'd have to wait for the official report from the coroner, but he could make an educated guess that she'd been strangled.

Had she been strangled while on her way to the most important event of her life? Or had she been killed, then dressed like a bride to provide some sick twist his fantasy? It was Tyler's job to find out.

This woman with her pretty blond hair and tragic end was now the new lady in his life. He could feel her need crying out to him, begging him to find justice for her untimely death.

He stood as he heard the arrival of more official vehicles. Jennifer joined him. "I didn't find a purse or any kind of identification. So where do we start?" she asked softly.

"We start with missing persons reports," he replied. "See if someplace out there there's a groom missing his bride." He stared back at the woman in the ditch.

Dinner with Annalise seemed a long time ago.

Chapter 4

They were everywhere. The dolls. Crowding her out of bed, hanging from the ceiling with their lifeless stares and porcelain limbs. "Help me," she cried as they drew closer, their cold, hard bodies hurting as they pressed against her, threatening to squeeze the air from her.

"Mommy? Mommy, help," she screamed as one of the dolls dropped from the ceiling and landed on her chest, the eyes boring into hers with a malevolence that was terrifying.

Sobs ripped from her throat. "Mommy, where are you?" she cried. She could hear the faint whir of the sewing machine. "Mommy, they want to kill me."

"Don't be melodramatic, Annalise. Go back to sleep. I'm working." Her mother's stern voice rose above the whir.

The dolls climbed all over her, pinching her skin and pressing against her chest, against her throat. They wanted her dead. They wanted to be her mother's only babies.

Annalise awoke with a gasp as she hit the floor next to her bed. She lay there for several moments, trying to still the frantic beat of her heart as the nightmare slowly faded.

The ringing of the telephone pulled her up off the floor as she fumbled on the nightstand for the cordless. "I thought we had a seven thirty appointment this morning." Danika sounded cranky, and as Annalise glanced at her bedside clock she understood why. It was quarter after eight.

"I'm so sorry. I overslept. It will take me at least an hour to pull it together and get to your office."

"Forget my office. I'm downstairs."

"I'll be right down to let you in." Annalise hung up, got off the floor and grabbed her robe. Not only had she overslept, but she felt as if she'd just sat through a double feature of horror films featuring Chucky, the killer doll.

She hurried down the stairs, and when she hit the lower level she could see Danika standing at the front door, tapping a foot impatiently as a frown of irritation furrowed her brow.

"I am so sorry," Annalise said as she ushered her friend into the store. "I can't believe I did this. You know I never miss appointments."

"Which is why I'm not going to cut out your tongue and roast it over an open fire." Danika stalked ahead of her toward the elevator. She always rode instead of walking up the stairs to the loft.

Annalise raced up the stairs, grateful that Samantha was opening the store that morning. Coffee. She needed coffee. Danika appeared to be in a bit of a snit, but if Annalise told her about the date the night before with Tyler, she had a feeling Danika would forgive her for her tardiness—and any other imagined transgressions of the past.

By the time she reached the top floor Danika was waiting for her, her briefcase clutched to her chest. "In here I have the new campaign for the fall. I must say I think it's totally awesome."

The two women went into the loft, and Annalise beelined to the coffeemaker while Danika got settled at the kitchen table. "In all the years we've been friends I've never known you to sleep in or miss an appointment. Are you sick?"

Annalise waited until the coffee had begun to fill the carafe before she turned to face Danika. "No, I'm not sick. I was out last night, and when I got home I was restless and couldn't seem to settle down. I sketched too late and forgot to set my alarm before I finally fell asleep."

"Where did you go last night?" Danika asked curiously.

Annalise got two coffee mugs from the cabinet, filled them, then joined Danika at the table. "I went to dinner with a date."

One of Danika's thin blond brows danced upward. "A date?"

Annalise smiled. "With a very handsome homicide cop."

"Shut up!" Danika exclaimed. "You went out with Tyler last night?"

"We had a lovely dinner at Joey's."

"And?"

Annalise laughed. "And nothing. Unfortunately before the date was over he got a call and had to leave to go in to work."

"So not even a kiss?"

"What makes you think I kiss on the first date?"

Danika grinned. "Because I was with you when you made out in the backseat of Johnny Mason's car with Danny Smith, and that was a first date."

"I was sixteen," Annalise exclaimed, "and just beginning to explore my power as a woman."

"Bullshit," Danika replied. "Everyone knew that Danny Smith was the best kisser at West High School. So, what did you think?"

"Danny was a good kisser."

Danika slapped her on the arm. "You know what I meant. What did you think about Tyler?"

Annalise took a sip of the coffee and leaned back in her chair. "He was nice."

"And he's not exactly hard to look at."

"He's definitely not that," Annalise agreed. A warm rush swept through her as she thought of the way his dark eyes had lingered on her mouth, then slid down the length of her in typical male fashion.

"So, are you going to see him again?"

Annalise shrugged. "He said he'd call. We'll have to wait and see what happens."

"I'll talk to him."

"No." Annalise grabbed Danika's arm. "Please don't do that. You did your job and we've had our date. Whatever happens now is between him and me, and I don't want you in the middle of it."

Danika sighed. "All right, I'll stay out of it." She smiled. "I'm just glad the two of you got together and things went well."

"I think things went very well," Annalise agreed. She hoped he'd call. The moment she'd laid eyes on him she'd felt a magnetic pull, a kind of sizzling excitement that she'd never experienced before.

"Now, why don't you show me what you've come up with for the new advertising campaign?"

For the next hour business took precedence over everything else. They discussed the ads and argued about what might work and what might not. Although Annalise had no idea what kind of doll would be the next Blakely product, the ad campaign wasn't geared toward a specific doll but rather the business as a whole. Finally all the kinks had been worked out, and Annalise gave the go-ahead for the ads to begin running as soon as possible.

"And before I go, I have a little present for you," Danika said. She pulled a tape recorder and two cassette tapes from her briefcase. "I took the liberty of contacting a local talent agent and told him we needed a voice for a doll. He called in a ton of girls and made recordings of their voices. Don't worry. I paid for it, and I know you haven't made a decision about Annalise having a voice, but would you just listen to the tapes and think about it?"

She wanted to fuss at Danika about overstepping her boundaries, but this was one of the few drawbacks of working with a friend. "I'll listen and I'll think about it," she said as she walked Danika to the door.

"Great! I'll call you later." She disappeared out the door, taking much of the energy in the room with her.

Minutes later, as Annalise stood under a hot shower, she thought about the winds of change that were blowing through her life. She knew Danika was right: It was time to bring something new to the dolls.

The competition for sales was fierce. Her mother's

vision of elegant dolls with exquisite clothing had been amazingly successful, but it was time to take things up a notch.

She didn't like the idea of a talking doll, but knew she had to make decisions based on business sense and not her heart or what she knew her mother would want.

By the time she'd showered and dressed for the day, she remembered she had a two o'clock appointment with George Cole to discuss renewing her insurance policies.

When she went downstairs to the store she found everything running smoothly. Samantha was waiting on a customer, and the back room was buzzing as everyone worked to finish the production of the Birthday Bonnie dolls.

"Ah, the queen bee finally decided to grace us with her presence," Ben said as his fingers nimbly worked to create a pigtail to perfectly match the one on the other side of the doll's head.

"I'm only here for a couple of hours; then I have an appointment with George Cole," she replied.

Ben made a face. "As far as I'm concerned there's only one thing worse than an insurance salesman, and that's the tax man."

Annalise laughed and sat at her desk. "George is okay. He never tries to sell me more than I need. How soon do you think we're going to be able to start on the fall edition?" She looked at Maggie Winters, who stood in front of a worktable attaching arms and legs to bodies.

"If all goes smoothly we should be finished with the Birthday Bonnies in a week to ten days. Have you decided what the fall edition is going to be?"

"Not yet." Annalise opened the sketchbook on her desk. She'd been drawing potential new designs for the last couple of months but had been unable to make up her mind what to do next. "If I followed the dream I had this morning the next doll would be a Chucky, complete with evil eyes and gnashing teeth."

Ben eyed her sympathetically. "You've been having that same dream for months."

"I know. I think it's stress." She turned the pages in her sketchbook, but her thoughts went back to the date she'd had the night before.

Maybe her father had been right. Maybe she needed something in her life besides the business. Since her mother's death she felt as if she'd been on a hamster wheel, running as fast as she could, spinning precariously out of control.

At two o'clock George showed up for his appointment with her, and together they went up to the loft. George was a nice man, unimposing and soft-spoken. She knew he'd lost his wife to breast cancer and had no other family.

"You know, both my wife and my mother loved your dolls," he said when they had concluded their business. "I still have them." He smiled at her shyly. "Whenever I have clients in I always tell them there's no doll better on the market."

"That's nice, George. I appreciate any free publicity that I can get."

"Have you considered a security system for this building?" he asked as she walked him to the door. "You know that would lower your rates a bit."

"To be honest, I haven't given it much thought,"

she replied. "In all the years we've owned this building, we've never had a problem with any break-ins."

"Still, it's something you might want to think about."

"I'll do that," she agreed.

When George had gone she walked over to the bank of windows and stared out at the park area below, watching as he made his way across the park and toward his apartment building on the other side.

A young man ran with a dog on a leash, the dog big enough that she wondered if he was walking the dog or the pooch was walking him. A couple of kids tossed a Frisbee back and forth to each other, and a woman sat on one of the benches reading a book.

John Malcolm sat on another bench, facing the direction of her building. Despite the fact that he was the apartment building maintenance supervisor, he spent a lot of time during the day on that bench. He'd explained to her that most of the tenants in the building had day jobs, and that the bulk of his work occurred in the evening hours. Many of them didn't want him in their apartment when no one was home.

She turned away from the window with a sigh. Would Tyler call and ask her for another date? She desperately hoped so. Maybe if she had something to look forward to she wouldn't feel the crazy sense of unease that had gripped her for the past couple of days, an unease she couldn't explain, an unease that worried her.

At the moment the last thing on Tyler's mind was the date he'd had with Annalise. He now sat at a conference table with four other members of the murder squad, discussing what they knew so far about the "bride" killing.

"We know the victim's name is Kerry Albright. She was twenty-three years old, and her roommate filed a missing persons report a week ago." Larry Crisswell looked up from his notes to make sure he had everyone's undivided attention.

"Go on," Tyler said, satisfied as he saw that everyone at the table was taking notes.

Larry nodded, then continued. "The roommate said she left their apartment at ten thirty at night to go to a convenience store for a pack of smokes. She never came home."

"What do we know about the roommate?" Jennifer asked.

It was Sam Goodwin who answered. "Her name is Faye Hazelton, also twenty-three. Works in billing at Saint Luke's Hospital. Nothing to indicate that there were any problems between the two women."

"And our vic had no fiancé, no wedding plans in her near future," Larry added. "When she went missing she was wearing a pair of jeans and a white T-shirt with a Budweiser logo on the front. She was not wearing a wedding gown."

"So our unsub strangled her, then dressed her like a bride." Jennifer popped her gum and shook her head. "What's that about? Are we looking for some creep with a wedding fetish?"

"Too early to tell," Sam replied. "We need more information. Maybe she jilted a boyfriend, who decided he was going to have her as his bride either dead or alive."

Tyler remained silent and let the others chew

over what little they knew so far. He listened as they shared their thoughts about the murder, and as they did he mulled over what the crime scene technicians had found, which had been damned little.

Kerry Albright had been killed someplace else and placed in the ditch. The killer had been careful not to leave behind trace evidence. They were waiting to hear whether the cell phone that had been found near the body had been used to call in the anonymous tip.

"I think she knew her killer," Larry said. "There was loving attention paid to her after her death. It just doesn't feel like a stranger kill."

"But we can't jump to that conclusion," Tyler said. "We simply don't have enough facts right now to jump to any conclusions."

"How do we proceed?" Larry asked. They all looked at Tyler.

"Larry, you follow up with the roommate. Get a list of everyone Kerry knew, old boyfriends, coworkers, whatever. See if there was a problem with drugs or gambling. You know the routine. Sam, you check her banking records. See if she owed anybody money. See if there has been any activity on her credit cards since the time of her disappearance. Jennifer, you talk to her family and follow up on that wedding gown. I want to know where it was bought and by whom. All of you report back here at six tonight."

Within minutes the detectives had all gone their separate ways. Tyler remained at the table and stared at the nearby wall-sized combination bulletin and dry-erase board.

The crime scene photos were there, and he stared

at them, seeking something, anything he might have missed before now. Larry was right: The killer had taken special care and attention with her. He'd not only dressed her, but Tyler suspected he'd carefully made up her face, given her a manicure and arranged her hair.

God, Tyler hoped Kerry Albright had known her killer. He hoped like hell this was a one-shot deal, that the perp had a personal hard-on for the pretty blonde and had settled the score in a drastic fashion.

Otherwise he was looking for a killer with a fetish, a madman creating fantasies from his twisted mind. And if that was the case, then this was just the beginning.

He stared at the photo tacked to the small bulletin board and drew a deep, shuddering breath. She'd been lovely—a perfect re-creation of the doll. But he'd had to get rid of her when she'd started to go bad.

He'd been so sad when he'd left her in the ditch. He'd wanted somebody to find her before his work was completely destroyed, so he'd called and told them where she could be found.

The display case now beckoned to him, and he stood in front of it, looking at the little women behind the glass. *Thump.* In his mind the sound of his mother's cane hitting the floor shot through him. *Thump. Thump. THUMP.*

Boy, can't you hear me? Get in here. I need you. Thump. Thump. THUMP.

A cold shiver worked through him. He wondered if he'd ever be able to get that noise out of his head.

The sound of her cane . . . the sound of her voice . . . it was a constant cacophony that ripped at his brain.

He knew she was in hell. He'd helped send her there, but she wouldn't shut up, and always, always it was about the dolls. The damned dolls.

His gaze landed on Fanny Flapper. How well he remembered when his mother had bought her. He'd gone without lunch money for a month so she could have her precious doll.

He opened the case, and his trembling fingers closed around her narrow waist. The gold fringe of her dress tickled his hands, her red Cupid's-bow lips smiling as if she shared a secret with him. Black hair curled riotously around her face, a headband across her forehead in traditional flapper fashion.

I should have been a young girl in the twenties. I'd be dancing and drinking bathtub gin and having a ball. I wouldn't have married your loser of a father, and I wouldn't have had no loser kid.

Noise. Such noise. He released his hold on the doll and clapped his hands over his ears, pressing hard to stop the noise.

"Stop," he whispered in desperation. "For God's sake shut up."

He didn't know how long he stood there, frozen with his hands shoved tight against his ears. Finally the noise stopped and he drew a deep, shuddering breath. Dolls. His mother had loved her dolls. That was all she'd ever loved.

He stared at the bulletin board, where the picture of his doll stared back at him. She looked so sad, so lonely there all by herself.

The doll case beckoned him, and his gaze lingered on the Annalise doll, with her long, dark hair and bright blue eyes. His mind filled with a vision of the real Annalise, so like the image her mother had created.

Annalise, who kept the dolls coming, who continued to destroy the lives of little boys and girls. His fingers trembled as they opened the case and curled around her little waist.

"Bitch," he hissed at her pretty little face. "It's all your fault." As his rage built he wondered how fast he could make the clothes that would turn the real, live Annalise into his own special doll.

Chapter 5

"Hi, my name is Annalise. Want to be my friend?" Annalise frowned at the tape recorder, where for the last half an hour she'd been listening to various voices all saying the same thing. The last one had sounded like a seasoned hooker.

She shut off the recorder and stared toward the windows, where the sun splashed brilliant pinks and oranges as it slid below the horizon. With a sigh she shoved the tape recorder aside and instead opened her sketch pad.

Inside, sketches of dresses and gowns filled the pages. She'd once dreamed of being a famous fashion designer, of sitting beside a runway with models clad in her latest creations high-stepping and posing for an appreciative audience.

She'd begged Lillian to let her go to fashion school, but her mother had told her a traditional college and a business degree were smarter, and, as in most things, Lillian Blakely had won.

Flipping through the pages she fought a vague sense of depression, then laughed at her own melancholy. She knew what was wrong with her. It was Saturday night and she was alone. It had been a week since she'd had dinner with Tyler, and he hadn't called. That was why she was feeling out of sorts.

It was obvious he hadn't enjoyed the evening as much as she had; otherwise surely he would have found a moment to call. *You'll never find Mr. Right sitting in your loft by yourself.* That was what Danika would tell her if she were here. But Danika wasn't here. In fact, Danika wasn't even in Kansas City. She and her newest boyfriend had flown to Las Vegas for the weekend.

"Viva Las Vegas," she muttered, and closed her sketch pad. She wasn't in the mood to sketch. What Danika didn't understand was that Annalise wasn't looking for Mr. Right. Boyfriends were nice, but she'd never considered anyone to be a permanent fixture in her life.

She blew a sigh of frustration. She was bored, and definitely not in the mood to go out. Maybe this was a good time to sort through some of the boxes that were stored on the second floor. She'd been meaning to do it for months.

Since it was Saturday the store had closed at six, and everyone had gone home. It was a perfect time to check out the boxes that had been packed up since she'd moved from her small apartment to the loft.

She went downstairs armed with her cordless phone and a box cutter. She flipped on the light switch and frowned as she realized several of the lightbulbs had burned out, leaving the only illumination in the center of the large room.

Frowning, she eyed the boxes stored one on top

of another. Some of them contained items for the business, but others held personal items that had belonged both to her mother and to her.

She located one of the boxes that was marked PERSONAL with a black Magic Marker, and pulled it out along the dusty floor into the center, where the light was best. She sat on her butt next to the box, knowing she'd get dusty and would have to shower before going to bed.

She was just about to open the flaps when her phone rang. "Annalise, it's Mike."

"Hi, Mike. What's up?"

"I got some papers in today that you need to sign, and I was wondering if you'd want to do it in the morning at the Corner Café. You know how terrific they are for breakfast."

He was the only lawyer she knew who tried to make every business event into a date. Why not? she thought. The store was closed on Sundays, and she'd been doing nothing but working all week. Certainly the thought of one of the Corner Café's awesome cinnamon buns was appealing.

"All right."

"Great!" he replied, obviously surprised by her capitulation. "Why don't I pick you up around ten?"

"How about I meet you there? I've got some errands I can run afterward, so I'd like to have my own car."

"All right," he agreed easily. "Whatever works best for you."

"Then I'll see you in the morning at ten." She hung up and for a moment wished she were attracted to Mike on a romantic level. She'd known him for years, and knew that he had both her personal and professional best interests at heart.

But he didn't make her pulse race. He didn't make her wonder what his mouth might taste like, what his hands would feel like holding her, caressing her.

There had been a moment at dinner last week with Tyler when she'd wondered those things about him. During that meal his gaze had held hers and her heart had actually ached with its frantic rhythm.

Maybe part of his allure had been that they'd spent the entire evening chatting and hadn't talked about dolls. It had been wonderful to spend the night without thinking about business.

"And he hasn't called," she muttered. She ripped open the box and instantly lost herself in memorabilia from her high school days.

She didn't know how long she'd sat there, lost in memories of school dances and adolescent crushes, when a noise came from nearby.

A faint rustling. A sound that didn't belong. She froze, her gaze shooting to the corner, where it seemed to have come from. It was too dark for her to see anything except the boxes stacked helter-skelter, making perfect hidey-holes for things that didn't belong.

She remained unmoving for several long moments, but heard nothing. Slowly her pulse returned to a more normal pace. Maybe she'd just imagined it.

Reaching the bottom of the box she began to stack back inside it the items she'd pulled out. The noise came again, a rustle like clothing brushing against a box.

This time she was positive she hadn't imagined it. She shot up from her seated position, the phone clutched tight in her hand. "Is somebody there?" All she could hear was the sound of her heart beating loud in her ears.

Was it possible it was a mouse? A rat? She'd never had problems with rodents before. Besides, it had sounded too big to be a rat. The noise came again, followed by a muffled cough.

Her fingers fumbled with the numbers on the phone, seeking the emergency number for help. "I have a gun and I'm not afraid to use it," she bluffed as she waited for an operator to pick up her call for help.

"Wait! Don't shoot!" The male voice sounded frantic as a young man stepped out from behind the boxes and raised slender arms up over his head. "It's me. Charlie. I'm your brother."

"Nine-one-one. What's your emergency?" The operator spoke in Annalise's ear, but she was trying to process the presence of the young man standing in front of her.

"Charlie?" she echoed.

"Hello? What is your emergency?" the operator repeated, and snapped Annalise from her momentary stupor.

"I'm sorry. I thought I had an intruder, but it turns out it's somebody I know," she said into the phone, her gaze not leaving the boy in front of her. What was he doing here? How had he gotten here?

"Are you in danger?" the operator asked.

"No. Everything is fine. It's all a mistake. I'm sorry to have called." As the operator clicked off the line, Annalise hung up.

As she stared at the half brother she'd never met, several things penetrated her mind. Though he was clad like a typical teenager in baggy jeans and an oversized jersey, she nevertheless saw the resemblance between herself and him.

They both had dark hair, although his was cut short. His eyes were the same bright blue as hers, and at the moment radiated intense nervousness.

"What are you doing here?" she asked.

He shrugged, picked up a backpack from the floor and stepped closer. "I decided it was time we met. I mean, it sucks to have a sister that I don't even know."

"Do your mother and father know where you are?"

He hesitated a moment. "Not exactly." He smiled, and it was a charming one, a smile that someday would break hearts. "We look alike, don't you think? Except you're prettier than me."

She didn't know what to say. She didn't know what to feel. She'd always known that eventually she'd meet Charlie. But she'd thought that it would be at a time of her choosing and under her own conditions. She wasn't prepared for this. She wasn't prepared for him.

"We need to go upstairs and call Dad."

His smile faltered. "But we can talk a little bit first, right? I mean, maybe we could have a Coke or something to eat and then call him."

Need. She felt it emanating from him. The need to connect to her. It surprised her, and it called to something deep inside of her, something she didn't know existed.

"Sure, we'll get something to eat, then call," she agreed.

The smile returned, lighting his features as he fell into step beside her. "This place is awesome," he said as they climbed the stairs to the loft.

"How did you get in?" she asked.

"I came into the store this afternoon, and when the woman behind the counter wasn't looking, I sneaked up the stairs. I went up to the third floor earlier, because Dad had told me that's where you lived, but I couldn't quite get up my nerve to knock on the door."

She opened the door to the loft and he walked in. "Wow! This is totally awesome. I knew you'd live in a cool place." His eyes shone brightly as he turned to face her. "I saw you on television a couple of times, you know, advertising your dolls. I kept asking Dad when I could meet you, but he always put me off."

"Why don't you sit at the table and I'll see what I can get you to eat?" she suggested.

He nodded and moved across the floor with a loose-limbed gait, his big, sneaker-clad feet threatening to knock into everything he came near. As he sat at the table Annalise opened the refrigerator and stared inside.

Up until this moment Charlie had always been an abstract in her mind, a piece of her father's life that had nothing to do with her. Now that piece was seated at her kitchen table, and she couldn't figure out why. What did he want from her?

"I knew you'd be cool, you know, with me just showing up out of the blue like this," he said.

She wasn't cool. She was in shock. She pulled a

bowl of leftover mac and cheese out of the fridge and put it in the microwave, then grabbed a can of soda and placed it on the table in front of him.

"So, you want to ask me some questions?" He looked at her eagerly, like a puppy awaiting a scratch behind the ears.

"Questions?"

"Yeah, you know, like what kind of a kid I am. What I like and don't like. Stuff like that."

She got the mac and cheese from the microwave, set it and a fork in front of him, then joined him at the table. Her mind still couldn't seem to wrap around his presence.

There had been a time years ago that she had resented his very existence, that she'd been angry that he was getting everything from her father that she had wanted, that she had needed when she'd been young.

He cracked open the top of the soda can and took a long, deep swallow. When he placed the can back on the table a burp escaped his lips. He grinned. "Sorry. Mom says I have the table manners of a goat."

Annalise checked the clock on the stove. It was just after seven thirty. "I really should call Dad and your mom and let them know you're here. They'll be worried about you."

"Nah, they think I'm at my best friend Jack's house. And they probably aren't home right now anyway. Whenever I spend the night with Jack they usually go to a movie or out to dinner. They call it date night." He rolled his eyes, as if he found the idea of his parents on a date disgusting. "Besides, we haven't really gotten a chance to talk yet. I've waited all this time to meet my big sister."

Big sister. She'd never thought of herself as that, but it was obvious that was the way Charlie thought of her. "So, tell me about yourself," she said.

He took several bites of the mac and cheese before answering. "I like sports, especially football. I love computer games, but my mom doesn't let me play them much. My favorite food is pizza, and my favorite place to be is at our cabin. Are you coming with us in August? I overheard Dad say he invited you."

Annalise remembered the key he'd given her for her birthday. "I don't know. I probably won't be able to take off from work."

His eyes darkened in obvious disappointment. He finished the macaroni and cheese, then gazed at her wistfully. "My friends all think it's weird that I have a sister right here in town and we don't know each other."

"And what do you think?" she asked.

"I think it would be cool if we could hang out together, especially in the summers, when I'm not in school. I think it would be cool if we could be close, you know. Like a real brother and sister." He laughed self-consciously. "You probably think I'm a dork."

"No, I don't," she protested. What she did think was that he was an unusually sensitive, lonely kid. And something about him touched her and made her uncomfortable at the same time. "You never told me how you actually got here. Did you have a friend drive you?"

"None of my friends drive. I took some of my

lawn-mowing money and took the bus." He leaned back in the chair, his arms and legs appearing too long for his body. "I just woke up this morning and decided that today was the day I was going to meet you, that it was stupid to have a sister and not know her. I know it makes Dad sad. He used to cry sometimes after he'd come to visit you."

She sat back, stunned by this revelation. He used to cry? She'd never known her father to be overly emotional. Standing up, she grabbed the empty bowl and carried it to the sink, needing a moment to compose herself.

"You know, I was thinking maybe it would be easiest for Dad to come in the morning and pick me up. I could sleep on your sofa, and I wouldn't get in your way."

Her first instinct was to say no, but there was such need in his voice. What would it hurt? a little voice whispered. He's already here, and what difference would there be if he's picked up tonight or in the morning?

"I'll tell you what. I'll call Dad now, and if he says it's okay, then you can bunk here for the night." Her words lit his eyes.

"Cool! They should be home from the movies by now." He got up from the table and walked over to the sofa, as if ready to go to bed before she changed her mind. Annalise dialed her father's number.

He picked up on the third ring. "Dad, Charlie is here with me." There was a moment of stunned silence, and she continued. "Apparently he took a bus to come here. He thought it was time we met."

"Jesus, I can't believe that kid. I'm so sorry. I can be there in about half an hour to pick him up."

"No, wait. Why don't you just let him stay here for the night and pick him up in the morning sometime before noon?"

There was another moment of stunned silence. "Are you sure?" he finally said. "I wouldn't want to impose."

Annalise looked over to where Charlie was bouncing on the sofa, as if testing its comfort. "It's okay," she said, and strangely enough it was. For years she'd dreaded meeting any member of her father's other family, but it was impossible, at least at the moment, to dislike Charlie.

"He's a good kid, Annalise," her father said softly.

That's because he was raised in a two-parent home. That's because he had you in his life. The old melody of pain began to rise up inside her, but she tamped it down. They agreed that he'd pick Charlie up around noon the next day; then she hung up.

At that moment the buzzer rang, indicating that somebody was at the shop door downstairs. Who could that be? she wondered. She wasn't expecting anyone.

"I'll be right back," she said to Charlie. She ran down the two flights of stairs and as she approached the shop's front door she saw two uniformed officers.

She knew why they were here: a follow-up on her 911 call. It was a good thing she hadn't been in imminent danger when she'd called. Their response time wasn't particularly reassuring.

"Annalise Blakely?" one of the officers asked as she opened the door.

"Yes, I'm Annalise," she replied.

"We're here to do a welfare check. Everything all right here?"

"Yes, I'm fine. I thought I had an intruder, but it turned out to be my brother."

The police officer who'd spoken stared at her features, while the other officer peered over her shoulder. She assumed they were checking that nobody stood in the shadows behind her coercing her into the statement that all was well.

"I appreciate your checking, but really, I'm fine," she assured them.

Moments later she climbed back up the stairs to find Charlie waiting for her.

"I just noticed, you don't have a television in here," he said as she locked her loft door.

"I've got a small portable one on the kitchen counter, but I don't do much television watching. I don't even have cable."

"Really?" For a moment Charlie eyed her as if she were from another planet. "I don't think I've ever known anyone who didn't have cable or satellite television. So, what do you do when you're up here?"

"I listen to music and mostly sketch," she replied.

"What do you sketch?" he asked. Curiosity rode his handsome youthful features. "Do you draw dolls?"

Annalise had never shown her sketch pad to anyone. She'd torn sheets from it to talk about doll designs, but nobody had seen the pages of clothing she'd drawn, clothing for a line she only dreamed of producing.

For the first time in her life she wanted to share. She had no idea what it was about this boy, this brother, that made her want to open her sketch pad, but that was exactly what she wanted to do.

"Sometimes I sketch dolls," she said. She walked over to the desk and grabbed her pad, then returned to the kitchen table and opened it. "But I also sketch clothing."

Charlie got up from the sofa and joined her at the table. "What kind of clothes?"

He smelled like boyhood, like sunshine and sweat and a faint scent that reminded her a little bit of a locker room. She hesitated to open the pad, wondering what had prompted her to mention it in the first place. A thirteen-year old boy who loved football couldn't be interested in ball gowns and tailored suits.

But he's interested in everything you do, she thought. From the moment he had stood up from his hiding place downstairs, his hunger to know her had been evident.

She opened the pad to display the first page and watched his features. He had an expressive face, one that instantly displayed the emotions inside him. As he gazed at the drawings, a look of awe swept over him.

"Wow, you're really good." He flipped one page, then another and another. "You're as good as any of those people on *Project Runway.*"

She frowned. *"Project Runway?"*

"That's right—you don't watch TV. It's a reality show where a bunch of designers try to win the prize of showing a collection in New York. Mom watches it every week. I draw, too. I want to be an artist when I grow up, but Mom says I need something to fall back on because there's too many starving artists in the world. But Dad said next year I could take some art lessons if I'm still interested."

He paused to draw a deep breath. "I'm talking too much, aren't I?"

She laughed. "No, not at all. How about I pop us some popcorn and we can sit on the sofa and talk a bit more before calling it a night?"

"Cool, I love popcorn."

Cool seemed to be his favorite adjective. It was funny—for years she'd told herself she had no interest in knowing anything about Charlie or his mother, but now that he was here, with his eyes so like hers and his youthful enthusiasm to know everything about her, she discovered she wanted to learn more about him.

"Are you a good student, Charlie?" she asked as they settled in on the sofa, the bowl of popcorn between them.

"I'm average. Mom says I'm an underachiever, and Dad says I'm a typical boy. I'll bet you were a really good student. Dad says you're really smart."

"I was a good student because I knew my mother would be upset if I brought home anything but As," she replied.

"She was tough?"

Annalise nodded. "She was tough."

They stayed on the sofa until almost eleven. Charlie filled the air with his energy and chatted about parents and his art, about best friends and all things important to a thirteen-year-old.

He asked her questions about her dolls, about how they were made and who did what in the production process. He seemed endlessly curious about her and her life, but at eleven she called a halt to the reunion.

"I've got to get to bed," she said as she walked over to the linen closet and pulled out a set of sheets. "There's a new toothbrush under the sink in the bathroom. You can use it to brush your teeth before you go to bed."

As he disappeared into the bathroom she made up the sofa for him and placed one of the pillows from her bed there. By the time he left the bathroom the sofa was ready. He got under the sheet, then shucked his jeans and laid them on the floor next to the sofa.

"Good night, Charlie," she said.

"Night, Annalise."

She turned off the overhead light, leaving only the dim light of the lamp next to her bed, then went into the bathroom to wash off her makeup and change into her pajamas.

Minutes later she climbed the platform to her bed and shut out the light. "Annalise?" Charlie's voice drifted toward her in the dark.

"Yeah?"

"Thanks for letting me stay."

"No problem," she replied.

"I'm glad you're my big sister."

The words wrapped around her heart and squeezed tight. "And I'm glad you're my little brother," she said. He must have fallen asleep then, for minutes later she heard his faint snoring.

Sleep remained elusive for her as she tried to process all the feelings Charlie's sudden appearance in her life had produced.

It was impossible not to like him, with his open,

giving nature. Despite the fact that she had never been a part of his life in any way, he was ready and eager to hand her his heart.

And what surprised her more than anything was that she wanted his heart. She wanted to be his big sister.

She squeezed her eyes closed, thoughts of her father filling her head.

Annalise, hurry and comb your hair and wash your face. Your father is coming to get you in fifteen minutes. He says he's going to take you out for a lovely dinner. Her mother's voice echoed from the cache of distant memories.

Daddy's coming! She remembered her excitement. She'd brushed her long hair a hundred times and scrubbed her face until her cheeks hurt; then she'd sat at the front window to wait.

And wait.

And wait.

Each minute seemed like an hour, and an hour felt like an eternity. She remained seated at the window until bedtime, her heart aching so badly she felt like she might die.

There remained a part of her that hurt, a part of her that was still that little girl with her nose pressed against the window, waiting for a daddy who had never arrived.

But somehow being with Charlie had helped. Knowing that her father had done—was doing— right by his son strangely enough eased some of that old pain.

Maybe this was what she'd been waiting for. Maybe this surprising event had been what she'd felt coming, what she'd worried might be something bad.

As sleep slowly overtook her she realized this had been one of the best Saturday nights she could ever remember.

He hated Saturday nights, but this one was better than most because he had a new project. She sat in his work chair awaiting her transformation.

Of course, things weren't perfect. Perfect would have been having Annalise in his chair. His need for her grew stronger and stronger with each day that passed, but so far he'd managed to control it and not let it control him.

It helped now that he had something to occupy his mind: the pleasure of a second creation. He'd already dressed her in the flapper clothes that had taken him hours to sew, but there was still so much to do.

He knew her name was Margie. He'd heard a friend call her by name just before she'd gotten into her sports car to drive home from the club.

He'd followed the vehicle to her apartment complex and strangled her as she'd come out of the car. It had been easy enough to load her dead body into his car and bring her here for her walk to immortality.

Glancing over at the photo pinned up on the wall, he smiled. Kerry had become immortal, forever pictured as Belinda the Bride doll. And now Margie would join his collection.

But first he had to cut her hair into the flirty fashion of the twenties, and her nails needed to be painted a fire-engine red. So much to do. At least the voices in his head remained silent, allowing him to focus on the task at hand without interruption.

Still, as he worked he thought of Annalise. He would see her tomorrow, as he did most days. He'd probably even talk to her, and as he talked, as he gazed at her, he'd be thinking about what a lovely addition she'd make to his collection.

The scent of her lingered in his head. The sound of her voice whispered through the darkest chambers of his heart.

"Soon," he whispered.

For the first time in years it wasn't a dead woman who occupied Tyler's thoughts, but rather a living, breathing one. He now sat in the room where he and his team had been working on the Albright murder case, but instead of being focused on the reports in front of him his head was filled with thoughts of Annalise.

It had been a week since he'd had dinner with her, a week filled with Kerry Albright's grieving family members, intense investigative work and far too many dead ends.

The wedding dress had been the first dead end. It had been discerned to be home-sewn, so Jennifer was now checking out fabric stores to see who might have bought yards and yards of white silk and pearl trimmings.

The security video from the convenience store had been useless. Whoever had taken Kerry from the location had done so out of the range of the cameras.

The investigation into her friends and lovers was

ongoing, but so far nobody had jumped to the top of the list as a meaningful suspect.

He glanced at his watch and realized it was just after midnight. Time to go home. As he walked out of the station and into the warm night air, his thoughts once again returned to Annalise. He liked her. He liked her a lot.

More than that, there had been an immediate sexual attraction to her. It had been a hell of a long time since Tyler had felt that kick of desire so strongly.

Tomorrow was officially his day off. If something was popping on the Albright case then he would have returned to the station at the crack of dawn. But there was nothing on his desk that wouldn't wait until Monday.

He'd call Annalise first thing in the morning, set up lunch or dinner with her if she were available. He was suddenly hungry to spend time with a woman who smelled like flowers, a woman whose eyes radiated warmth and light.

He only hoped that tonight when he closed his eyes he'd dream of Annalise and not be haunted by visions of Kerry Albright, her dead eyes pleading with him for justice.

Chapter 6

The scent of frying bacon teased the edges of Annalise's consciousness. She loved bacon and eggs for breakfast but rarely took the time to fix them. What a wonderful dream, she thought as she snuggled deeper beneath the bedcovers. A dream complete with the smells of hickory and freshly brewed coffee.

The loud clink of dishes brought her fully awake. Her eyes flew open and she immediately saw Charlie. His sleep-tousled hair stood on end and his face radiated deep concentration as he set the table. She quickly closed her eyes once again.

The kid was making them breakfast. Heck, her own mother had never taken the time to make her breakfast. Myriad emotions danced through Annalise as she remained unmoving beneath the covers. The emotion that danced the fastest in the spotlight in her head was regret.

It seemed silly now, how closed off she'd kept herself from the very idea of her father's family. She cracked open an eyelid and watched as Charlie carefully poured orange juice into two glasses and set them on the table, then whirled back to the stove to flip the bacon slices.

Was this normal behavior for a thirteen-year-old kid? Somehow she thought not. She suspected Charlie Blakely might just be an extraordinary young man. "Do you cook at home?" she asked.

He looked up, obviously startled by her voice, then grinned. "Sunday mornings and Wednesday nights. Mom thinks it's a good idea for guys to know how to cook. Don't tell any of my friends this, but I like to cook."

"Don't worry; your secret is safe with me." She grabbed her robe from the end of the bed and pulled it around her as she stood.

"I was going to surprise you with omelets, but you don't have much stuff in your fridge."

"I don't eat here much, Charlie," she replied, then remembered she had a breakfast date to meet Mike at the Corner Café at ten. She needed to call and cancel. She grabbed the clothes she intended to wear for the day and her cordless phone. "I'll be out in a few minutes," she said as she disappeared into the bathroom.

The loft bathroom had been where much of the renovation money had gone. It was huge, with an oversized Jacuzzi bathtub on a raised platform in front of a big window. This side of the building caught the morning sun and had no neighbor to allow anybody to see her in her bath.

A shower was in order, but first she had to call Mike. She sat on one of the steps that led up to the bathtub and punched in his number.

"Seeing your name on my caller ID doesn't bode

well for our breakfast together," he said when he answered.

"I'm sorry, Mike. Something has come up and I'm going to have to cancel. I'm assuming the papers I need to sign can wait."

"Of course. I was more interested in sharing breakfast with you than getting them signed. Everything all right?"

"Everything is fine. My thirteen-year-old half brother showed up on my doorstep last night. He spent the night, and my father is picking him up sometime this morning," she explained.

"Was this unexpected?"

Annalise smiled. "About as unexpected as you can get, but I'm glad he showed up. We've had a nice visit."

"When are you and I going to have a nice visit, Annalise?" His voice was deeper than usual. "You have to know that I'm not just interested in being the Blakely Dolls lawyer. I'd like to be something more to you."

Although she had suspected Mike's feelings, this was the first time he'd spoken of them aloud, and for a moment she was lost for a response.

"Annalise, you need a life other than the dolls. I'm afraid you're slowly being consumed by the business. Your mother was, and you know she wasn't a happy person."

That was the understatement of the year, Annalise thought. "Mike, believe me, the last person I want to become is my mother. Why don't we go to dinner tomorrow evening? I can sign those papers and we can talk."

"That would be great. Why don't I pick you up

around seven?" His enthusiasm was evident in his voice.

"Okay, I'll be ready."

She clicked off and undressed, then got beneath a hot shower spray. Maybe she should give Mike a chance. Love didn't always come with fireworks and infernos. Didn't it sometimes creep in softly, build slowly and stay forever?

Certainly Allen hadn't generated explosive desire in her. She hadn't loved Allen. She'd recognized that when she'd so easily kicked him to the curb when she felt he'd disrespected the business.

Annalise wasn't sure she knew what real love was, didn't know if she was capable of truly loving another human being. To love meant being vulnerable.

"Been there, done that," she muttered as she shut off the water and reached for a towel.

And had the scars to prove it, she thought ruefully. She'd loved only once, with a child's open heart and trust. More than once she'd sat on the front stoop waiting for the man she believed had hung the moon. When she got older she vowed her heart would never again be that open to disappointment, to pain.

That didn't mean she would mind a man in her life. She missed cuddling and the kind of inane conversations that lovers often shared. She missed sex. God, did she miss sex.

Dismissing all thoughts of romance from her mind, she finished dressing. She had a thirteen-year-old boy waiting on her to eat.

Charlie's conversation at breakfast was as animated as it had been the night before, much of it in the form of questions.

"When you were my age did you have a bunch of friends?" he asked as they cleared the table.

"Not a bunch, but there was one girl who was my very best friend, and she's still my best friend." Annalise smiled as she thought of Danika. If it hadn't been for Danika's friendship, Annalise's childhood would have been too lonely to bear.

"I'll bet you were a cheerleader and a homecoming queen."

She laughed. "Charlie, I hate to disillusion you, but I was neither of those things. And now you'd better get showered, because I have a feeling Dad is going to show up here sooner rather than later."

As Charlie disappeared into the bathroom, Annalise grabbed the dish cloth and wiped down the table, her thoughts traveling back in time.

She hadn't dated much in high school and hadn't participated in extracurricular activities. Even then her life had revolved around the dolls.

She'd rushed home from school each day to stitch and sew, to plait hair and box dolls for mailing. Getting out the orders, that was what mattered to her mother, and therefore to her. Working together on the dolls was the only time Annalise felt close to her mother, the only time she felt as if she had her mother's undivided attention and love.

The dolls are your legacy, her mother would tell her. *My life's work, Annalise, and someday they will be yours.*

The ringing phone interrupted her mind's journey. "Hello?" she answered.

"Annalise." The smooth, deep voice shot a rivulet of pleasure up her spine.

"Tyler," she replied.

"Look, I'm sorry I haven't called, but I've been swamped at work. I know this is short notice, but I'm free for lunch today and was wondering if you were, too?"

"I'd be free for a late lunch," she replied, unsure exactly what time her father would arrive to get Charlie. "Say around one?" She moved to the window and looked outside.

"One would be fine," he said. "Any particular place you'd like to go?"

"How about a picnic in Riverfront Park?" she asked impulsively. "Why don't you just show up around one and I'll take care of the rest."

"I can't let you do that," he protested.

"Why not?" she countered.

There was a moment of silence; then he laughed, that low, sexy rumble she remembered from last time they'd been together. "Okay, a picnic sounds like fun, and I'll leave it all up to you."

They agreed to meet in the park at one, then hung up. She wasn't sure why a picnic had popped into her head, other than that it was a gorgeous day and the idea of a leisurely meal outside was something she wouldn't ordinarily do by herself.

She mentally made a list of what needed to be done to prepare for the picnic, and by that time Charlie was out of the shower and once again filling her space with boyish energy.

"While we wait for Dad to come and pick me up could you show me around downstairs? You know, where you do all the work to make the dolls?" he asked.

"Sure," she agreed. She grabbed her cordless phone and motioned him toward the door.

They left the loft together, Charlie heading for the elevator and Annalise toward the stairs. "Doesn't the elevator work?" he asked.

"Yeah, it works. But I never use it," she replied as he joined her at the top of the stairs.

"Why not?" Charlie asked as they descended.

"I don't know; it's a silly phobia," she confessed. "I guess I'm a little bit claustrophobic, and being in an elevator always makes me feel like I'm in a small box." Or a coffin, she thought.

"I don't like bugs and I don't like fire," Charlie said, his feet clomping on the stairs as if to punctuate each word.

"Then you must not be much of a camper."

"Staying in the cabin is as close as I want to get to camping." He shot her a sideways glance. "This is cool."

"What's that?"

"Having a sister I can tell stuff to."

He seemed determined to head-butt his way into her heart, and the heart she'd kept closed for so long opened to allow him in just a little bit.

When they reached the first floor she gave him the tour of the workroom, explaining the production process that created each of the Blakely dolls.

He appeared interested in every aspect. Whether his interest was genuine or feigned didn't matter. She found it charming either way.

Her phone rang as she was showing Charlie around the retail store. It was her father, letting her know that he and Sherri were parked outside. It appeared that an impromptu family reunion was about to occur.

Meeting Charlie had been a shock, albeit a pleasant one, but that didn't mean Annalise was prepared to meet Sherri. Even though she knew it was silly and probably Freudian, she'd always been a little jealous of the woman who had managed to garner her father's devotion and love.

"Dad and your mother are out front," she said to Charlie, and tried to ignore the swift stab of disappointment that flashed on his features.

"I'm probably going to get my butt chewed royally."

"Why don't you run up and get your backpack, and I'll go see if I can smooth any troubled waters?"

He shot her that charming smile of his. "Thanks," he said as he headed toward the stairs.

Annalise drew a deep breath and unlocked the shop door. The sunshine warmed her shoulders as she stepped outside and saw her dad's car parked along the curb. He stepped out, his expression concerned.

"Annalise, I'm so sorry for all this—" he began.

She held up her hand to halt his apology. "It's okay, Dad, really." She smiled, and the worry that had lined his face fell away.

"Where is he?" he asked.

"He went upstairs to get his backpack. I told him I'd come out and see if I could circumvent the butt-chewing he's figuring on getting."

A small smile curved one corner of Frank's mouth. "His mother was ready to show up here last night and ground him for the rest of his natural life.

He didn't have permission, and what he did was foolish."

Annalise looked toward the car and saw the woman in the passenger side. "Isn't Sherri going to get out of the car? I think maybe it's time we said hello."

He stared at her for a long moment, as if trying to assess her state of mind. "She'd like that," he finally said, and walked over to the car and opened the passenger door.

Annalise wasn't sure what she expected, but the tall blonde with the strong features and confident walk couldn't have been more different from Annalise's mother.

Lillian Blakely had been pretty and petite. Physically she was the type of woman men wanted to protect, a woman who oozed vulnerability . . . unless you knew her.

As Sherri approached her, an unexpected panic welled up in the back of Annalise's throat. *It's probably that woman he married who keeps him from seeing you.* Her mother's voice played in her head, evoking a trace of bitterness that still had the audacity to linger in Annalise even after all these years.

"Annalise." Sherri held out her hand and smiled. It was Charlie's smile, with the same generosity shining from her eyes, the same warmth of spirit radiating to embrace Annalise. All the years of self-imposed isolation suddenly seemed ridiculous.

"Hi, Sherri, it's nice to finally meet you," Annalise said. She began to reach for Sherri's hand, but instead Sherri threw her arms around Annalise and hugged her as if they were long-lost friends.

"It's taken far too long for us to get to know each

other," Sherri said as she finally dropped her arms and stepped back. "I hope my son didn't cause you any grief."

Annalise smiled. "He was fine. He's a neat kid."

Sherri beamed with a mother's love. "We think so. I've tried to teach him to be independent, but I had no idea he'd hop on a bus to come and meet you."

"We should have seen it coming," Frank said. "Charlie has been asking questions about you for months. He's gotten it into his head that having a big sister is better than Disneyland and Christmas all rolled into one."

"I think having a little brother is going to be cool," Annalise replied, using one of Charlie's favorite words. At that moment Charlie came out of the store.

"I know, I know—I'm grounded for life," he exclaimed as he eyed his mother, then his father. "But I knew if I asked you to come here you'd put me off, like you have for the last year."

"I'm glad you came," Annalise said to her brother. "And you're welcome to come back again."

His face lit up. "Cool." To her surprise he threw his gangly arms around her neck and gave her a hug. "Can I call you?" he asked as he released her.

"Sure. Dad has my number."

"And now it's time for us to get out of here," Frank said, and looked at his son. "And you're going to spend the rest of the day and evening cleaning the garage, young man."

"Dad," Annalise protested softly.

"It's okay," Charlie said. He flashed that grin that

could penetrate body armor with its charm. "You were worth it."

The lump in Annalise's throat couldn't have grown any bigger as she watched the car pull away from the curb. Lillian Blakely had not been a demonstrative person. Hugs and kisses hadn't been her style; nor had Annalise ever figured her father as a man who showed his affection through touch.

Funny how deeply the hugs she'd received from the two people she'd thought she wanted nothing to do with had affected her.

She went back into the shop and up the stairs to get her purse. She'd hit the city market and put together a picnic that Tyler King would find hard to forget.

Two hugs and a date all in the same day. Maybe the stars were aligning for something wonderful. The thought perched a smile on her lips as she headed out to shop.

Chapter 7

Tyler hated his house. Oh, architecturally it had been just what he'd wanted when he'd bought it seven years ago. The ranch boasted three bedrooms, two baths, a big kitchen and a large family room complete with wood-burning fireplace.

The house was located in a neighborhood that was typical suburban. Almost every house had an SUV in the driveway and neatly manicured lawns that seemed to be issues of subtle competition.

On the weekends most of the males in the households wielded Weed Eaters like weapons and rode around on lawn mowers that did everything but bring them a beer when the men were finished.

For the first year he'd lived here Tyler had tried to keep up. On his time off he mowed and weed-whacked, raked and bagged and learned the fine art of weed and feed and fertilizer. But during difficult cases and long work hours the lawn would get away from him, and he'd suffer faint disapproving glances from his neighbors. He'd finally decided he didn't need the pressure and instead had hired a lawn service.

Still, he liked the fact that it was a friendly place, that the people seemed to value their neighbors. In fact next Saturday the neighborhood association was holding an ice-cream social in one of the cul-de-sacs.

What he hated about his house was the decor, a mishmash of half-finished projects that his last girlfriend, Stacy, had begun before she'd proclaimed him unfit for human consumption and left.

He now stood in the kitchen, where one wall was painted puke green and another one baby shit yellow. Both walls had hammerhead-size holes in the Sheetrock, courtesy of Stacy's temper fit when Tyler had given his honest opinions about the new colors.

Stacy had been a Martha Stewart wannabe without taste or follow-through, and the remnants of her manic decorating were in every room of his house.

He should be using this downtime to repair the Sheetrock and invest in about ten gallons of white paint. He should be steaming off the wallpaper border in the master bedroom that had never made it to all four walls. He should have been doing a million things besides going on a picnic. But a picnic with Annalise Blakely held far more appeal than any home-improvement project.

He grabbed his car keys off the counter and headed for the front door. Minutes later, as he drove toward Riverfront Park, where he was to meet Annalise, he tried to imagine what her living space was like.

Was she a frills-and-lace kind of woman? Was she into antiques and Tiffany lamps? Or was she simple and elegant in her home furnishings? The truth was, he didn't know her well enough to even make an educated guess.

He didn't know her, but he knew himself well enough to know that what he was doing was filling his mind with anything to keep it from dwelling on Kerry Albright in that damned wedding gown.

A bride with no wedding. He knew that the way she'd been dressed, the care that had been taken with her after death held a clue, but damned if they'd been able to figure it out.

The staging of a scene such as what they'd found at the Albright murder was always disturbing, whispering of perverted fantasies, twisted obsessions and subliminal messages in every nuance.

Tyler didn't like unfinished business, and Kerry was definitely unfinished. Her family lacked closure, and her friends mourned a death that offered no explanation, no reason.

He shoved aside these disturbing thoughts as he approached the city market area. Parking was at a premium on the weekends, and it took him several minutes to finally find a space.

He cut the engine, and a ridiculous flutter of nervous tension went off in his stomach. What was it about the prospect of seeing Annalise Blakely again that made him feel like a teenager?

The park where they had agreed to meet was across the street from the Italian place where they'd eaten. It was easy to guess that these were familiar stomping grounds for her.

She must live nearby, he thought as he walked toward the park. In the last five years this area had exploded with condos and lofts.

The minute the park came into view he saw her,

and the nervous tension inside him skyrocketed, along with an intense burst of pleasure.

The blanket she'd spread out looked like a piece of sunshine cast down amid the lush green grass beneath a large oak tree. Wearing a pair of white shorts and a white-and-yellow-striped tank top, Annalise looked cool and casual.

She saw his approach and stood, a bright smile lighting up her face. In that single moment of a shared smile, his nerves calmed and he was left with only a sweet anticipation.

"Wow, you look amazing," he said.

She laughed, and a light, warm breeze rippled the long, dark hair across her shoulders. "Amazing would be a little black dress with strappy sandals. This is just okay."

He grinned. "Okay looks pretty amazing to me."

She gestured him toward the blanket and sat. "I hope you brought your appetite as well as your flattery."

"I did; in fact, I didn't eat any breakfast in anticipation of your dazzling culinary skills."

She laughed again, the low, melodic sound blowing a swift wind of desire through him. "Thank goodness you don't have to rely on my questionable culinary skills; otherwise you'd be sorely disappointed."

"Not much of a cook, huh?" He eased down on the blanket next to her.

"If it comes frozen or in a box, I'm good. If it's delivered to my door then I'm even better. What about you? Are you a master chef?"

"I'm afraid we share the same lack of interest in cooking. Personally I'm a junk-food junkie. If it's fried and comes in a paper wrapper, then I'm satisfied."

"Well, today you're going to sample the flavors of the marketplace." She placed a hand on the large picnic basket and stretched her legs out before her.

She had great legs, with slender ankles and shapely calves. Tyler had always been a leg man. His mother said he took after his father, who had enjoyed a long-standing obsession with Betty Grable's legs. As far as Tyler was concerned, Betty Grable had nothing on Annalise Blakely.

"How about something to drink?" she asked, and opened the basket. "I have soda, juice and bottled water."

"Bottled water is fine." He took the chilled bottle from her and she grabbed one for herself. "Do you live around here?"

She pointed across the street, and for the first time he noticed the building whose large window boasted her name. " 'The Dollhouse.' So that's where all your doll magic happens?"

"First floor, retail and production; second floor, storage; and third floor, personal living space," she said. "This area has always been home to me. I lived with my mother in an apartment a couple of blocks from here when I was growing up. Then about ten years ago she bought that building and opened the store, but continued to live in the old apartment. When she passed away three years ago I had the top floor renovated and moved in."

"You like it in this area?"

She shrugged. "I don't know anything different. It feels comfortable, familiar. What about you? I know you live someplace close to Danika."

"Just down the street. It's a great house, but it needs some work. Most of the time all I manage to do when I get home is sleep, shower and change my clothes. The last week has been particularly hard."

"Big case? I'm sorry to admit I usually avoid the news."

"That's refreshing. Generally I like to make it a rule that I don't talk about my work." He didn't want to offend her, but he wanted to set the ground rules up front. "My work is ugly and filled with the worst things that people do to one another."

Her blue eyes gazed at him thoughtfully. "Then I understand why, when you aren't at work, you don't want to talk about it."

The issue was resolved that easily. As she began to unpack the basket they chatted about a variety of things, and he tried to ignore the simmer of want that warmed the pit of his stomach.

The scent of her perfume filled the air around them, a fresh floral that stirred in his head fantasies of rumpled sheets and hot sex.

The food was as erotic as his thoughts. Chunks of a variety of cheeses, plump olives dripping juice, a hunk of Italian bread thickly buttered and pepperoni and salami sliced into bite-sized pieces.

Finger food, and each time he saw her lick one of her fingers he felt that lick right down to his toes. It had been a very long time since he'd felt this kind of attraction to a woman.

As they ate he tried to stay focused on the conversation and not on how her mouth might taste or if her legs felt as sleek as they looked.

Any thoughts he might have had about Kerry Albright and the case he was working couldn't be sustained as his head filled with all things Annalise.

She pointed out people sharing the park with them, neighbors who sat on benches or strolled around the perimeter. There was an insurance salesman, a building supervisor and a woman with a stroller who all waved to her.

Just after three, Joey, the owner of the restaurant where they had eaten the week before, hurried toward his establishment.

"This is a busy little park," he observed after they had eaten and were just lounging on the blanket.

"That's one of the things I like about it. When I get lonely all I have to do is step outside and I'll find somebody to talk to."

"You get lonely?" he asked.

Those beautiful blue eyes of hers looked at him for a long moment, then gazed off at some indefinable point just over his shoulder. "Sometimes. Most of the time I'm too busy to be lonely, but there are those moments late in the evening when the quiet gets to me." She looked back at him. "What about you?"

He shrugged. "Like you, most of the time I'm too busy to think about it. But sure, I have my moments of loneliness."

It was hard for Annalise to imagine him as a lonely man. He appeared so self-contained. There was an aura of strength that surrounded him, and to her he appeared a man who would have need of nobody.

Still, his nearness caused her heart to beat a little faster, her mouth to be a bit dry. There was no denying it: Something about him stirred her hormones into a frenzy.

She didn't know if it was the scent of him, that clean male smell that emanated from him. Or maybe it was just that the man had chest and arm muscles that looked capable of dealing with anything, and a tight butt and long legs.

Certainly his eyes attracted her. Sometimes dark and enigmatic and at other times lit with humor and warmth, she suspected they mirrored a complicated soul.

"I had an unexpected visitor this weekend," she now said. He crooked a dark eyebrow upward in question. "My thirteen-year-old half brother decided it was high time we met and so took a bus and appeared here last night."

"You'd never met him before?" He rolled over on his side, closer to her than he'd been before. He was now in her personal space, close enough that she imagined she could feel the heat from his body, feel the warmth of his breath as he spoke. "Does he live out of town or something?"

"Or something," she replied drily. "Actually, he lives twenty miles from here." She frowned thoughtfully. "I'm ashamed to admit that for the first few years of his life I didn't want to have anything to do with him, or the woman my father had married. Over the years my father was very careful to keep me and his other family separate. My relationship with him has always been complicated."

He reached out for a strand of her hair that had fallen forward and tucked it behind her ear. "So, how was it to finally meet your brother?"

She smiled and tried to ignore the sweet sizzle of

heat his touch had evoked. "It was actually pretty great. Charlie is a terrific kid, and I'm looking forward to developing a real relationship with him."

"And I'm looking forward to developing a real relationship with you," he replied.

Tremulous laughter escaped her lips. "Are you always so forward about what you want?"

"Always." His charcoal eyes gleamed. "As far as I'm concerned, life is too short, too uncertain not to grab what you want."

"And what, exactly, do you want?" She held her breath as his gaze slid slowly, appraisingly down the length of her, then finally settled on her lips. "A kiss would be a good start."

Her heart fluttered an uneven rhythm. "I think a kiss would be a great start."

He leaned forward and barely touched his lips to her own. The soft-as-a-whisper touch sparked electricity through her veins.

With demand and hunger he increased the pressure of his mouth against hers. She opened to him, allowing his tongue to dance with hers. He tasted of the strawberries and orange slices that had been their dessert, and she'd never savored anything quite so wonderful, quite so erotic in her life.

She wanted him to wrap her in his arms, to press the length of his body against hers, but he didn't touch her at all except with his sinfully wonderful lips.

When he finally broke the kiss she opened her eyes and sighed. "That was nice."

He grinned. "Nice for an appetizer."

The words held the promise of better things to come, and Annalise found herself eagerly anticipating the next step. Someplace in the back of her mind she recognized that the relationship might be moving a little quickly, but she didn't care.

She would take a page from Danika's book of life, the page that said, "Live for the moment and to hell with the consequences." As Danika would say, Why worry about finding a Mr. Right, when Mr. Right Now stood directly in front of you?

Tyler sat up and stared off in the distance for a moment, then looked back at her. "I've been told I make a crappy boyfriend."

"Really? And why is that?" She sat up as well, noticing that the park had begun to empty as people headed home for their evening meal.

"I'm undependable," he replied. "You saw that for yourself. Even when I'm off I'm usually still on call."

"Dependability is overrated as far as I'm concerned." She gave him a hint of a smile.

"I'm demanding," he continued. "And I've been told I'm not always sensitive to other people's emotional needs."

"Do you always kiss a girl until her toes curl, then spend the next few minutes telling her all your terrible qualities?"

"Nah, I usually ambush the woman with the bad qualities much later in the relationship," he said with that sexy grin of his.

"Then why are you telling me about them now?" she asked curiously.

"Because I like you, Annalise, and I figured it was only fair of me to give you a heads-up."

"If you're expecting me to reciprocate, then don't hold your breath," she said drily. "I don't intend to

warn you about any of my bad traits." He laughed
and she continued. "Seriously, Tyler, let's just take it
one day at a time, okay? No expectations and no
promises."

"That sounds good to me," he agreed, then
glanced at his watch and frowned. "We should
probably call it a day." His voice held a wealth of regret. "Even though I'm officially off duty, there are
some things I need to check on down at the station."
He stood and held out a hand to her.

Although she knew she had tons of things to do
before the next workday, she hated to see this time
with him end. She grabbed his hand, and he pulled
her to her feet and right into his arms.

Acutely conscious of each point of body contact,
from the press of his firm thighs to his muscled
chest against her breasts, she let a small gasp escape
her.

Then he was kissing her the way she'd wanted to
be kissed, long and hard, with his arms wrapped
tightly around her and his heartbeat pounding
against her own. When he finally released her she
sighed and smiled up at him. "You do that very
well."

He winked at her. "If you think that's good, wait
until I show you my other talents." He gestured toward the picnic blanket. "I'll help with these things
and walk you to your door." As he picked up the
picnic basket she quickly grabbed the blanket and
folded it, trying not to think about his other talents.

"Next Saturday my neighborhood is having a
block party, you know, ice cream and burgers," he
said as they began to walk toward her place. "I'd
like it if you'd go with me."

"Sounds like fun. What time?"

He frowned. "I can't remember the specifics. I'll have to check the flyer and call you."

They stopped at the door of the shop and she pulled keys from her pocket and unlocked it. "Annalise, thanks for a great day." He set the basket down. "I don't often get a day just to relax and enjoy the company of a beautiful woman."

She had no idea what thoughts filled his head at that moment, but his eyes grew darker and his lips thinned as a frown creased his forehead. "And now it's back to the ugly reality of the world."

She wanted to place her palms on either side of his face and remind him that the conversation and laughter they'd shared, the pleasant passing of time, was part of the real world, too. But before she could give action to her thoughts he stepped back from her. "I'll call you, and unless all hell breaks loose between now and then we'll set up the details about Saturday."

She could tell he'd already made the mental transition from pleasant afternoon to whatever unpleasantness his evening might hold. As he said good-bye he touched her cheek, then turned and walked away.

Watching him go, she was warmed by his touch and the time spent in his company. She liked him. She liked him a lot, and she couldn't wait to see him again.

She watched until he disappeared from her sight; then she turned to unlock her door and it was at that moment that the heat that had warmed her seemed to suck right out as a cold wind of unease blew through her.

The hairs on the nape of her neck stood straight up, and she had the feeling that somebody was watching her. She whirled around and looked out at the park, where the last straggler, a woman with a toddler, was hurrying away in the distance.

There didn't appear to be anyone lurking in the evening shadows that had begun to be cast across the area, no dark figures peeking out from the alleyway, and yet the disconcerting feeling continued. Her heart banged against her ribs, and her breath came in frantic little pants.

Fear. Without rhyme, without reason. It sputtered through her as she quickly got her things inside. She relocked the door, heart racing, and moved to the window to once again look outside.

Nothing. She released a small, hesitant laugh. Crazy. Somebody had definitely walked over her grave.

There was absolutely no reason for her to feel the way she did, and yet the prescient feeling of doom continued as she climbed the stairs to her loft.

Max woke up as the sun died in the West, streaking the sky with the last of the colors it had to gasp out. As always when he opened his eyes his gaze locked on the picture. It was stuck on a nail inside the wooden crate Max called home.

And always in that first glance after sleeping the day away, he remembered—he remembered the life he'd once lived before this one he'd chosen.

Sam and Mickey. His sons. They smiled at him from the faded photograph. They had been such good boys, filled with laughter and life.

There had been a mother once, Max's wife. She

had died when the boys were two and four. Try as
he might Max could no longer remember her name.
But in this rare moment of clarity, with sleep just
barely left behind, the memories of his sons filled
him.

Mickey had been the oldest, a good-looking kid
who'd grown up loving all things sports-related,
and his younger brother, Sam. Sam had been qui-
eter, less physical. He'd been shy and found his
pleasure in reading and music.

They had been the Three Musketeers, laughing
together and loving one another through the ups
and downs of life. The boys had been Max's reason
to get up in the mornings, their laughter the sound
that sustained him through the days.

His hand trembled as he reached to take the picture down. They had been fourteen and sixteen
when the picture had been taken, seated on the sofa.
Sam wore shorts and a T-shirt, and Mickey wore
jeans and was shirtless. Nothing posed about it;
Max had simply grabbed his camera on impulse
and snapped the photo. He'd had the roll of film de-
veloped and got the pictures back the day before
their deaths.

Pain . . . excruciating pain coupled with devastat-
ing grief crushed him. His chest constricted, so tight
it threatened to shut off his air, and he wanted it to.
He wanted to die as he thought about all he'd lost.

But somewhere in the distant past he'd been
taught that it was a sin to take your own life, that
the consequence of such an act was to burn in hell
forever. And although someplace deep inside he
suspected he was already in hell, he was afraid to

chance that there could be something worse than what he lived right now.

He shoved the photo in his back pocket, and that quickly the pain and grief subsided as the memories tumbled away. With a grunt he crawled from the crate, bones creaking and muscles groaning as he stretched to his full height.

It would be a good night. The market had been filled with people all day long. That meant good Dumpsters and, with a little luck, enough dropped change on the sidewalks and in the parking lots to buy a bottle of booze. That would assure that the memories stayed away.

Night shadows moved in quickly. Max had a routine, and the first place he headed was the parking lot next to the city market, where Crazy Betty had arrived before him. He raised a hand to greet her. She scowled and hugged a shopping bag filled with pinecones close to her chest as she scurried away.

The parking lot yielded four dollars and twelve cents, promising sweet oblivion in the form of a bottle of cheap gin. His next stop was the liquor store, where he bought his bottle and tucked it into a pocket inside his jacket.

He moved on to the Dumpster behind the Italian restaurant. Even on the worst nights there was usually bread to be found there.

As he left the Dumpster behind Joey's and walked across the park he saw the lights go off in the upstairs of the doll lady's place. Anna. No, that wasn't right. Annalise. He liked her. She had kind eyes, and when there was nothing in the trash worth eating he knew she'd have a little something for him.

It took him hours to check all the Dumpsters in the area and gather anything he thought might be edible or usable. When he was finally finished he settled at the base of a large oak tree in the park to drink away any vestige of memory that might attempt to be known.

The night deepened, the moon climbing higher and higher in the sky. He'd grown accustomed to judging the time of the night by the position of the moon in the sky.

Max had stopped getting drunk years ago. Years of abusing alcohol had built up a tolerance inside him. Now he got numb night after night.

It was after two in the morning when Max saw him. Max's bowels cramped in fear as he tried to melt into the tree behind him.

The devil, that was who Max saw creeping through the shadows of the night. He was dressed all in black, and Max didn't look at his face. He'd seen the face only once before, a face stripped of all humanity. Max couldn't tell anyone if the devil's eyes were blue or black or brown, for the one time he'd looked in them all he'd seen was the flames of hatred and burning hell.

Max held his breath as the devil stole past him, as silent as a stalking cat. He held a box in his arms, and Max watched in horror as he approached the doll lady's home. The devil placed the box just outside her door, then turned and came back toward Max.

Max squeezed his eyes tightly closed and held his breath as the devil went by. It was only when the demon had gone back to hell or wherever he came from that Max opened his eyes again and hurried toward his crate.

When he was safe inside his little home he curled into a fetal ball. As he thought of that box sitting just outside Annalise's door he began to weep, because he knew his friend was in trouble. The devil was after her, and the worst part of all was that Max was too afraid to warn her.

Chapter 8

Annalise found the box when she opened the store the next morning. It was one of her own, a Blakely Dolls box. She thought of the strange feeling she'd had the night before when she'd gone inside, and as she picked up the box that same fear struck her again.

She carried it into the back room, where Ben was already busy at his workstation. "What's that?" he asked.

"It was by the front door." She set it on her desk.

"A return of some kind?" Ben got up from his chair and joined her.

"I don't think so." She opened the lid and parted the tissue paper.

"It's a Fanny Flapper," Ben said, stating the obvious.

As before, a note was folded and tucked in next to the doll's smiling face. She grabbed the note and opened it and read it aloud. " 'Soon people won't be talking about your dolls anymore. They will be talking about mine.' " She looked at Ben. "It's signed 'The Real Dollmaker.' "

"Weird."

"I got another one before. It was a Belinda the Bride doll, and the note said something like, 'I don't need your dolls anymore. I have my own.'" She frowned thoughtfully. "You haven't heard of a new dollmaker in town, have you?"

"No, but that doesn't mean there isn't one," Ben replied.

"I'll be right back. I'm just going to run this upstairs." She tucked the note back into the box, replaced the lid, then carried the whole thing back to her loft. She placed the box in her linen closet right next to the one she'd received before.

She moved to the window and stared outside, an edge of frustration welling up inside her. As if business hadn't been bad enough the last few months, now it appeared that a new doll store was in town and was determined to compete with her for sales.

The business will never let you down, Annalise. Her mother's voice rang in her head. *Men will come and go, and love never lasts. It's the dolls you can count on.*

She whirled away from the window with a vague sense of guilt niggling at her. When she'd opened her eyes that morning it hadn't been the doll business that had filled her thoughts. It had been Tyler King.

She should be making a decision about what the next doll was going to be. She should be spending all her spare time listening to that tape Danika had made to find a perfect voice for a new, improved doll.

It was silly to waste a lot of time thinking about Tyler. It was said that you could predict future behavior by past behavior, and if that was the case Annalise knew how things would go with Tyler.

They'd date for a while, they'd share some good times and laughter and they'd have sex. Eventually the passion would wane, or he'd ask more of her than she was willing to give, and that would be the end of it. It would be great while it lasted, but it never lasted long.

By the time she got back downstairs the production area was in full swing. The whir of a sewing machine competed with Ben's hair dryer as they worked to complete the last of the Birthday Bonnie dolls.

Annalise sat at her desk and punched her computer on. If there was new competition in town, maybe she'd find out about it on the Web.

An hour later she gave up on the Internet. If there was a new doll business in the area it apparently wasn't advertising online yet. She moved onto the task of updating her inventory list.

She was still seated at the computer working on the inventory when Danika arrived unexpectedly. "I had an appointment cancel on me, so I thought I'd take a chance that we could do lunch."

"I really shouldn't," Annalise replied. "I'm behind on the inventory, and I need to finish up some sketches, then make a final decision on what the next project is going to be. I blew off way too much of the weekend."

Danika eyed her curiously. "That's not like you. Were you sick or something?"

"Or something. I met Charlie this weekend." Danika looked at her blankly. "You know, Charlie, my half brother?"

Danika's eyes widened. "You mean the little bastard who managed to get your dad's love when he had none to give to you?"

Annalise was aware that all work in the room had screeched to a halt as everyone waited for Danika and Annalise's conversation to continue. "Back to work, people," she said as she got up from her desk and grabbed Danika's arm. "I don't have time for lunch, but I'll take a fifteen-minute break upstairs."

As Danika headed for the elevator Annalise raced up the stairs, trying to decide whether she was going to tell her friend not only about Charlie's visit but also about her picnic with Tyler.

By the time Annalise reached the loft, Danika was already in the kitchen with her head stuck in the refrigerator. "Don't you have anything besides bottled water?"

"There should be a couple bottles of sodas in the door. Why don't you grab me a Coke?"

Danika grabbed the drinks; then the two sat at the table. "Tell all," Danika demanded.

Annalise did just that, beginning with the moment she'd discovered Charlie hiding on the second floor until she'd met Sherri and told them all goodbye.

"And how was it, meeting the wicked stepmother? Did she offer you a nice, shiny apple?"

Annalise laughed at the reference to the old fairy tale. "Actually, she seemed nice. I think if I gave it half a chance I might like her."

Danika took a sip of her drink and eyed Annalise wryly. "So, you've made nice with your stepbrother and stepmother, but you still hate your father."

"I don't hate my father," Annalise protested.

"You have major issues with your father, and if you don't resolve them you'll never find true love with any man. I've always been surprised that you aren't a big slut. Isn't that what happens a lot with girls who didn't have their fathers in their lives?"

Annalise laughed. "I didn't have time to sleep around. My mother kept me on a short leash."

"Don't get me started on your mother. You know my opinions where she is concerned piss you off."

It was true. Lillian Blakely was the one topic of conversation they couldn't discuss without one of them getting hurt or angry. They could talk about religion and politics and everything else under the sun—except Annalise's mother.

"Are you going to the block party in your neighborhood next Saturday?" Annalise asked in an effort to change the subject.

"How did you know about that?" Before Annalise could reply Danika leaned forward. "You've talked to Tyler again, haven't you?"

"We had a picnic yesterday; then he invited me to go to the neighborhood party with him."

"I don't know why I get excited by the prospect of you actually enjoying somebody, especially a nice guy like Tyler. It won't be long before you'll find a reason to kick him to the curb." Danika shot her a look of disgust. "Face it, Annalise: When it comes to relationships and men, you have a huge self-destructive streak."

"For God's sake, Danika, can you give it a rest?" Annalise didn't even try to hide her irritation. "It seems like every time we talk lately you spend all your time pointing out my character flaws."

"I'm sorry," Danika replied softly. She reached out and touched Annalise's arm. "It's just that I think I've finally found the one." Her eyes took on an excited glow. "Danny and I had a wonderful time in Vegas, and he's asked me to marry him."

Annalise stared at her in stunned surprise. "That's wonderful, but isn't it kind of quick? You've only been dating him a month."

"One month and six days, and I told him it was way too fast." Her smile was dreamy. "But it's right, Annalise. I know in my heart that he's the man for me."

"Then I'm happy for you."

"I'm happy for me, too," Danika replied with a laugh, then sobered. "But I worry about you. I want you to be happy."

Annalise smiled. "I am happy. I don't need to get married to be happy. My life is fine just the way it is."

Danika frowned. "I just don't want you to end up like your—" She caught herself. "I don't want you to wind up being lonely and bitter."

"I don't have time to be lonely, and I don't have any reason to be bitter. Besides, I'll never be alone. I have Birthday Bonnie and Flapper Fanny and all the other girls."

"They aren't girls, Annalise. They're dolls."

"I know that," Annalise scoffed.

Danika leaned forward once again. "Why don't you take some classes in fashion design? I remember a time when all you wanted to do was start your own label of clothing."

"Childish dreams. I have a business to run."

"Your mother's dream. When do you get the chance to pursue your own dream?"

The very idea of letting the doll business go caused a hard knot to form in the center of Annalise's chest. Her mother had depended on her to continue the business she'd spent a lifetime building. Lillian Blakely had sacrificed all her life for her dolls, and if Annalise let it go then her mother's work and sacrifices meant nothing.

"This is my dream," she finally said firmly. She stood. "And now I need to get back downstairs. We usually have a staff meeting about this time on Mondays."

Minutes later she was back downstairs and had the people she considered family around her.

"The last of the Birthday Bonnies on order will be shipped by the end of the week," Sarah said. "That leaves us almost a hundred to sell in the store."

Annalise nodded and hid her disappointment. Usually by the time the orders were filled there were only about a dozen dolls left to sell in the retail shop. She turned to Samantha. "I'm a little behind on the inventory records. Anything we need to order?"

"The beds have been selling very well. I think I only have two left in stock."

"And don't forget we're running a Web special on the tea sets," Sarah said.

Annalise inwardly cringed. The tea sets had been her idea, miniature chinaware stamped with the Blakely Dolls logo. It had bombed big-time.

"All we're really waiting on is your announcement of what's next," Ben said. "And whatever you decide, I'm hoping for a girl with marvelous hair."

"And not too much embroidery work on the clothes," added Sammy, her head seamster.

"I know everyone is waiting for me to make up my mind. I'll have a decision by next Monday, I promise," Annalise said.

Later that evening, as she got ready for her dinner with Mike, Annalise wondered why she was having so much trouble deciding what the next doll creation would be.

Soon people won't be talking about your dolls anymore. They will be talking about mine. The words from the note echoed in her head and increased the pressure to make certain that her next doll creation was spectacular.

A little competition was healthy, but the grinding weight of too much pushed down on her. Always when she thought of the business failing a sickening panic welled up inside her. In her mind she could see her mother's forehead wrinkle in disapproval, feel the coldness of her disdain.

As a child Annalise had dreaded disappointing her mother in any way, and it seemed that even in death Lillian had the same kind of power.

An hour later she sat across from Mike in a Chinese restaurant. She'd already signed the papers he'd brought with him, and now they were waiting for their meal to be served.

"I heard we're supposed to get some storms tomorrow night," he said to break the awkward silence that had descended.

She smiled. "You know what they say about Missouri weather. If you don't like it, just wait a few minutes and it will change. We could definitely use the rain."

"Have I mentioned that you look pretty tonight?" he asked, his eyes radiating a warmth that gave her a sinking feeling.

She'd hoped to get through the meal with pleasant, innocuous chitchat and nothing too personal, but apparently Mike had a different agenda.

"Thank you." She picked up her glass of plum tea and took a sip, wishing the waitress would arrive now with their orders.

Mike looked down at the table as if summoning courage to speak, and she steeled herself for what was to come. When he looked at her again there was a wealth of emotion in his eyes, emotion that made her want to jump up from the table and run.

"Annalise, I've enjoyed working for you as your lawyer, but you have to know that I'm interested in pursuing another kind of relationship with you, a personal one."

"Mike, you know I cherish our friendship."

A flash of pain darkened his eyes. It was there only a moment, then gone as he grinned wryly. "Ah, the dreadful words that no man ever wants to hear."

"It's nothing personal," she said hurriedly, hoping, praying she wasn't hurting his feelings. "To tell the truth, I've met somebody."

Surprise lifted his eyebrows. "I didn't know. I had no idea you were seeing anyone."

"It's relatively new. We've just had a couple of dates."

"But you aren't the kind of woman to date two men at the same time." It was more a statement than a question, and she nodded.

"That's me," he said with a touch of self-deprecation. "Always a day late and a dollar short." Annalise remained silent, unsure what to say. "If it doesn't work out with this new guy, maybe you'd give me a chance?"

"Perhaps," she hedged, grateful that the issue had been resolved that easily and nobody had gotten hurt feelings.

Their orders were delivered, and as they ate the conversation remained light and pleasant. They lingered over cups of hot tea, talking about her mother and the business and Annalise's concern that she wasn't doing a good enough job.

"You know how much all of this meant to my mother. I have this terrible feeling of letting her down each time the daily sales figures come in and they're so bad."

"Sales are always depressed in the summer months," he reminded her. "Lillian worried from May to November; then the pre Christmas orders would begin to come in and she'd calm down."

"I can't imagine my mother being anything but calm and in control," she replied drily.

Mike smiled. "She looked as soft and sweet as cotton candy on the outside, but she had a will of steel and a drive to succeed that would put Donald Trump to shame."

A shard of grief stabbed Annalise as she thought of her mother. Lillian had often been difficult, and she could be cold and distant, but she was practically all Annalise had had, and there were still times when she missed her mother desperately.

"Have you decided on the fall doll yet?" Mike asked.

"No, although I've promised the staff that I'll have a final decision by next Monday. I want to be sure that my choice will have people excited about Blakely Dolls again."

Once again Mike smiled. "I'm certain that it won't be long before everyone will be talking about the Blakely dolls again," he said with a wealth of conviction. She could only hope that he was right.

Blakely Dolls had become old news. Danika was even having trouble booking her on any more news shows as a local human-interest story. Her mother had managed to compete with the ever-popular American Girl dolls, but Annalise felt that with each day that passed, she was losing ground and the business was slowly sinking.

She was back in her loft by eight, and at eight fifteen Tyler called. "The ice-cream social starts at four on Saturday," he said. "Shall I pick you up around three thirty?"

"It's silly for you to drive all the way over here to get me," she replied. "I can get there under my own steam. All I need from you is your address."

"And you promise you won't make fun of the peculiarities of my home decor?"

She laughed, that crazy warmth flooding through her, the one she always got when she was talking to him. "I'll try my best, but I'm not making any promises."

They small-talked for a few more minutes, but she could tell he was at work, and it didn't take long for him to say he had to go.

As she got ready for bed an hour later she was still warmed by the conversation and the sweet pleasure of anticipation of the weekend to come.

It was only when she got into bed that night and the loft was cast in darkness that she remembered the doll and the note that had arrived that morning, and the warmth seeped away, replaced by the faint chill of apprehension.

Chapter 9

All hell broke loose at three seventeen Tuesday afternoon, when an anonymous caller reported a body behind the Dollar General store at North Oak and Eighty-third Street.

As Tyler and Jennifer headed to the scene, angry storm clouds gathered in the distance. The air was thick with humidity, and a preternatural stillness prevailed, a portent of severe storms by dusk.

"Maybe it was a prank phone call." Jennifer flipped the air-conditioning vent so it blew directly on her face. "The dispatcher said the caller didn't indicate that he was a store employee. You'd think that if there was a body behind a business, somebody who worked there would know about it. Of course, maybe all the employees enter through the front door and nobody has gone out the back today."

Tyler said nothing and as usual allowed Jennifer to verbalize every single thought that popped into her head. When they'd first been partnered together her chattiness had driven him crazy. Now he realized that Jennifer processed things by talking them out. He spent much of his time with her only half listening to the often inexplicable twists and turns of her thoughts.

"Used to be a time every business had an employee who smoked, and the back door was their best friend. Nowadays it's politically incorrect to smoke almost everywhere." Jennifer puffed a sigh. "Before you know it there will be smoke detectors in every house, and Big Brother watching to make certain nobody lights up."

She'd told him she'd quit smoking a month before, but there had been several times Tyler had smelled the telltale scent of tobacco smoke on her. She hadn't quit; she'd just become a sneaky smoker.

"Thank goodness you don't have to worry about that anymore." Tyler flashed her a quick grin, but the smile didn't last as he pulled into the parking lot in the strip mall where the Dollar General store was located. A small crowd was gathered in front of the store, and two uniformed cops appeared to be trying to maintain control.

The sight of a news truck parked in front caused a cold, hard knot to form in the center of Tyler's chest. "Doesn't look like a false alarm," he said as he pulled into a parking space.

Together he and Jennifer got out of the car. "Detective King, can you tell me what's going on here?" Reuben Sandford, a cheeky young reporter who loved to needle Tyler, hurried toward them.

"Don't know, Reuben. As you can see, we just got here," Tyler replied as he headed toward the business.

"I heard there was a body back there," Reuben said, hurrying to keep up with Tyler's long, determined strides. "I just thought maybe you'd heard voices in your head, you know, the dead talking to you, and you'd already have the full scoop."

"Lay off, jerk-face," Jennifer exclaimed.

"Bite me," he retorted.

Tyler nudged Jennifer, afraid that she just might do as Reuben had challenged. "Ignore him; we've got work to do."

A uniformed officer stopped Reuben when he attempted to follow them into the store. Inside Tyler was grateful to see Ben Ranier, another uniform he'd worked with before. Ben stood in one corner, where all the employees seemed to be gathered. One girl was crying as an older man patted her shoulder.

Ben left the small group and walked over to Tyler and Jennifer. "Afternoon, Tyler . . . Jennifer."

"Ben." Tyler nodded.

"I was the first one on the scene," Ben said, his features grim. "I spoke to the manager." He pointed to the older man consoling the young woman. "I asked him if anyone had gone out the back door at all today, and he told me he didn't think so. He unlocked the back door for me and I went to check it out."

Tyler wouldn't have thought it possible for Ben's features to get any grimmer, but they did. "We found her on the other side of the Dumpsters. It's just up your alley, Tyler, freaky as hell."

Jennifer nodded toward the crying woman. "Does she know the vic?"

"No. The owner had all the employees step outside to see if anyone could make an identification, but before I got here they all said they'd never seen her before."

Terrific, Tyler thought irritably. That certainly compromised the crime scene.

"Time will tell if that's really the case," Jennifer exclaimed.

"I've got two officers securing the scene," Ben said.

"Let's go see what we have," Tyler said. As he left the air-conditioning of the store, the humid air hit him like a punch in the chest. He glanced upward, where the storm clouds had darkened and filled the southwestern sky. Thunder rumbled, barely audible, but for Tyler the sound was the beginning of a ticking clock.

"Let's hope the crime scene people get here quickly and process fast, before we lose evidence to a storm," he said. He and Jennifer nodded to the cop standing at the edge of the large industrial-sized Dumpster, then passed him to reach the other side.

Jennifer saw the body first, and the sharp gasp that escaped her steeled Tyler for his first view. And it was bad. The sight of the girl propped up against the Dumpster nearly caused his breakfast to come up. Not because the scene was so ugly, but rather because it was just as Ben had described—freaky as hell.

She looked as if she'd just stepped out of the roaring twenties. Her gold dress was covered with matching fringe, and her legs had been positioned to one side, as if she had been in the middle of doing the Charleston when death had claimed her unexpectedly.

Her short, curly dark hair was perfectly coiffed

beneath the gold headband that crossed her fore-head. Pouty Cupid's-bow lips were bright red with lipstick, and her eyelids were sooty dark, lashes spiky with mascara.

"Jesus," Jennifer murmured faintly. "It's just like the bride. Posed and perfect."

And that was what had twisted Tyler's gut: the fact that he immediately thought of Kerry Albright. He'd hoped like hell that Kerry had been an isolated case, that somebody had killed her for a specific reason and the wedding dress had been part of that reason. But unless this young woman had been killed on her way home from a costume party, the particulars of this case made Kerry's murder something altogether different.

The first thing he did was survey the area, noting that it would have been relatively easy for some-body to pull up in a vehicle, position the body, then leave again without anyone seeing anything. Unfor-tunately the asphalt didn't show any tire tracks that could be used to identify the specific vehicle used.

"Check and see if you can find anything that might give us an ID," he said to Jennifer. "Officer, perhaps you can look in the Dumpster and see if you find a purse or something like that in the trash."

While they got busy, Tyler knelt beside the dead girl, his mind clicking and whirling with first im-pressions. She was young, probably between the ages of twenty and twenty-five. Just like Kerry, this victim appeared to have no defensive wounds. Her fingernails were painted fire-engine red and had no chips.

Her throat held the same dusky bruises as Kerry Albright's. That, coupled with the petechial hemorrhages in this new victim's eyes, was a sure sign of strangulation.

"We've got a fruitcake on our hands, don't we?" Jennifer said from beside him. Her search of the area had apparently yielded nothing.

"You know me; I hate to jump to conclusions, but let's just say that I have a bad feeling about this . . . a very bad feeling." Tyler stood, and as he continued to stare at the dead woman he wondered what kind of fantasy the killer was playing out.

So far he appeared to be highly organized and smart. If they didn't figure out what motivated him, what prompted the costumes and staging, he had a feeling this unsub was going to be a hard one to catch.

"Dumpster is empty," Officer Mathis reported a few minutes later. "I spoke to the manager, who said it was picked up late yesterday afternoon."

"So, we know for sure that she was left sometime last night," Tyler replied. "If she'd been here when the trash had been picked up, somebody would have seen her."

The crime scene unit arrived, and a large tarp was erected over the immediate area in case the weather turned nasty before they finished.

Tyler supervised the evidence gathering as Jennifer took notes, and overhead the thunder got louder and now flashes of vivid lightning could be seen in the black, roiling clouds.

It was just after seven when they finished up. They'd gathered everything they could, and the victim had been zipped into a body bag, her next stop the coroner's office for a full autopsy.

As Jennifer and Tyler headed back to their car, the

Carla Cassidy

wind gusted as the first raindrops began to fall. Before they could reach the car Reuben caught up with them.

"I heard we've got a dead girl dressed like a flapper," he said. "Can you confirm that?"

"No comment," Tyler said.

"I heard she was dressed in fringe and had been strangled." Reuben's short legs struggled to keep up with Jennifer's and Tyler's longer strides. "Is there any connection between this one and the girl who was dressed like a bride last week?"

"I said, no comment," Tyler said sharply. "I imagine there will be some sort of press release available by morning."

He got into his car and slammed the door as Reuben continued to yap. As Jennifer got in he started the engine, grateful that the noise of a knocking valve in the police-issue vehicle made it impossible to hear Reuben's high-pitched voice.

"I was hoping nobody would make a connection between our flapper and our bride," he said as he pulled away from the Dollar General store and headed toward the police station.

"Maybe there isn't a connection," Jennifer replied, although he knew from her tone that she didn't believe her own words.

"Reporters start writing stories about connected murders, that always makes people nervous." Tyler frowned and tightened his grip on the steering wheel as the rising wind fought for control.

"That always makes the chief nervous," Jennifer observed.

"Hell, I'm feeling pretty nervous at the moment." Thunder boomed overhead. They had heard while at the scene that the Kansas City area was under a severe-thunderstorm warning and a tornado watch.

Tyler wasn't worried about the inclement weather. He had a feeling the storm they were about to face with these two cases would make a cyclone look like an irritating wisp of wind.

Annalise paced in front of her windows, wincing each time the lightning flashed and thunder boomed. She didn't mind thunderstorms, but when she heard the local weatherman more often than she heard music on her favorite radio station, it made her edgy.

Spring and early summer weather could be volatile in Kansas City, and tonight Mother Nature seemed to be particularly pissed off.

She moved away from the window as another crack of thunder boomed overhead. She returned to the kitchen table, where a cup of hot tea was cooling and the small portable television on the counter was turned on.

This was one of those nights when she wished she didn't live alone, when she wished there were somebody to talk to, to take her mind off the crashing noise of the storm and the frantic beeps that emitted from the television, indicating dangerous weather.

She sipped her tea slowly, knowing she wouldn't go to bed until all the severe storms and tornado warnings in the area had expired.

Charlie had called her that afternoon, his bubbly friendliness breaking up the monotony of the day. The phone had nearly vibrated with his energy, and once again she'd found herself entertaining the regrets of a closed heart where her father's family was concerned.

She'd hung up, making a mental note to set aside another Saturday for him to come and spend the night. But not next Saturday. She'd be spending that day with Tyler. At least thoughts of him momentarily banished any worries about the storms.

She didn't remember feeling this excited when she'd first started dating Allen. In fact, she could never remember a man stirring in her such a delicious sense of anticipation.

What she didn't understand was why she continued to suffer moments of irrational dread—a subtle portent of bad things to come?

She'd felt it again that afternoon when she'd walked across the park to grab some lunch at Joey's. It was an unpleasant tickle up her spine, an acute feeling of being secretly watched. It was a nebulous emotion that had her holding her breath and waiting for a catastrophe to strike.

Maybe it had just been a sensitivity to barometric pressure changing due to the storms, she thought. Maybe she had a weird PMS thing going on.

She finished her tea and got up from the table, the frequent flashing of electrical impulses creating a light show in the window. In the back of her mind she knew what was making her more nervous than usual.

Those dolls. Why was somebody sending her dolls that had obviously been purchased years ago?

Although the dolls were tucked away, out of sight wasn't necessarily out of mind. She walked over to the linen closet and grabbed both the boxes off the shelf, then carried them back to the table.

She took the lids off both of the boxes, pulled out the dolls and the notes, then spread them all out over the top of the table and stared at them.

These two dolls would be far more valuable than any that had been produced under Annalise's time as head of the company. Both the Belinda the Bride doll and the Fanny Flapper had been early models and would have fetched a healthy price on eBay as collectibles.

Annalise didn't like things that didn't make sense, and somebody sending her these two dolls definitely didn't make sense. Even after reading each of the notes again she didn't understand.

On impulse she undressed each of the dolls and looked them over, checking to see if anything had been changed about them. But everything was as it should be, right down to Lillian Blakely's signature across their lower backs.

She redressed the dolls and placed them into their boxes, then once again tucked the notes back inside. Would she receive other dolls? Would new notes explain what was going on?

Having no answers, she put the dolls back into the linen closet next to her towels and washcloths. When she returned to the kitchen table she saw that the worst of the storm had dissipated and the tornado alerts had all been downgraded to severe-storm warnings south of the city.

She could now go to bed and not worry about being blown to Oz. Now if the rest of her worries could be as easily dispatched, she might sleep without dreams.

*   *   *

He loved storms. Maybe it was because his mother had always hated them. It was the one thing in the world that frightened her. When he was young and she wasn't yet bedridden, at the first hint of storms she'd prepare to go to the basement.

Boy, get my dolls and be careful with them. We've got to get them downstairs. The rest of this shit hole can blow away, but I want those babies safe.

The shit hole was the small two-story house where they had lived until his mother's death. Surrounded by crack houses and abandoned places, the house had been left to his mother by her father.

Even as a young boy he'd often prayed that a tornado would hit the house before his mother and her precious dolls could make it down the stairs.

He'd dropped one of her dolls once. Walking down the narrow stairs to the dank, concrete-block basement, he'd tripped on the last two stairs. He'd slammed his knees down so hard on the floor he thought he'd broken both his kneecaps. The doll, a Kimono Kim, had left his hand and slid across the floor.

His mother had screeched. *What have you done? Sweet Jesus, what have you done!* And for just one crazy moment he'd thought she was going to run to him and check to make certain he was all right. But she ran to the doll. The damned doll.

Now, with the sound of her voice creating painful chaos in his mind, he left his place and went out into the storm. The thunder banished the sound of his mother's voice from his head, and he lifted his face to the rain, imagining that it was washing all thoughts of her out of his life.

Restless, he headed for his car. He'd drive for a while; driving often calmed him. He headed north, toward the Dollar General store on North Oak, where last night he'd said good-bye to his latest creation.

And that was what made him restless tonight. He was alone again, with only the pictures of his dolls for company. He needed a new project. His desire pulsed inside him with a fevered rhythm. He'd find no new doll tonight, not with the rain peppering down and lightning slashing across the black skies.

He reminded himself that he wasn't ready for another doll. He had to decide what he wanted to re-create; then there would be hours of sewing clothing and studying hair and makeup styles.

He wasn't an expert seamster. He'd been self-taught with library books and practice. He'd taken up sewing in a direct act of defiance against his mother, who thought that a boy sewing meant he was gay.

Kimono Kim. The pretty doll in her elaborate costume and geisha makeup had been on his mind since the first rumble of thunder. She would be a challenge. He'd have to find the perfect Asian girl, and the costume would take hours to get right. As his mind whirled with the details of the new doll he began to relax.

It would be nice if he could quit his real job and devote himself to his artistic talents. But that just wasn't possible.

He slowed as he approached the strip mall where

the Dollar General store was located. The stores had closed hours ago, and there was nothing to see from the front. He didn't dare drive around the back of the store. He wondered if Margie had been found. Of course, she hadn't been Margie when he'd finished with her. She'd been Flapper Fanny.

Surely somebody had responded to the anonymous call he'd made. He'd wanted—no, needed—somebody to see his work, to appreciate and admire his talent.

Still restless, and with the storm passing, he turned the car around, knowing where he wanted to go. Minutes later he parked his car and headed for the Dollhouse . . . *her* house.

Annalise. Her name thundered in his head as he stood in the park and stared at the building, where all the lights were off.

He stood for a long time, staring up at the third-floor windows where she lived. As he thought of creating her doll, desire began to pulse inside him once again. It nearly took his breath away, his need to have her, to create her.

But he wasn't ready. It was too soon. He needed to make sure everyone understood about his dolls, about his genius, before he ended it all with her.

Still, he needed to get closer, close enough that he could imagine the scent of her perfume, that soft, flowery scent. He crossed the street and went around the side of her building. The occasional lightning flashes that lingered behind the storm aided his vision.

He knew what the inside of the building looked like; he'd been inside once when the renovations were taking place. He knew that the store was on the first level, storage was on the second and her living space was on the top floor. . . . He reached the back of the building, not yet ready to leave and go home.

The rain still trickled out of gutters, and the wood of the building had a wet sheen. Was she lying in bed now, planning another doll?

Soon she'd know about him, about his work. Would she be fascinated by his genius? Would she be intimidated by his talent?

He hoped so. He hoped she was afraid, just like he'd been afraid when his mother had mentioned that a new Blakely doll was about to be released.

He walked around the last side of the building and froze, a tingling excitement racing through him. The metal fire escape had once been painted a bright red, but now was a rusty, weathered brown. But it wasn't the fire escape stairs that caught his attention.

It was the open window on the second floor, just to the right of the stairs. Open just a couple of inches, the window called to him, a siren song that promised fulfillment and euphoria.

A man standing on the fire escape could reach that window. He could raise it up just enough to slither inside. His entire body trembled as he thought of taking her, of walking right into her loft and standing over her bed while she slept.

The thought made him hard as he imagined her shock, her horror just before he strangled her. He could immortalize her tonight, but he wasn't ready.

"Patience," he whispered, and drew a deep, shuddering breath. His mother had always called him an impatient little pig, but he had the patience to wait until it was right. And wait he would have to.

As he walked away from the building his heart sang because she hadn't closed the window against the rain. And that meant she didn't know the window was open.

Chapter 10

It had taken them two days to identify the victim found behind the Dollar General store, and they'd spent the past twenty-four hours trying to reconstruct the last hours and days of her life.

The victim's name was Margie Francis. She was twenty-four years old, lived alone and at the time of her death had been between jobs. Her family resided out of town, and in the small apartment where Margie lived they couldn't find an address book or anything else that listed the names of any friends or relatives.

They'd made their identification when somebody had turned in a purse they'd found along the street a block away from the Dollar General. The purse had contained her driver's license. Although in the picture she'd had longer hair and had been without makeup, it was still easy for the officials to match the picture with the dead girl.

They'd caught a break ten minutes ago, when Wendy Robertson had walked in after seeing the news story about Margie's murder. She'd indicated to the desk cop that she wanted to talk to the detective in charge of the case. Tyler now sat across the table from Wendy, a mousy blonde with faint acne scars.

"I left town Monday morning," she explained as she twisted a damp tissue in her hands. "I drove to Parsons, Kansas, to spend the week with my parents. I got back this morning and thumbed through some of the newspapers, and that's where I saw the story about Margie—" She broke off as her eyes began to fill with tears.

"You and Margie were friends?" Tyler asked.

She dabbed at her eyes with the tissue. "I was probably one of her only friends. Margie is . . . was painfully shy."

"And how did you know her?"

Once again she twisted the tissue in her lap. "She worked at the same place where I worked for a couple of months."

"And what place is that?" Tyler asked.

"The Price Chopper supermarket at Oak and Barry roads. I work as a cashier and Margie worked in the deli."

"Did she quit or get fired?"

"She quit. She wanted to find a job where she wouldn't have to work with the public so much. Like I mentioned before, she was really, really shy."

"When was the last time you saw Margie?" The conversation was being taped, but Tyler still took the time between each question to take notes.

"Last Saturday night." Again tears began to form in her hazel eyes. "I forced her to go out with me. I told her she'd spent way too long cooped up in her apartment and she needed to get out." A sob escaped her. "If I hadn't insisted, then she wouldn't be dead."

She began to cry in earnest then. Deep, wrenching sobs tore from her as Tyler got up from the table and got her a glass of water.

He placed the water in front of her, shoved the tissue box closer, then waited. Fortunately it didn't take long for her to pull herself together once again.

"I'm sorry," she said, then blew her nose and grabbed a handful of fresh tissues.

"So, you and Margie went out last Saturday night. Where did you go?"

"We went to Red Lobster for dinner; then I talked her into going to Rum Island." Tyler frowned and looked at her blankly. "It's a brand-new club off Vivian Road."

"What time did you arrive there?"

She took a sip of the water before answering. "We left Red Lobster about eight and met at Rum Island right after that."

"You drove separate cars?"

She nodded. "We always drove separately, because we didn't live that close to each other. It was easier that way for both of us."

"What time did you leave Rum Island?"

She frowned. "It must have been just after midnight."

"And you left together?"

"We did. We said good-bye in the parking lot, and she headed toward her car and I went to mine."

They went over all the details a second time; then Tyler thanked her for coming in and walked her to the door. When she'd gone he walked back down the hall to the small room that had been declared the war room specifically to deal with this and the Albright murder.

Nobody else was in the room. Everyone on his team had either gone to grab a quick lunch or were out in the field. Tyler sank down at the table and stared at the photographs of the two women, Kerry Albright in her bridal finery and Margie Francis in her flapper costume.

Costumes. That was what they were, and there was no doubt in his mind that the same unsub had committed both crimes. Although nobody had said the term, all of the team recognized that they were probably hunting a serial killer.

Tyler rubbed a hand across his forehead and opened the files that held all the reports they'd gotten back so far on both victims. He'd read them at least a hundred times already and knew that before they found the killer he'd read them another thousand times.

Someplace in the crime scene photographs or in the forensics was a clue to the killer, but damned if Tyler had been able to find it yet.

They now knew that Margie had made it home from Rum Island last Saturday night. Her car had been parked in the lot of the apartment complex where she lived. But he doubted that she'd ever made it into her apartment that night.

The coroner had been fairly sure that she'd died sometime between Saturday night and Sunday afternoon. But her body hadn't been found until Tuesday. That meant somebody had kept her for two days after her death. And in those two days the unsub had dressed her, cut and styled her hair and done her makeup. She'd been tended to after her death with loving care.

He'd never admit it to anyone else, but it scared him that the perp had managed to kill two and leave nothing behind. It scared him that there had only been a week between the two murders.

Their killer was not only highly organized; he was also apparently on a short timetable, which left the team little time to find him before he killed again.

As he stared at the reports, his eyes blurred. Exhaustion weighted him down like a pile of bricks on his shoulders.

Since Margie had been found he didn't think he'd had more than a total of five hours of sleep. Even for him that was far too little. Someplace in the back of his mind he knew he couldn't keep up the pace, that if he wasn't careful he'd crash and burn and be of no use to anyone.

"Hey, boss," Jennifer said as she entered the room, the scent of fried onions and cigarette smoke clinging to her.

"Let me guess: Sonic lunch and a sneak smoke after."

She scowled at him. "Sometimes you're scary."

"Nobody has onions on their burgers like Sonic, and no matter how much you spray that cheap perfume you wear, that smoke stays with you."

She threw herself into the chair opposite him. "Okay, so I confess I haven't quite managed to quit."

"At the moment your sucking on the end of a cigarette is the last thing I'm worried about. I now know where Margie Francis spent the last night of her life."

"Where's that?"

"A bar called Rum Island."

"Great place," Jennifer replied. "They've got the whole thatched-roof/beach thing going on."

Tyler stared at her. It never failed to surprise him how many places his partner hung out, how many people she knew. "Is there any bar in town that you haven't visited?"

She leaned back and eyed him with a touch of wry humor. "I'm single, Tyler. I have a life outside of this place, unlike some people I know."

"I have a life outside of this. In fact, I was supposed to go to a block party tomorrow with a beautiful woman, but it looks like I'll have to cancel."

"Don't you dare," Jennifer exclaimed as she leaned forward. "Tyler, you're the first one to tell all of us that we need downtime. You've been here almost around the clock since Tuesday. You look like hell, and I can see cranky starting to show on your face."

"I don't get cranky," he protested. She raised an eyebrow. "Okay, maybe I get a little cranky at times," he conceded. "Finding the creep responsible for these deaths would go a long way toward keeping me from getting cranky."

"You know we'll get him," Jennifer exclaimed with the bravado of a young detective who so far had worked only one major case in her short career. "We got David Abbott last winter, didn't we?"

"He wasn't a serial killer," Tyler replied.

"He killed three people and tried to kill Vanessa Abbott."

"Yeah, but he had a specific personal reason for wanting those people dead. He thought they were all in some way responsible for his brother's suicide."

For a moment Tyler allowed himself to think about the old case. Vanessa Abbott had been a young widow of a talented artist who had jumped off a bridge into the Missouri River. His body hadn't been found after his suicide, and two years after his jump off the bridge people who had been in his life had begun to be murdered.

At each of the crime scenes was a slash of red paint that had been his artistic signature, making both his widow and Tyler wonder if somehow he'd managed to survive the jump. As it turned out it was his brother who had committed the crimes.

Tyler looked at the photographs on the bulletin board. "This is altogether another kind of animal. So far we haven't been able to establish any kind of a connection between the two victims, and I don't think we're going to find one."

"So you think they were randomly chosen?"

Tyler leaned back in his chair, fighting a bone-deep weariness as his gaze remained on the crime scene photos. "Oh, no, they were specifically chosen by the killer because physically they match whatever sick fantasy he's playing out. But I seriously doubt if either victim knew the killer."

"Which makes our job even more difficult," she observed. She followed his gaze to the board. "At least they weren't raped."

"What we need to figure out is what a bride and a flapper have in common, and what they might mean to our unsub."

"Thank God we've managed to keep the details of their appearances away from the press," she said as she looked at him once again. "That creep Reuben has been hanging out, trying to get somebody to confirm the rumors he's heard about their odd clothing."

At that moment several of the other detectives came in with reports to discuss and notes to compare. They worked until nearly midnight; then Tyler headed to Rum Island to question the people who worked there.

He stayed until closing time, flashing a photo of Margie and asking anyone if they remembered her being in the bar the previous Saturday night.

Nobody remembered seeing her, and given what Wendy had said about her extreme shyness, Tyler wasn't surprised. Disappointed, but not surprised.

He headed back to the station and stayed until almost noon. Then, recognizing that Jennifer had been right—that he needed to take a break before he crashed completely—he headed home.

A long, hot shower did nothing to quiet his mind. All the details of the murders whirled around and around, puzzle pieces seeking a fit, rhymes with no reason.

He tumbled into bed and desperately sought sleep, but the faces of the two women flashed again and again in his head. Kerry, who had loved to party and had an endless supply of friends and acquaintances. She'd loved animals and had volunteered two weekends a month to work the malls with an Adopt-A-Dog foundation. Kerry had been addicted to chocolate, laughter and clubbing.

Margie's shyness had been torture for her; the evidence of that had been in the poetry they had found in her apartment, poetry about isolation and loneliness. She'd been an old-movie buff, and he could easily imagine her curled up on her sofa, a bowl of popcorn in her lap as she watched *Gone With the Wind* for the fiftieth time.

His need to solve the crime grew exponentially as he learned the details that made the victims more real to him. They became like family members who needed his help to rest in peace.

As he finally drifted off to sleep he worried that if they didn't get a break soon, there would be more victims.

Chapter 11

Annalise had half expected a phone call from Tyler canceling their date. It didn't come. She let herself get excited about seeing him again.

She drove into Danika's subdivision, squinting against the bright sunshine. The rain had left on Tuesday night and ushered hot air flooding in from the South. The temperature today was supposed to reach near ninety.

A perfect day for a block party, she thought as she passed Danika's neat little ranch house. She'd dressed for the occasion, wearing a new sundress in a bright turquoise and matching sequined sandals. In a small tote bag she had sunblock, several bottles of water and a visor. The only thing she had forgotten was her sunglasses.

She couldn't remember when she'd looked forward to an afternoon more than she was looking forward to this one. It had been a week of small frustrations. The last of the hair order to finish the Birthday Bonnie dolls had come in, and it was the wrong color. One of her most valuable seamstresses had decided to retire, and Danika had been missing in action for the last two days.

A meeting with her accountant had let her know that profits were lower in the last six months than they'd ever been. And she'd had her doll nightmare twice in as many nights.

Today she was putting all the stresses, all thoughts of dolls and bookkeeping and work pressures behind her. Her stomach tingled as she approached Tyler's house. She pulled into the driveway of a neat white ranch with hunter green shutters.

The lawn looked freshly mowed and still retained the bright green of spring grass. A leafy oak tree stood in the front yard, casting welcome shade over half the sidewalk. As she got out of the car her stomach again danced and jumped with nervous tension.

She was anxious to see him. It was ridiculous how much he'd been in her thoughts during the past week. She'd be talking to a distributor on the phone and suddenly get a vision of his sexy smile in her head. Or she'd be brainstorming new hairstyles with Ben and remember the taste of Tyler's kiss.

She shut off the car engine, grabbed her tote and stepped out of the car, and in typical feminine fashion had a flash of panic that she was overdressed. She should have worn shorts and a shirt.

Laughing at the self-consciousness that gripped her, she walked up to the door and knocked with a confidence she didn't feel.

He opened it immediately, as if he'd been standing on the other side just waiting for her knock.

"Hi." His smile was warm as he opened the door to allow her entry. "As usual, you look terrific."

She stepped inside and smiled. "Thanks. You look pretty terrific yourself." And he did. He was in a pair of beige shorts that showed off his long, tanned legs and a short-sleeved white and beige dress shirt that fit across his broad shoulders as if tailor-made.

"I figured I'd better clean up better than usual to make nice with my neighbors. Come on in. Remember you promised not to laugh at my awful decorating."

She wasn't sure what to expect, but the living room looked perfectly presentable to her. Neutral beige carpeting matched the walls. The sofa and chair were a dark green, the coffee table a solid-looking mahogany and a television stood on a stand in one corner.

If she were to make an assessment of the space it would be that the person who lived here didn't spend much time in it. There were no books, no stereo, no pictures on the walls. It was as impersonal as a lobby in a motel.

"I don't know what you're talking about," she said. "It looks fine to me. A little plain, but there's nothing wrong with that."

"You haven't seen the worst of it. Come on into the kitchen and I'll fix us something cold to drink before we head outside again."

She stopped short in the kitchen doorway and bit her bottom lip as she saw half-painted walls in the ugliest colors she could ever imagine. "Oh, my. This is . . . interesting." She noted the holes in the wall. "I see you're fond of the early demolition style."

He grinned. "Actually, those holes are compliments of my last girlfriend. They were her reply when I told her my opinion of her color scheme."

"Did all your old girlfriends have bad tempers? Because if you like dangerous women I'm afraid you're going to find me pretty boring."

His eyes smoked as his gaze slid from the top of her head down to the tips of her manicured toes. When he raised his gaze to meet hers, a sexy smile once again curved his lips, and her body temperature spiked by at least ten degrees. "I don't know; you look pretty dangerous to me in that dress. You look like the kind of woman who could make a man forget his name."

The air between them sparked with sexual tension and dried Annalise's mouth. For just one insane moment she wanted to tell him to blow off the block party and instead take her to bed and make love to her for the rest of the evening.

She didn't. Instead she released a small, unsteady laugh. "And I have a feeling you're a man who would never let go of reason long enough to forget your name, and I'd love something cold to drink."

That seemed to dissipate some of the heated tension in the air, at least for the time being. "Have a seat," he said, and gestured to the table as he went to the refrigerator. "We have about a half an hour before we need to walk down the block." She sank down at the table. "I have cold beer, soda and milk."

"A soda would be great. Diet Coke if you have it." As he fixed their drinks she looked around the kitchen with interest.

Aside from the awful paint it was a nice room, big, with a bank of windows that would allow in the early morning sun. The countertops were white and held only a coffeemaker. Again the impersonal air the room contained—as if nobody really lived here—struck her.

"You must not spend much time here," she said as he joined her at the table.

"I don't. Looks like a motel, doesn't it? Stacy—that was my last girlfriend—couldn't wait to get her hands on things, to make it feel like a real home, she said." He grimaced. "Unfortunately, her idea of what a home looks like was very different from mine. I'm not into walls painted the color of bodily fluids."

Annalise laughed. "But it's a nice kitchen, big and airy."

"That's one of the things that attracted me to it when I bought it. I have lots of fond memories of the kitchen in my parents' home. We spent a lot of time there. I wanted a kitchen like that in my own home, where a family could come together."

"So, you want a family?"

He shrugged. "At one time I thought I did. But it's tough to make a family when you barely have time for a girlfriend. Besides, I've already told you what terrible boyfriend material I am. Imagine how horrible I'd be as a husband." He paused to take a sip of his soda, then asked, "What about you? You want a family?"

"I don't think about it much," she replied. "My mother always taught me not to depend on a man to fulfill me, that I can be my own best friend. I always figured if fate decides I get a family, that's wonderful, but if it doesn't happen I'm okay with that, too."

"It seems like the older I get, all the women I meet talk about their biological clocks ticking inside. You don't have one?"

She laughed. "If I have one it's ticking very softly and not bothering me a bit."

"That's a change." He leaned back in his chair, and once again his gaze seemed to caress rather than to look at her. "I had seriously considered canceling the plans for today."

Her heart dropped. Maybe he wasn't as interested in her as she was in him? "And why is that? You didn't like my picnic lunch?" She was glad her tone remained light.

"No, I liked it very much." A shadow passed across his face, momentarily darkening the gray of his eyes and tightening his features. "I'm in the middle of two big cases and wasn't sure I could in good conscience take the time off. But I'm glad I did. I think you're just what I need right now, Annalise Blakely."

Her heart fluttered. If he asked her to strip naked and lie down on the kitchen table at that moment, she'd seriously consider it. "I've certainly been looking forward to today." She gave him a teasing grin. "You did mention there would be ice cream."

"And here I thought it was probably my natural charm that had you anticipating the day."

"That, too," she admitted with a small smile.

Once again the tension was back between them, a thick, heady energy like she'd never experienced before. He took another drink of his soda, and she wondered if his mouth was as dry as hers.

When he lowered his glass back to the table, he

looked at her intently. "We'd better get out of here
before I try to take advantage of you."

So, he felt it, too. She was grateful that it wasn't
just her. "We'd better get out of here before I *let* you
take advantage of me," she replied, and nearly shivered at the look he cast her.

"Why don't you leave your things here? There's
a cabana set up and plenty of shade. All we need to
bring are chairs."

She left her bag and followed him outside to the
garage, where he opened the door and retrieved
two fold-up deck chairs. "Want me to carry one of
those?" she offered.

"Nah, it's a man thing. I'll carry the chairs."

They fell into step together. As they walked down
the sidewalk he talked about his neighbors.

"The Walkers live there. They have two little
kids, and he works for Kansas City Power and
Light. They like to barbecue, and sometimes bring
me ribs they've cooked." He pointed to the house
on the opposite side of the street. "And the Ander-
sons live there. She's a nurse, and whenever I run
into her she lectures me about the importance of
getting enough sleep and eating right."

"Sounds like you have good neighbors," she said,
surprised at a small sense of wistfulness that suddenly reared its head.

"They're good people," he replied. "What about
you? You have good neighbors?"

"Not like this. There's a faint sense of community
where I live. People meet in the park and small-talk
but nobody brings me food or gives me advice. I
guess it's just different living in a neighborhood like
this."

"I think this is an unusual neighborhood. The president of our association plans lots of community events and encourages all of us to attend. I try to go whenever I can."

They followed the sidewalk into a cul-de-sac that had been blocked off from car traffic with wooden sawhorses. A large bright blue cabana stretched between two houses, and a refreshment truck gave off the scents of hot dogs and popcorn.

"Quite a fancy setup," she exclaimed.

"Frank Knight owns the hot-dog stand. He works it downtown during lunch hours and always donates his time and supplies for these shindigs."

As they approached everyone greeted Tyler, and for the next fifteen minutes he introduced Annalise to his neighbors. By the time they finally sat down with glasses of tea in their hands, her head spun with the new names and faces of the people she had met.

They sat with a couple Tyler introduced as Cindy and Dave Swanson. They had been chatting for about fifteen minutes when Cindy snapped her fingers. "I knew I'd seen you before. You're Annalise of Blakely Dolls, right?"

"Yes, I am."

"I saw you on some noon news show a couple of weeks ago. Tanya, my little girl—she has one of your dolls. Of course, we don't let her play with it; it's way too pretty and fragile for that," Cindy exclaimed. "She's nine. She isn't much into dolls anymore, anyway."

"What kinds of toys does she like?" Annalise asked.

"To our delight, she likes anything that's educational."

Before Annalise could reply another couple joined them, and the conversation turned to other topics. At five it was announced that the ice cream was being served in the kitchen of one of the houses, and together Annalise and Tyler went inside with the others.

"I think I've died and gone to heaven," Annalise said as she surveyed the table. There were three kinds of ice cream and dozens of toppings, including nuts, chocolate chips and whipped cream.

As she and Tyler created their sundaes, she was intensely aware of his nearness and the overwhelmingly clean male scent that emanated from him. He touched her frequently, little casual touches that stoked a simmering burn inside her.

What was wrong with her? She knew little about him, had shared no real meaningful conversations with him, and yet felt as if she knew everything about him that was important.

It was obvious he was liked by his neighbors. She knew he was committed to his work, and both those things went a long way in telling her what kind of man he was.

Besides, he'd chosen chocolate ice cream and had doused it with chocolate syrup, just like her. Now, that was a man after her heart.

The mood was lighthearted, and laughter filled the air. Children played tag and raced around, chastised by both parents and friends when they got out of hand.

There was no way she could compare her friendly talks in the park to the camaraderie that existed among these neighbors. There was a sense of genuine caring here that she'd never experienced before.

The festivities lingered until after dusk, and it was almost nine when they walked back to Tyler's place beneath a sky of starlight and a moon that looked so plump it threatened to burst.

"Come in for coffee?" he asked.

She knew with a woman's instinct that he wasn't just inviting her in for a cup of Maxwell House, and that tingle in her stomach reappeared.

"Coffee sounds wonderful," she replied.

They went back into his kitchen, where she sat at the table while he filled the coffeemaker and then joined her as they waited for it to brew.

"My neighbors liked you," he said.

"I like all of them," she replied.

"Jim Walker pulled me aside to let me know that if I let you get away he'd never bring me another slab of ribs again."

"Hmm, that's a pretty serious incentive to see me again."

He flashed her a teasing grin. "Yeah, I'd do just about anything for Jim's ribs."

The coffee finished, and he got up to pour them each a cup. "Cream or sugar?" he asked.

"No, black is fine."

"How about we take these into the living room?" He carried the cups and she followed him. He set the cups on the coffee table; then they sat side by side on the sofa. The tension between them was like a third person in the room.

"I had a wonderful time," she said.

"It was fun, wasn't it? I needed some time with

decent people to remind me that they exist." Again that shadow darkened his eyes. "Sometimes I get so immersed in my work I forget how much good there is in the world."

"It must be hard. What made you decide to become a cop?"

He reached out and picked up his coffee cup. "When I was fifteen I found a dead body. It was a man who'd been shot and left in the woods near where we lived."

"That must have been horrible," she exclaimed.

"It was," he agreed, and paused to take a sip of his coffee. "But as traumatizing as it was, when the cops arrived and began to investigate I found their work fascinating, and it was then that I decided I wanted to do what they did. What about you? Did you always want to make dolls?"

"I don't remember ever having much of a choice. My mother started training me to take over her business before I could walk. My birthday parties were really marketing meetings for her. She'd gather all my little school friends and ask them about their favorite dolls and take notes."

"And you like what you do?" He set his cup back down.

"I don't think much about whether I like it or not. I just know it's where my mother would want me to be, and I can't in good conscience walk away from her dream. At the moment I'm concerned, because the dolls have lost a lot of their popularity and the business is struggling like it never has before."

"I'm sure you'll manage to turn it all around." He reached out and brushed a strand of her hair off her shoulder. His hand lingered just a moment too long against her bare skin. "You know I didn't invite you in because I wanted a cup of coffee."

His touch sparked a glowing heat inside her. "Oh, no? Then why did you invite me in?" Her heart beat so strong with anticipation, she wondered if he could hear it.

"Because the whole time we were sitting and talking to people and eating ice cream, all I could think about was kissing you."

"Then maybe you should. I wouldn't want to keep you from doing something you want to do."

He didn't need a second invitation. He pulled her into his arms and took her mouth with his. He kissed her with slow determination, with an intensity that swept every thought from her head.

His tongue met hers as his hands rubbed up and down the back of her dress and onto the bare skin of her shoulders. She was lost in him, lost to the taste of him, the feel of his broad chest against her breasts and the touch of his hands against her flesh.

She'd simmered with desire for most of the afternoon, and now it flared out of control. She wanted him. She didn't want just a kiss, a simple touch. She wanted him naked against her.

If she'd been thinking rationally, the depth of her desire for him would have stunned her. But she wasn't thinking rationally. She wasn't thinking at all. Sheer emotion and physical yearning drove her, and she allowed these basic instincts to overwhelm her.

She tangled her hands in his hair, loving the feel of the silky strands against her fingers. When his mouth once again found hers there was a raging hunger there, and she welcomed it.

When the second kiss ended, he raised his head to look at her, his eyes smoky with intent. "I want you, Annalise. I want to make love to you."

"I'd like that," she said simply.

He stood and held out his hand to her. His eyes held enough heat to melt the clothes right off her. Heart crashing against her ribs, she stood and took his hand. Neither of them spoke a word as they walked down the hallway and into the master bedroom.

A small lamp glowed on the nightstand, but Annalise got no other impression of the room. Her total focus was on Tyler.

"I want you in my bed, Annalise."

The words shot a shiver of delight up her spine. "I want to be in your bed," she replied, surprised to find herself half-breathless.

He smiled then, a smile of wicked sensuality and promise, then pulled his shirt off and flung it carelessly onto a chair nearby. Instantly he pulled her back into his arms, holding her so intimately against him she could feel that he was already aroused.

"I've been spending far too much time lately thinking about you," he said.

"Really? And what have you been thinking about?" She raised her hands to his bare shoulders, loving the feel of the muscles beneath his warm skin.

"I've been wondering how you taste right here." He leaned forward and placed his lips against the sensitive skin just below her ear. A sigh of sheer pleasure escaped her lips.

"I've also wondered how silky and soft your legs are," he whispered, and at the same time one of his hands slid from her knee up her inner thigh, stopping just short of touching her intimately.

"And I've spent all evening long wondering how you'd look without this dress." He reached behind her and unzipped the back of her dress. When it was unfastened he pushed it off her shoulders and it fell to the floor.

He stepped back and stared at her, his gaze lingering first on her lacy turquoise bra, then on her matching panties. Her nipples hardened beneath the heat of his gaze.

"I knew you'd look amazing." He unfastened the button at the waist of his shorts.

Annalise's heart beat fast as her body ached with the need to be touched—not just by his gaze, but by his hands and lips. As he stepped out of his shorts she took off her bra and panties, and by that time he was as naked as she.

Once again he took her by the hand, this time to lead her to the side of the bed. He kissed her again, and there was no mistaking his hunger as he took full possession of her mouth.

His tongue battled with hers as his hands slid down her back to cup her buttocks and pull her against his hardness. She moved her hips against him, weak-kneed at the contact.

"If we keep this up we'll never make it to the bed," he groaned against her mouth.

She laughed as he released her, half-giddy with her own desire for him.

Then they were in the bed, arms and legs tangled as they kissed with a fervor that left her breathless. As he kissed her, his hands cupped her breasts, thumbs raking her erect nipples until she wanted to scream with pleasure.

His hardness pressed against her thigh, and she wanted—no, needed—to touch him. She reached down and wrapped her fingers around the length of him. He gasped against her mouth. She stroked him with her hand, and he froze against her.

"Annalise, honey, you might not want to do that, or we're going to be done here way before I want us to be," he said, his voice thick with emotion.

She laughed. "We certainly don't want that." She pulled her hand away and instead kissed the underside of his jaw, loving the slightly rough feel of his five-o'clock shadow against her cheek.

She didn't want things to go too fast. She wanted to take time to explore him, to learn what touches he liked, what made him moan and tightened his muscles.

He seemed to have the same desire. He found each and every place that made her sigh and shiver with wild delight. When he cupped her between the legs, his fingers dancing against her, the tension inside her built to explosive levels.

When she thought she couldn't stand it any longer, when she thought that if he didn't take her she'd scream, he rolled over and grabbed a condom from the drawer in the nightstand. Her breaths came in pants as he put on the condom, then rose up on top of her.

She raked her hands down his back as he slid into her moist heat as if he belonged there. She wrapped her legs around his back to hold him tight against her, inside her.

"God, you feel so good I'm almost afraid to move," he whispered into her ear.

"You feel amazing, and I'll kill you if you don't move," she replied.

He laughed, a husky, rough sound that thrilled her; then he moved his hips, stroking in and out of her with a slowness that sent electric sensation through her entire body.

Within minutes he increased his speed, and she arched her hips to meet each of his frantic thrusts. Wild with abandon, she raked her fingernails down his back, grabbed his butt, and when her climax finally came it shuddered through her with the force of an earthquake.

His release followed almost immediately, and he stiffened against her and cried out her name. He collapsed to the side of her, his breathing ragged as she gasped for air, waiting for her heartbeat to return to a more normal pace.

"Wow," he finally said, and propped himself up on his side to look at her.

"You can say that again," she replied.

"Wow."

She laughed, then for the first time noticed the wallpaper border that stretched partially around the ceiling of the room. "You have fairies on your ceiling."

He winced. "I was hoping you wouldn't notice."

"I guess the fairy wallpaper wasn't your idea."

He reached out and traced a finger down the side of her cheek. "What self-respecting homicide cop would put fairies in his bedroom?"

"You have a point there." She gazed at him

somberly. "I don't often fall into bed with a man as quickly as I've done with you."

"You don't have to tell me that. Danika told me you weren't a party girl who got into bed with a guy easily."

She smiled. "I just didn't want you to think that I'm easy."

"I don't think you're easy. I think you're pretty terrific."

She laughed again. "Ah, spoken like a satisfied male."

"Trust me, my attraction to you isn't just physical. I like you, Annalise. I like you a lot." He frowned. "And I think maybe you came into my life at one of the worst possible times."

"You mean because of the cases you're working on?"

He nodded. "I have two dead women, and I need to find the bastard who killed them, and that requires long hours and leaves me little free time."

She ran her fingers lightly over his chest. "Then I'll take whatever little free time you have to give me."

He raised a dark brow. "Most women wouldn't be satisfied with that."

"Then I'm not most women," she replied. "I have a pretty full life myself, Tyler. I'm not going to sit by the phone waiting for you to call. I have a business to run and a half brother who wants to get to know me better. I'd love to spend more time with you whenever you have it, but I'm not going to pressure you for something you can't give."

"I think I've died and gone to heaven."

"Trust me, I'm no angel," she exclaimed. At that moment the phone rang. "You need to get that?"

"Nah, I'll let the machine pick it up. If it was work they would call my cell number."

There was a moment of silence; then a female voice came from the answering machine on the nightstand. "Tyler, this is your mother. You might not remember me, but I'm the one who gave birth to you after twenty-three hours of unbelievable pain. It's been over a week since your father and I have heard from you. A phone call to let us know you're still alive would be nice."

"Sounds like you're in trouble," Annalise said when the machine shut off.

"No more than usual. She pulls out the painful-birth guilt on a regular basis when she hasn't heard from me often enough."

"So you're close with your parents?"

"Very."

Annalise sat up. "I need to get home."

He grabbed her arm. "You could stay the night." He dropped his hold on her as she slid out of bed and stood.

"That's a sweet offer, but I don't want to get used to sleeping in any bed I might eventually get kicked out of," she said with a smile.

"Only a fool would kick you out of bed," he replied.

After they dressed she grabbed her bag, and he walked her to the front door.

"I feel like a heel letting you drive home alone," he said as he took her into his arms.

"Don't; I'll be fine. I had a wonderful time, Tyler."

"So did I." He held her tight for a long moment. "Just being with you pulls me back from the bad places my work takes me." He kissed her softly, tenderly; then he released her. "Call me when you get home? Just to let me know you got there safely?"

"I will."

He walked her to her car and delivered one last searing kiss; then she left. As she drove home she felt that for the first time all week the stars had aligned in her favor. Her body still tingled from their lovemaking, and already she looked forward to seeing him again.

This could work out to be the best relationship she'd ever had. The sex was terrific, and Tyler seemed to be the kind of man who wouldn't want a deeply intense emotional bond, something Annalise wasn't at all sure she was capable of giving.

It had been a wonderful day, but she wondered where Danika was. She'd hoped to see her friend at the party. She hadn't heard from her since they'd had their talk on Monday. It was uncharacteristic of Danika to stay out of touch for so long.

The clock on the dashboard read ten fifty-three as she parked her car in her usual place in front of her building. Despite her mild concern about Danika, her heart felt lighter than it had in months.

Not only was Tyler smart and fun, but just thinking about their lovemaking curled her toes and made her heart race. Hopefully he'd been telling the truth when he said he wanted to spend more time with her.

A smile curved her lips as she headed around the building to the front. She was almost to her door when she sensed a presence behind her. She whirled around to see Max.

"Max! You scared me."

He was obviously already drunk. His breath

reeked of alcohol, and his eyes were glazed and red. "Anna . . . Annalise." Her name slurred from his lips. "Gotta tell you."

"Tell me what?" She pulled her keys from her purse, assuming he was going ask her for money again. "Are the Dumpsters bad tonight?"

"No. No. No." He shook his head from side to side in a frenzy, then staggered back a step as he nearly lost his balance. He frowned as if he'd momentarily forgotten what he wanted to tell her. He seemed agitated as his gaze shot first over his right shoulder, then over his left. When he looked at her again his eyes were filled with fear.

"What, Max? What is it?" As ridiculous as it was, something about his demeanor stoked a quiet fire of nervous tension in her.

"It's the devil," he said.

Annalise relaxed once again. Poor man—he was suffering from some sort of frightening delusion. "Max, it's okay. There's no devil around here."

This time his head nodded up and down, fast and frantic. "Yes, yes, there is. I gotta tell you. You gotta know."

"Know what, Max?"

His eyes widened once again. "That the devil is after you. He's after you, Annalise."

Chapter 12

"I know you've all been eagerly awaiting the announcement of our next project," Annalise said to her staff on Monday afternoon. "And I think you're going to be shocked by my decision."

"Let me guess," Ben said. "We're doing a bald biker doll with leather chaps."

Annalise laughed. "No, we aren't doing anything that drastic, but we are going in a totally different direction. First of all, our new doll isn't going to be porcelain; it's going to be plastic."

"Blasphemy!" Ben exclaimed. "Your mother is probably rolling over in her grave."

Annalise refused to allow his words to deter her from the decision she'd made in the middle of the night on Saturday. It had taken her hours to get to sleep after Max's startling announcement, and she'd used those hours of sleeplessness to realize the immediate future of Blakely Dolls.

"My mother isn't here," she said firmly. "And as you all know, sales have been steadily declining over the last couple of years. If we don't make some changes we're all going to be out of our jobs."

"So what's this new doll?" Sammy asked. Sammy had been one of the first people Lillian Blakely had hired when she'd no longer been able to do all the sewing herself. He'd been with Blakely Dolls for years.

"I was at a block party on Saturday and met a woman who had a young girl." Annalise tried to keep her mind focused on business and not thinking about Tyler. "Anyway, this woman told me her daughter had a Blakely doll, but she didn't play with it."

"Our dolls were never meant to be played with. They were collector items to be on display," Jennifer Welk, one of the production people, interjected.

"I know. And we're going to change that with this new doll. We'll call it a special edition, and she's going to be geared toward girls five to twelve years old. One of the things this mother told me was that her daughter was really into educational toys. With this new doll, we're going to address the needs of kids who like to learn."

Annalise opened her sketch pad to show her concept of the product. "We're going to call her Anniversary Annalise, a special doll commemorating thirty years of Blakely Dolls. She'll not only have three complete outfits, but will also speak three different languages."

A stunned silence greeted her words. Was the brainstorm that had sounded so promising in the middle of Saturday night nothing more than a stupid idea?

"I think it's a great idea," Jennifer said, breaking the silence. "What languages is she going to speak?"

"English, French and Spanish," Annalise replied,

relaxing as she felt the acceptance of the small group of staff. "And I know I'm going to be asking a lot of all of you, but I want the doll to come with two extra sets of clothing, one a traditional Spanish and the other something that looks French."

"What about hair?" Ben asked.

"I was thinking maybe shoulder-length for our American girl, a long luxury fall for the Spanish and maybe detachable braids for the French version."

Ben frowned. "I don't know. It's sure a big change. I'm not sure change is good. Eventually sales will increase."

"Change is vital if we intend to stay in business," Annalise replied.

"If we just stay the course things will turn around. They always do," he protested with a stubborn jut to his chin.

Annalise was surprised by Ben's negative reaction to her new idea. He'd always been one who supported her no matter what her decisions.

The rest of her team were all taking notes, and despite Ben's reluctance to embrace the idea, Annalise's confidence began to rise. "I know I'm asking a lot from you all, especially you, Sammy. I'm asking you to produce three outfits per doll in the same time you normally sew one. Ben, that means we need three hairstyles in the same time you've been doing one. Hire whatever help you need to get the job done, and I'll have the final sketches of what I want each one to look like by the end of the day."

The meeting progressed better than Annalise had anticipated, as they all seemed receptive to her new ideas. By the time the meeting broke up she was feeling more than a little optimistic that by Christmas-time they would turn around the declining sales.

Needing a break from the people and the place and having not yet eaten lunch, she decided to go to Joey's and order a salad to go.

It was another unusually warm day, but a slight breeze kept it from being intolerable. As she walked across the park she couldn't help but think of Tyler. He'd called her yesterday from the police station. He'd told her he'd had a minute to himself and was thinking of her.

Their short conversation had held a new intimacy, and when the call had ended it had been an hour before she'd stopped smiling.

When she entered the restaurant the first thing she noticed was that Joey wasn't the one to greet her. Instead a tall young man she'd never met welcomed her. She told him she was ordering to go, then asked him about the chubby owner.

"Where's Joey? I don't think I ever remember a time when he wasn't here on a Monday."

"He's taking a couple of days off. I'm Mark, his assistant. I'll be taking his place for the next few days."

"He certainly deserves a little break," Annalise said. "No matter what time of the day or night I come in here he's working."

"That's Joey," Mark replied. "He's a driven man."

They small-talked until her salad was ready; then she left and headed to the park, deciding to eat outside before heading back into the shop to continue the finalization of the new doll.

As she approached the bench where she usually

sat to eat lunch, she saw John Malcolm already sitting there. "Hey, John," she greeted him.

"Afternoon, Annalise." He gestured toward the other end of the bench. "Going to join me?"

"I think I will." She sat and opened her lunch sack. "I decided I needed a little break from the store and thought I'd eat lunch out here."

"I just finished my lunch," he replied. "In another hour or two I think it's going to get too hot to be outside."

Annalise opened her salad container and grabbed the plastic fork. "I think you're right. It's way too early in the summer for us to be having such hot days."

He smiled at her. "We'll be wishing for these days come January."

She laughed. "You're absolutely right. So, how's the maintenance business?"

"Nothing ever changes there. People complain about their water pressure, their furnaces or air conditioners, and I try to make it right for them. What about the doll business? How's it going?"

"Not bad." She speared a piece of boiled egg.

"I need to come in and buy one of your dolls. I have a little girl who has a birthday coming up."

She looked at him in surprise. "I didn't realize you had kids."

"She's not mine. She's the daughter of a friend of mine. She's going to be seven, and I figured one of your dolls would make a nice present."

She grinned. "I'm certainly the wrong person to ask about that. I'm definitely prejudiced. But if you want to come in later this afternoon, I'd be more than happy to help you find something special."

"Will do. And now I'd better get back to the building. My lunchtime is officially over." He stood. "How about around four?"

"That would be fine, John," she agreed.

She watched as he walked toward his building. John wasn't a big man, but she'd seen him enough times in a T-shirt to know he was as solid as a rock, with muscles that looked like they saw regular use.

Her mind suddenly filled with thoughts of Tyler's muscles, sleek and firm and amazingly sexy. The thought of their lovemaking raised her internal temperature a couple of degrees. The fact that she also liked him out of bed was a definite bonus.

When he'd called they'd made tentative plans for dinner Thursday night. She'd offered to cook for him at her place, and already she couldn't wait to see him again.

There was nothing better than the first flush of a new relationship. She intended to enjoy every minute of it, because she knew there was no way the wonderful, delicious feeling she now had could possibly last.

She finished her salad, then returned to work. The afternoon flew by as they all brainstormed outfits and talked about potential problems. Annalise spent a lot of time on the phone, talking with the manufacturer responsible for the doll parts she'd used in the past.

Now that her decision had been made she was eager to begin production. At four John came into the store, looking ill at ease as he studied the different dolls that they had to sell.

"This is our most recent one," Annalise said as she showed him the Birthday Bonnie. "And since you said it was for a birthday, she would be very appropriate."

He frowned and walked in front of the display case. "I don't know, the Belinda the Bride doll sure is pretty. Don't all little girls like bride dolls?" he asked.

"That one's quite a bit more expensive," she explained. "It's a collector's item."

"Okay, then I'll take one of those birthday dolls," John said.

As he paid and she wrapped up the doll for him, they chatted about little girls and birthday parties, and she told him about the new doll that should be on the market just in time for Christmas.

"Three languages," John mused. "Maybe I should buy one of those for myself. I've always wanted to learn how to speak French."

She laughed. "You'd probably do better taking a class or buying one of those CDs that teach you the language. The doll isn't going to address the entire French language."

When John left Annalise went to the back area, where everyone worked in quiet concentration. The next few days would be busy ones, as she and Sammy brainstormed the best materials and colors for the outfits he and his team would begin sewing. She hoped to have production up and running on the new doll by the end of the week.

By six o'clock everyone had gone home, and Annalise was in the process of closing down the shop when she thought of Danika. Picking up the phone she quickly dialed her friend's number, but after three rings got the answering machine. She then called Danika's cell phone, but it went to voice mail.

She tamped down an edge of worry. It was so unlike Danika to go so long without talking to her. Her head suddenly filled with her encounter with Max on Saturday night.

Even though she knew his ramblings were nothing more than those of a drunken lost soul, there was no denying he'd unnerved her. He'd seemed so intent on telling her that she was in danger, that the devil was after her.

Despite the warmth of the shop a shiver crawled up her back, and she shook her head in an attempt to dispel the vision of Max's frantic words and terror-filled eyes.

It was weird that his words had played into the feelings she'd had too often over the last couple of weeks—that something was about to happen, that somebody was watching her.

"Don't be silly," she muttered to herself as she climbed the stairs. Max's words had nothing to do with anything except that the poor man drank too much and suffered from mental illness.

As for the rest of it, the strange emotions she'd been having had been nothing but stress, and with the most pressing business decision made, she hoped she wouldn't suffer that odd, unsettling feeling again.

By Wednesday night Tyler knew he was going to have to cancel his date with Annalise for the next evening. Aside from the two murders he and his team had been working on around the clock, somebody had decided to shoot a city councilman in the head.

The latest murder had taken precedence over

everything as the team scrambled to get out from under the political heat of the case.

It was just after seven on Wednesday night when he called her. The sound of her voice when she answered instantly picked up his spirits.

"Hey, it's me."

"Tyler."

He liked the way his name sounded on her lips, and he smiled despite the fact that he was exhausted and mired in reports that reminded him of how evil human beings could be.

"I'll bet I know why you're calling," she said. "Tomorrow night is off."

"I'm sorry—" he began, but she cut him off.

"I heard about Councilman Gentry's death early this morning and saw you on the news. It was one of those rare times that I decided to turn on the television."

"Don't remind me." He grimaced as he thought of how the ABC reporter had caught him leaving the scene and had broadcast his terse "No comment" reply.

"You looked good," she said.

He laughed. "I looked pissed-off and older than my thirty-five years." His laughter died and he sighed. "I can't tell you how sorry I am. I was really looking forward to seeing you again."

"Is it possible you could get away for a quick dinner someplace near the police station?"

For a moment he was too stunned to speak. He wasn't accustomed to the women he dated being so accommodating, so understanding.

She must have mistook his silence for something

negative. "I mean, I'm not trying to be pushy . . ." she said uneasily.

"You aren't, and yeah, that might work. Of course, it won't be the same as you cooking for me."

"No, the food will definitely be better," she replied. "Just tell me where and when and I'll be there."

"There's a bar and grill a block away from the station. It's called Harry's. How about six?"

"Sounds perfect," she agreed.

They talked for a few minutes; then he hung up. He was still seated at the conference table in the war room when Jennifer came in.

She stopped short at the sight of him. "You look like the proverbial cat who just swallowed a canary."

"I think I'm finally dating the most rational, reasonable woman in the world."

Jennifer flopped down in the chair opposite him and grinned. "Don't worry; I give it a couple of weeks before you do something stupid and screw it all up."

"Thanks. It's nice to know I can always depend on you for emotional support," Tyler replied drily. "And now let's get back to work."

Chapter 13

Harry's Bar and Grill was located in a strip mall and flanked on one side by a tattoo parlor and on the other side by a coin-operated Laundromat.

As Annalise got out of her car at quarter till six on Thursday evening the air outside smelled of frying onions and Downy softener.

She'd looked forward to this all day long. As she'd argued with Sammy about fabrics and gotten opinions on colors, she'd reminded herself that no matter how stressful the day got, she had tonight with Tyler.

The interior of Harry's was dark and smoky, and it was obvious when she looked around that this was a favorite place for off-duty police officers.

She felt horribly self-conscious as she stood inside the door. A busty blond waitress approached her. "Hey, honey, you looking for somebody? I don't recognize you, and you sure as hell look too classy to be a regular."

"I'm looking for Detective King."

"Ah, Tyler. He requested the use of our private

dining room in the back. He's already there." She motioned for Annalise to follow her.

The "private dining room" turned out to be a card table set up in the storage area. As she entered, Tyler stood from the table, his smile so warm she figured he could light candles at a single glance.

"It's not exactly the Ritz," he began.

She moved right into his arms and kissed him, then danced away before he could grab her and turn the light kiss into something much different. "It's fine," she assured him. "I'm just glad you had time to meet me."

He held out the chair for her and she sat, then waited until he was seated in the chair opposite her. "You look tired," she said softly.

He nodded. "Exhausted, but you look great."

"Thanks." For a moment she wasn't sure what to say next. The natural flow of the conversation would be for her to ask him about his work, about the cases that had the skin beneath his eyes shadowed with fatigue and the lines in his face a little deeper than usual. But he'd made it clear on more than one occasion that talking about his work was taboo.

She realized that while she'd been looking at him, he'd been looking back. She flushed and laughed. "Sorry—I think I was staring."

"So was I," he replied easily. "Just looking at you makes me feel good. Tell me about your day. Talk about ordinary things so I can get grounded back into the real world."

She told him about her new doll, about all the elements that went into getting a new product out. She shared the stresses of the lack of sales and the pressure to get back on top of things. She talked to him about eating lunch the day before in the park, and about Charlie's latest phone call to her.

She stopped only when the waitress arrived to take their orders. When the waitress left, their conversation turned to their childhoods.

Over dinner Tyler shared with her some of his memories of growing up, and she found herself envious of the pictures he painted. It was obvious his parents adored him and had indulged him as a child.

Annalise had always felt as if she had to work hard for her mother's love, that Lillian's affection was conditional on Annalise's behavior. Certainly her father's absence hadn't given her any sense of being loved or cherished.

"Whenever things calm down a bit, I'd like to take you to meet my parents," he said. "I think you'd like them, and I know they'd like you."

"I'm sure they're terrific people, because they raised a terrific son," she replied.

Although the meal was short, she felt as if she'd gotten to know him better. They believed in the same things, shared the same rather traditional values. It was almost scary how much she liked him.

"I'm a little worried about Danika," she said as they walked out of Harry's together. "You haven't seen her around the neighborhood, have you?"

"No, but I haven't been home much. Why are you worried about her?"

They stopped at her car and she pulled her keys from her purse. "I haven't heard from her since last week, and that's really unusual. I've tried to call her, but she's not answering the calls."

"Was everything all right the last time you saw her?" he asked.

Annalise frowned, remembering that the last conversation she'd had with Danika had been a little testy. "We got a little tense with each other, but nothing we haven't done before, and I thought everything was all right when we parted."

"If it will make you feel better I'll run by her house on my way home from work tonight and see what I can find out." He pulled her into his arms. "What good is it to be dating a cop if he can't find a missing person in your life?"

She laughed, her heart quickening at his nearness. "I'm not sure she's missing. Maybe she was more irritated with me than I thought."

"I can't imagine being irritated with you," he murmured before his mouth took hers in a kiss that didn't just scream of desire, but also whispered of something deeper.

She molded herself against him, wishing they were someplace else, someplace private. It surprised her how much she wanted to make love to him again.

When he released her it was with reluctance. "It's crazy; we've only had a couple of dates, but somehow I feel like I've known you forever."

She knew exactly what he was talking about. From the night of their first date she'd felt something different with him than she'd felt for any other man in her life. "It scares me just a little bit," she admitted.

"Me, too. My partner is certain that given enough time I'll screw things up with you."

Annalise laughed. "That's funny. Danika thinks the same thing about me."

He dropped a light kiss on her forehead. "I guess time will tell who is right. Thanks for coming down here to meet me."

"Tyler, trust me: I understand about the demands of your job. I know all about dedication and commitment. I suffer from the same beasts myself." She unlocked her car, then turned back to him. "Call me when you get a chance."

"I'll make a chance," he replied.

As she drove home she had that same familiar feeling that she got when she tried to ride in an elevator, a tightness in her chest, a feeling of being half-suffocated.

She knew what it was: the fear of things moving too fast, of Tyler getting too close. It was the underlying psychological baggage that her father had left behind when he'd deserted her. Danika would have a field day if she were here right now and could peer into Annalise's heart.

"You're being foolish," she said aloud. After all, it wasn't like either of them was thinking or talking about love or commitment. At the moment they were just having fun and enjoying each other's company whenever possible.

She got back to her loft at seven thirty and found a message from Charlie waiting for her on her answering machine. "Hey, sis. It's me, your brother, Charlie. I was just kind of wondering when I could come and visit you again. Mom told me not to be a pain and bug you, but I told her it was cool. It is cool, isn't it? I mean, I'm not being a pain, am I?"

There was a long pause. "Well, call me when you get time, okay?" The line went dead.

As usual Charlie's need to connect touched something deep inside her, a place where she'd vowed long ago that nobody would ever touch her again.

She changed into her pajamas, then picked up the phone and called her brother. Knowing how much she had to do over the week, she made plans for him to spend the night with her the next weekend.

He was thrilled, and after finalizing the plans with her father she hung up. She'd decided to head to bed when the buzzer rang to let her know there was somebody at the door downstairs.

She hurried downstairs to see Danika knocking on the door. She was absurdly relieved to see her friend and hadn't realized until that moment just how worried she'd been.

She opened the door and pulled her inside. "Where in the hell have you been?"

Danika held up her hand to display not only a gorgeous engagement ring, but a wedding band as well. "We got married!"

"What?"

"We eloped to Vegas, got married, then had a glorious honeymoon." Danika spun in a circle, obviously delirious with happiness. When she'd finished three rotations, she stopped and grabbed Annalise in a hug. "Be happy for me, Annalise."

"Of course I'm happy for you," she replied, and gave Danika a fierce hug, then released her. "But the last time I talked to you, you told me things were moving too fast and you were going to take some time."

"I know, I know." Danika grabbed her by the arm. "Let's go upstairs and I'll tell you all about it. I had convinced myself that Danny and I needed to slow down, but when it's right, it's right. And I decided, why waste time?"

The two climbed the stairs, and Danika chattered like a magpie as she talked about the tacky wedding she'd had in one of those Vegas wedding chapels.

"Where's Danny now?" Annalise asked when they were settled in on her sofa.

"He's at my place. We're going to sell his house and keep mine. I told him I couldn't wait another minute to tell my best friend that I'd gotten married. He wanted to come and meet you, but I told him it would be best if I came alone tonight." Danika frowned. "Are you mad at me?"

Annalise looked at her in surprise. "Why would I be mad at you?"

"Because when we were in grade school we promised that we'd be each other's maids of honor."

"Oh, Danika, I could never be mad at you." Annalise gave her another hug. "I just hope I'll be invited to your fiftieth anniversary party."

They talked far too long into the night. It was like a final slumber party. At eleven Annalise popped popcorn and they sat at the kitchen table drinking soda and eating while talking about the merits of marriage and Annalise's decision for the new doll.

Danika called Danny five times while seated at the table, each time giggling like a schoolgirl as she told him how much she loved him. When she finally left after midnight, Annalise realized her friendship with Danika would never again be the same.

Danika was no longer a single woman who would want to go out for a drink or spend an occasional night over. She was now a married lady, and her first loyalty, her first commitment, would be to Danny, as it should be.

Somehow the idea depressed her just a little bit. Danika was moving on with her life, and Annalise somehow felt she was stuck in hers, working her mother's business, resenting her father, and refusing to commit her heart to any other human being.

She needed to call Tyler and let him know that Danika had surfaced safe and sound. The thought of hearing his voice brought a smile to her face.

He'd worked extrahard the last couple of days, sewing the clothes that would transform an ordinary woman into Kimono Kim. As he worked he'd tried to keep his mind off that open window on the second floor of the doll shop. But the thought of it tantalized him, excited him.

Soon, he thought. Soon he'd take Annalise and make her his final creative masterpiece. And just before he carried her out of her building he'd set fire to the place.

Flames momentarily danced before his eyes, making it impossible for him to focus on the hand stitching he'd been doing.

A conflagration, that was what he wanted, a total fiery destruction of Blakely Dolls. He could almost smell the smoke, hear the crackle and roar of the flames, feel the blistering heat on his face. He closed his eyes and lived in that moment of fire and soot and utter obliteration of the dolls that had ruined his life.

He finally opened his eyes and stared at the red-and-black silk he'd been stitching. Kimono Kim. That was who he was supposed to be thinking about.

He'd found his Kim by accident. He'd been in his car stopped at a red light and had glanced at the driver of the car next to his. There she was. Her sleek black hair had glistened in the sunshine, and her Asian features were absolutely stunning.

He'd followed her for the last three days, learning her routine and deciding how best to take her. She lived in an apartment with two roommates, worked as a dental assistant, and was attending night classes at Maple Woods Community College. He had no doubt that he'd find a place to grab her. He'd have his Kimono Kim doll very, very soon.

The bulletin board displayed his genius, and he glanced over at it, smiling at the photos of the two life-sized dolls he'd created. His smile faded, and instead a frown of dissatisfaction tugged at his features. What good was it to be a genius when nobody seemed to notice?

The news accounts of the women's murders, both in the newspaper and on the television, had been sketchy. Nobody had even mentioned the intricate work that had been done by him on the clothing and makeup and hair.

Someday I'll be famous, he'd told his mother one day when he was about ten years old.

She'd snorted with laughter, making him inwardly seethe. *You're nothing now, boy, and if you live to be a hundred you'll always be nothing.*

"Shut up," he now said aloud. "You shut up, you old stupid, fat cow." It felt good to talk to her in a way he never would have spoken to her when she'd been alive.

He glanced over to the chair, where a spill of lavender material awaited him. The Annalise doll was clad in a pretty lavender dress, and he'd already begun work on it. He wanted to be ready for her.

Once again flames flickered in front of his eyes. His fingers tingled as he thought of wrapping them around Annalise's soft neck, then squeezing the life from her. As the flames subsided he saw in his mind that open window in her building. It was a sweet invitation to accomplish his ultimate goal.

Suddenly he needed to see the window in reality, not just in his mind. As if in a daze he got up and left his work behind.

He was driven by an uncontrollable impulse, and his mind went blank. The blankness didn't pass until he found himself outside her building and staring up at the open window.

He climbed up the first five steps of the fire escape, just to see if he could reach the window. His heart raced as he managed to grab onto the window ledge. With one hand he pushed the window, and it rose without making a sound.

Maybe he'd just see if he could get inside. It was ridiculously easy to swing his leg from the fire escape into the open window and hoist himself up and over the sill.

He dropped to the floor behind a large stack of boxes, and for a moment he couldn't believe he was there. His exhilaration level was at fever pitch.

Standing perfectly still he listened, but could hear nothing but his own ragged, excited breathing.

He was just a staircase away from her. He closed the window he'd come in so that it was open only a mere inch, enough for him to get a fingerhold to raise it back again and yet not enough to be visible from the street below.

He scooted out from behind the boxes, grateful for the moonlight that drifted in through the windows. The storage room was huge, but filled with enough boxes and old furniture to create an obstacle course.

Carefully he maneuvered his way to the stairs. I'm not ready for her, he thought. It's not time for her yet. Still his hand clutched the stair railing and he began to climb.

Impatient little snot. His mother's voice rang in his ears and halted him midstep.

He gripped the railing more tightly and willed the voice away. He climbed the stairs slowly, heart pounding in anticipation. When he reached the top he found himself in the small foyer, the door to her loft just ahead.

He imagined that he could smell her. The light floral scent she wore eddied in his head and made him half-dizzy. She would be sleeping now, lying in bed and unaware of how close she was to immortality.

Stepping closer to the door he placed a hand on the wood. She was just on the other side. He could feel her life force warming the door.

He leaned his entire body against the door and closed his eyes. He could feel her. Her heat radiated through the wood, warming him and making him hard as a rock.

Take her now, a little voice whispered inside his head. Open the door and take her right now. He leaned back, breaking his contact with the only barrier that kept him from her.

His hand shook as he caressed down the door and gripped the brass knob. Holding his breath he turned it, excitement sizzling through him as he realized it was unlocked.

He jerked his hand back and drew in several deep breaths in order to control his frenzied need. Not time, he reminded himself.

Slowly, without making a sound, like a shadow moving through the night, he backed away. Now he knew how easy it would be when he was ready. Now he knew he could take her without having to plan any further.

She didn't know it yet, but she was his . . . his beautiful doll.

Chapter 14

He hunched down between two cars in the Maple Woods Community College parking lot, his heart pounding as loud as the cicadas singing in the trees nearby.

He'd known if he were patient eventually a time would present itself when he could get his Kimono Kim, and now the time had come. He had everything he needed to take her: duct tape, rope, and a crowbar. But more important, he had the cover of night and a relatively deserted parking lot.

She'd stayed late at the library, studying for tests she'd never take, talking to friends she'd never see again. But she would forever be immortalized as the perfect Kimono Kim, a far better doll than Annalise Blakely could ever make.

It was almost ten when he heard her coming, her flip-flops slapping rhythmically against the parking lot pavement. She was alone, as he knew she would be.

He tensed, his excitement at a fever pitch he'd never reached before. He waited until he heard the jingle of keys and her driver door opened; then he sprang and jumped behind her.

He crashed the crowbar down on the back of her head. She didn't make a sound as the books she held slid to the ground and she fell to her knees.

She was half-conscious when he slapped the duct tape across her mouth and bound her hands together behind her back. It was only then that she seemed to know the danger she was in. Her dark brown eyes widened and she struggled against him. But by that time it was too late. He was in control.

Looking around the parking area he saw nobody who might give him any problems. He scooped up his next creation in his arms and put her in the trunk of his car.

Minutes later, as he drove back to his production room, his hands shook with the excitement of the task at hand. Certainly she would be his biggest challenge. While her Asian features were beautiful it would take a particularly deft hand to transform her into the geisha doll. But he was up to the challenge.

It only took fifteen minutes for him to drive from the college to his place, where he unloaded her from the trunk and carried her to the special room where he did all his work.

He tied her into the chair, ignoring the pleading in her almond-shaped eyes. She grunted against the duct tape, and he knew she was begging for her life.

"Shh, it's okay," he said, and offered her a smile. He went to the small refrigerator and pulled out the ice-cube tray. He placed several cubes into a plastic bag, then carried it over to her and held it against the back of her head where he'd struck her with the crowbar.

She winced as he pressed the ice against the wound. It wouldn't do for her to have a lump. Perfect dolls didn't have lumpy heads.

She strained against the ropes that held her arms and legs in place. "You might as well stop fighting," he said. He was finding it a novelty having her alive with him. The others had been dead when he'd brought them here.

He could share with her his genius. The idea delighted him. As he held the ice against the back of her head he told her about the dolls and pointed to the photos on his bulletin board.

She screamed against the tape, but he ignored the sound, thinking how beautiful she'd be as Kimono Kim.

Sulee Hwang smelled the madness emanating from him, and she knew she was going to die. She didn't understand why this was happening. She should be at home in her apartment with her roommates. She should be wearing her pink and blue pajamas and getting ready for bed.

She'd never seen this man before. What had made him choose her? What did he intend to do to her? Oh, God, her heart felt as if it were going to burst from her chest.

As he began to brush her long, dark hair with loving strokes, chills of revulsion joined the stark terror that sizzled through her. Even worse, as he pressed against her she could tell he had a hard-on.

Although she'd tried not to cry, knowing that she

could choke with the tape across her mouth, the tears now began to flow.

"Stop it," he commanded. "Stop it or you're going to make your eyes all red and swollen." He threw down the brush, his face red with rage. "Don't cry!"

She blinked, frantically trying to contain her tears as he stalked across the room and picked up a doll dressed in a kimono. He held it out to her, his hand trembling. "Look at her. Are her eyes red? Does it look like she's been crying?"

She shook her head back and forth, wanting to agree with him, to do whatever it took to take the rage from his eyes, but her tears refused to stop.

He drew a deep breath and closed his eyes for a long moment. When he opened them again he stared at her with a dispassion that was even more terrifying than his rage.

Without saying a word he placed the doll back on the nearby table, then approached her. "I can't have it. You're going to ruin everything. I'd hoped you'd be able to be a part of your final transformation, but I'm afraid that's not going to happen now."

He wrapped his hands around her throat, and he leaned his face so close to hers she saw the madness flaming in his eyes.

She tried to fight, but within minutes she could get no breath, and as the black edges of unconsciousness closed in she heard him whisper, "You're going to make a beautiful doll."

"Shit," Jennifer said, verbalizing Tyler's initial thought as they stared at the dead woman lying in a grassy area directly behind a pizza place.

"Looks like what we have here is a genuine geisha girl," Jennifer said.

The young woman was beautiful even in death. Her delicate features were enhanced by the traditional Japanese makeup, and there was no sign of the beginnings of decomposition, despite the fact that it was just after nine in the morning and already eighty degrees.

"She may look like a genuine geisha, but we both know it's our sick bastard's work," Tyler replied tersely.

They already knew the victim's identification. A call to missing persons had given them the name of Sulee Hwang. Her roommates had filed the missing persons report late last night.

Sulee had left her apartment on Tuesday evening to attend a night class at Maple Woods Community College. She hadn't returned home after class.

The roommates had called the police then, but had been instructed that a report couldn't be officially filed until the subject had been missing for twenty-four hours.

Sulee wasn't missing anymore, but what concerned him more than anything was that the killer seemed to be on a much shorter timetable than before.

The other two women had been dumped after decomposition had already begun. This one appeared to have been dumped almost immediately after death.

As with the other two, *dumped* wasn't really the word. Sulee had been gently laid in the grass. Not a wrinkle marred the red-and-black silk kimono she wore. Her arms were extended out at her sides, as if she had intended to make an angel in the snow.

It was tragic. It was obscene and it was frustrating as hell. As with the last two, an anonymous call had been made as to where to find Sulee. Unfortunately the call hadn't been made to the police but rather to a reporter, Reuben Sandford, who had decided to check it out before calling the police.

He'd found the body and promptly thrown up, contaminating the area to the left of the victim. He now stood, pale and somber, next to a police officer.

Tyler had yet to interrogate him. He was too pissed to be civilized and was waiting for some of his anger to pass before questioning the man.

Things would have been far less complicated if Reuben had called the cops and let them be the first on the scene. Tyler wasn't at all pleased that a reporter had seen the body. He had a feeling that was going to make things even more difficult than they already were.

"Strangled, just like the others," Jennifer observed, pulling Tyler from his thoughts. "Scratch marks around her neck. She tried to tear his hands from her throat. Maybe she managed to scratch his hands."

Tyler looked at the perfectly manicured nails of the victim and frowned. "Even if she did, it's doubtful we'll get any evidence." The perp was smart, way too smart to give them his skin under the victim's fingernails.

He blew out his frustration on a sigh as the crime scene techs began their work. "Guess I'll go have a little chat with Jimmy Olsen." He pointed a finger at Reuben.

"And I'm going to talk to the coroner and see if he can pin down time of death," Jennifer replied.

Reuben seemed to melt into himself as he saw Tyler's approach. His shoulders slumped and he ducked his chin. His skin still held the pasty hue of a man with an unsettled stomach, and he breathed through his mouth as if aware the air smelled of death and vomit.

"Why didn't you call the police the minute you got the tip?" Tyler asked without preamble.

"Because I figured it was probably bullshit," Reuben replied.

"You get a lot of bullshit calls involving dead women?"

Reuben straightened his shoulders. "I get a lot of bullshit calls involving lots of things. Aliens on the roof, hit men on the corner, neighbors dealing dope—people like to talk to reporters."

"And you always check out these tips?"

"I don't climb on rooftops looking for aliens, but yeah, if I think it's legit I try to check it out." Some of the color returned to his chubby cheeks.

"What made you check this call out?" Tyler asked.

Reuben frowned. "Slow night. I had nothing better to do."

"Tell me exactly what the caller said to you."

"He asked if I was the reporter who had written the story on the murders of Kerry Albright and Margie Francis. I said I was, and then he said that I would find his next creation behind the pizza place at Ninety-fourth and North Oak."

"Creation? Are you sure that's the word he used?" Tyler asked.

"Definitely sure. I thought it was a weird word to use."

"What else did he say?"

"Nothing. That was it. He hung up as soon as he told me where to find her." Reuben held out his cell phone. "I suppose you're going to take this from me."

Tyler nodded, took the phone, and slipped it into his pocket. "Can you tell me what he sounded like? Any accent? Any speech impediment that you noticed?"

"Nah, just a deep male all-American kind of voice."

"Did you hear any kind of background noise, something that might indicate a location where he was calling from?"

Reuben frowned. "It all happened so fast. But no, not that I remember." He glanced over to where the body was being placed in a bag. "Sorry about the puke," he said. "She looked so peaceful; then a fly crawled out of her nose and I lost it." He grimaced.

"Just makes things a little more unpleasant for the crime scene techs," Tyler replied. "You think of anything, you call me." Tyler turned to leave.

"Detective King?"

He turned back to look at Reuben.

"It's the same guy, isn't it?"

Tyler kept his expression carefully schooled. "What are you talking about?"

"The same guy did this one and those other two who were dressed funny . . . the bride and the flapper. He killed them; then he dressed them up."

Tyler cursed inwardly. He'd been hoping to have a little more time before anyone made a connection between the victims. But it had been an unrealistic hope. Victims dressed in costumes were too weird for somebody not to make the connection.

"What makes you think the killer dressed up this one?"

"Because while I was waiting for you all to arrive, I talked to her roommates, and they told me she doesn't own a kimono. You got a serial killer on your hands, don't you?"

Tyler walked back to Reuben and threw an arm around his shoulders, trying not to think about how pissed off he was, about how Reuben could screw things up if he printed information before the police wanted it released. "Reuben, you know the press has always been a valuable tool for the police department."

"Oh, no, don't even try to get all chummy with me." Reuben stepped away from Tyler. "This is a huge story. Freedom of the press and all that."

"All I'm asking is that you give us a couple of days before you break the story," Tyler said. "Give us a couple of days and I'll give you an exclusive."

Reuben's eyes narrowed in speculation. "You'll give me everything? The details and where the investigation is going?"

"I'll give you everything I can without compromising the investigation."

Reuben stared back to the crime scene, then looked at Tyler. "If I think I'm going to be scooped, then all bets are off and I'm going with what I have."

Tyler swallowed a sigh of frustration as he left Reuben. He'd hoped to keep the fact that somebody was killing pretty young women and dressing them up in costumes from the public a little bit longer. But he had a feeling he wasn't going to get his wish.

"Coroner estimates time of death sometime after midnight," Jennifer said as she joined Tyler next to the crime scene van. "He'll be able to pinpoint it more closely after autopsy."

"There's nothing much more we can do here. We might as well head back to the station and wait for the preliminary reports to come in," Tyler said.

"At least we don't have to worry about Councilman Gentry's murder anymore," Jennifer said once they were in the car.

Fortunately that murder had been solved remarkably easily when it had been discovered that William Gentry was having an affair. He'd tried to break it off, his young lover had been enraged and in a fit of temper had shot him. She'd been arrested, and the end result was a devastated widow who now knew of her husband's unfaithfulness and a respected city official whose reputation had been forever tarnished. Case closed.

As Jennifer fiddled with the air-conditioner vents, Tyler's thoughts went to Annalise. Over the past week they'd managed to meet for dinner twice at Harry's Bar and Grill.

Those dinners had been beacons of light for him. Annalise had entertained him with stories about her workweek and her staff, who obviously meant a lot to her. She'd told him about Danika's impromptu marriage and that she'd met her friend's husband for the first time three days after the happy couple had returned from their honeymoon.

Each time he'd met Annalise the conversation had been about ordinary things. What was extraordinary was how much he looked forward to seeing her again. And with this latest murder he had no idea when he might find time for her.

He knew better than to expect his relationship with her to last. Eventually she'd get tired of the impromptu dinner dates and his inability to commit to anything. She was bright and beautiful and certainly deserved better than what he was giving her at the moment.

He shoved thoughts of her away. What he needed to do at the moment was focus on the case. He now had three dead women, all killed by the same unsub.

He had just pulled into a parking lot at the station when Reuben's cell phone rang. It played some noisy tune that Tyler didn't recognize. He dug it out of his pocket and checked the caller-identification box. It read, PRIVATE CALLER. He flipped it open, aware of Jennifer watching him intently from the passenger seat.

"Hello?"

There was silence, but Tyler knew somebody was on the other end of the line.

"Hello? Can I help you?"

"Where's the reporter?" The voice was deep and male.

Tyler pressed the phone more tightly against his ear, hoping to hear something, anything that might pinpoint a location where the call was coming from. "He's unavailable at the moment. Maybe I can help you."

"Who are you?"

"Detective Tyler King. Who am I speaking to?"

"Did you find my work?"

Excitement pumped through Tyler. "Yeah, and I'd like to talk to you about your work."

There was a momentarily pause. "I don't think so." The phone line went dead.

"Who was that?" Jennifer asked as Tyler muttered a curse.

"That was our man." Tyler got out of the car, his frustration a living, breathing entity inside him. The dead girls weren't talking to him, but he had a feeling he'd hear from the killer again.

Chapter 15

Annalise stood at the shop door on Friday night and watched for her father's car. She'd talked to Tyler a few minutes earlier, and he'd told her he was going to be working through the weekend, and she'd said that was fine, that Charlie was going to spend the weekend with her.

"I feel like I met the right woman at the wrong time," Tyler had told her. "I keep expecting you to tell me that you're already tired of my crazy schedule."

His words had unexpectedly warmed her. "Tyler, I'm fine with things the way they are right now. I'm spending every spare moment I have trying to figure out ways to save my mother's business. I'm certainly not spending any time sitting by the phone and crying because you can't work me into your busy schedule."

While her words to him had been true, as she stared out the shop window she had to confess to herself that she wouldn't have minded spending more time with Tyler.

The memory of their lovemaking made her hungry for him. It wasn't just a physical hunger, but also the desire to be held in his strong arms, to see the light in his eyes just before he lowered his mouth to hers.

She liked the sound of his laughter, and the keen intelligence he possessed. She liked that she felt as if she could confide in him, share things that she'd shared with nobody else.

She knew there were things he didn't share with her, that there were pieces of himself he kept close to his vest. Hopefully in time he'd realize he could tell her anything about his work, his thoughts, his dreams.

There was no denying her feelings for him were stronger than she'd ever had for any man. But she told herself that the relationship was moving along in a way that was comfortable. No demands. No messy needs. No risk of heartache.

And speaking of heartache . . . her father's car came into view. As always she steeled herself for seeing him. As the car pulled up to the curb in front of the shop, she stepped out the door and into the humid early evening air.

Sherri got out of the car first, a bright smile lifting her lips. "I can't believe you want to put up with this kid for the whole weekend," she said as she took Annalise's hand in hers, gave it a squeeze, then released it.

Annalise smiled, unable to help liking the woman who exuded warmth and friendliness. "It's not all going to be fun and games," she replied. "I intend to put him to work tomorrow in the shop."

"That's cool with me," Charlie said as he climbed out of the backseat with his backpack. He bounded like an eager puppy to where his mother and Annalise stood. "I brought my portable DVD player and some movies for us to watch," he said.

"I suppose they're blood-and-guts movies," Annalise said.

Charlie grinned. "Nah, they're comedies. I figured you wouldn't appreciate blood and guts."

Frank joined them on the sidewalk. "Hi, sweetie," he said to Annalise.

"Dad." She nodded stiffly. He looked casual and relaxed in a pair of jeans and a T-shirt.

"Sherri and I are going to the movies, but if you need to reach us for anything I have my cell phone with me."

"I'm sure we'll be just fine," she assured him.

"We'll be home all day tomorrow if you decide you've had enough teenage testosterone," Sherri said.

Charlie rolled his eyes. "She said we'll be fine."

"You just make sure you mind your manners," Sherri exclaimed, her words making Charlie roll his eyes once again.

"We'll be back to pick you up on Sunday morning around ten," Frank said. He leaned down and kissed Charlie on the cheek, then tousled his hair affectionately. "You behave yourself."

A stab of emotion pierced through Annalise as she saw her dad's interaction with Charlie. So light and easy, without any of the tension that marked his relationship with her. It wasn't envy she felt. She was glad Charlie had a loving relationship with his father. What she felt was simple, raw need.

She mentally commanded her inner child to stop being such a baby and threw an arm around her brother's shoulder. "Come on, brat brother; let's get upstairs and veg out with a movie and some popcorn."

"Cool," he exclaimed in typical Charlie fashion. As Frank and Sherri headed back to their car, Annalise and Charlie went inside.

As they climbed the stairs side by side Charlie told her what movies he'd brought and which was his favorite. "I know you told me you didn't watch much TV," he said, "but watching a movie is different, especially if you've got somebody to watch it with you."

They ate popcorn and watched movies until midnight; then she reminded him they had an early morning and they called it a night.

They were up and dressed by eight the next morning. Annalise was manning the retail store for the day, although several of the production people had decided to come in and work on the prototype for the new doll.

She and Charlie ate cold cereal and fruit for breakfast, then headed downstairs, where Annalise showed him how to make a sale on the cash register.

"You're going to let me work the register?" he asked, his blue eyes gleaming with excitement.

"I told you that I was going to put you to work today," she said.

"Yeah, but I thought you'd have me doing something dumb like sweeping the floor."

"There's nothing wrong with sweeping floors, Charlie, but I thought you might prefer making sales."

"Cool."

She showed him once again what keys to push for a cash sale and how to do a credit sale. When she thought he had it down pat it was time to open up the doors.

She saw the box the moment she unlocked the front door, a Blakely box that she knew contained one of her dolls and a note from whoever was leaving them. She carried the box to the counter.

"What's that?" Charlie asked curiously.

"Somebody has been anonymously returning dolls." She pulled off the lid and pushed the tissue aside to reveal Kimono Kim.

Charlie frowned. "She looks okay. Why would somebody return her, and even if they wanted to return her, why didn't they come inside to get their money back?"

"I don't know." She dug around in the tissue and found the folded note. She didn't want to open it. She wasn't sure why the dolls with their strange notes bothered her so much, but they did.

"I'm just going to run her upstairs," she said to Charlie. "Can you hold down the fort for a few minutes?"

He straightened his shoulders and puffed out his chest. "Sure, take your time."

She carried the doll upstairs and put her on the table along with the note she hadn't yet read. On impulse she got the other two from the linen closet and added them to the table as well. She unfolded the first two notes and laid them side by side, and only then did she open the new note.

YOUR TIME AS THE DOLLMAKER
IS COMING TO AN END.

She stared at the words for a long moment, a creepy-crawly sensation just under her skin. In and of itself the note felt oddly ominous, but taken with the previous notes it seemed to be some sort of crazy competitive challenge.

Somebody was trying to play mind games with her, and she couldn't help but believe it was somebody poised to make a big splash on the market with a new doll. As if there wasn't enough competition already, she thought with a touch of depression.

Aware that Charlie was downstairs alone, she placed the lids back on the doll boxes, left them on the table, and hurried back down to the shop.

When some of the production crew began to arrive Annalise introduced each of them to Charlie, and for the remainder of the day he split his time between the retail area and the back, where he was treated like an indulged mascot.

At six o'clock they closed up shop and walked across the park to Joey's. Mark met them at the door. "Joey isn't here?" Annalise asked.

"No, he's extended his time off," Mark replied.

"I was going to introduce him to my brother, Charlie," she said.

Mark smiled. "Well, I'm not Joey. My name is Mark, and it's nice to meet you, Charlie." He held out his hand.

"It's nice to meet you, sir," Charlie said as they shook.

"Dinner for two?" Mark asked as he picked up two menus from a stack nearby. He motioned for them to follow him.

"Do you eat here a lot?" Charlie asked once they'd been seated and their orders had been taken.

"Way too much," she admitted. "It's so much more convenient just to walk across the park rather than to cook."

"It was fun today, especially meeting Ben and Sammy and the gang. They were all really cool."

She smiled. "I depend on them a lot when it comes to business."

"I forgot all about it last night, but I brought you a present." He dug into his pocket and pulled out a small object wrapped in a clean white handkerchief.

"A present? Why did you get me something?"

He shrugged. " 'Cause I felt like it. Besides, I didn't get you anything for your birthday." He pushed the present closer to her. "Go on, open it."

She unwrapped the handkerchief to reveal a small porcelain elephant with blue jeweled eyes. "Oh, Charlie. It's beautiful."

"I know you have a collection of elephants, and I didn't see any like this one, so I thought you might like it." He smiled at her with a hint of uncharacteristic shyness. "So, do you like it?"

"I love it, Charlie. I'll treasure it always." She carefully rewrapped it, then placed it in her purse. "You know, Dad started my elephant collection. When I was seven he gave me my first one, and he's been giving them to me ever since." She took a sip of her water. "I'm not sure why he thought I needed an elephant collection."

"I know why," Charlie replied. "He told me that when you were a little girl he took you to the zoo, and when the day was over you told him you loved two things more than anything else in the world—him and elephants."

She stared at him, unable to speak around the lump that had formed in her throat. She was thankful that at that moment the waitress arrived to serve them their meals.

She didn't have to talk much through the meal. Charlie, with his usual exuberance, kept up a running monologue about everything and anything that entered his mind.

She tried not to think about that long-ago visit to the zoo, but Charlie's words had unearthed faint, half-buried memories. The pungent smell of the animals mingled with the scents of freshly popped popcorn and sweet spun cotton candy. The sound of her father's deep laughter combined with the bleat of a baby lamb eager for a handful of grain.

But it had been the elephants that had fascinated her, especially when her dad had explained that elephants were big but sensitive creatures that played and laughed and often grieved deeply when a family member died.

She'd told her dad she loved him and elephants and he'd given her elephants, but soon after that day he'd removed himself from her life.

The residual bitterness of his choice now chased away her appetite, and she only picked at her veal. Charlie cleaned his plate, then eyed her leftovers longingly.

She pushed her plate toward him. "Knock yourself out, kid." He not only finished her meal, but also ate a large piece of cheesecake while she nursed a cup of coffee.

When he was just about finished, she pulled out

the envelope she'd prepared earlier in the day. "This is for you," she said, and shoved it across the table.

He looked at her curiously as he picked up the envelope. He opened it, and when he saw what was inside his eyes widened. "It's a check. Why are you giving me a check?"

"I always pay my help," she replied. "You were a good worker today, Charlie. You earned every penny of that. And the key is to my place. I think a brother should have the key to his sister's house."

He put the key and the check back into the envelope and tucked it into his pocket. When he looked at her again his eyes were filled with deep emotion. "I knew you were awesome before I ever met you. I just wish . . ." He looked down at his plate.

"Wish what, Charlie?" she prompted.

He looked up at her again. "I just wish we would have met sooner."

His words squeezed her heart. She swallowed against a knot of emotion and reached across the table for his hand. "We'll have lots of time together, Charlie. We're going to make so many memories you won't have room in your heart for all of them."

It was after dusk when they left Joey's and walked back across the park toward her place. "I've got one more movie I brought that we didn't watch last night. Want to watch it now?" he asked as they reached the front door.

"Sure." She dug her keys out of her purse, but before she could unlock the door Max stepped out of the alleyway and beelined toward them.

Charlie stepped in front of her, as if to protect her from danger. "It's all right," she said. "I know him." She smiled at Max. "Hi, Max."

Max ignored her and stared at Charlie. "Mickey?" he said softly, his voice thick and hoarse with emotion.

Charlie took a step back as Max reached out a trembling hand toward him. "Mickey, where have you been? Where's your brother?" Max asked. Hope lit his eyes as he stared at Charlie.

This time it was Annalise who stepped between her brother and the homeless man. "Max, this is my brother, Charlie. His name isn't Mickey; it's Charlie," she said for emphasis.

The old man stared at Charlie, then at Annalise, his rheumy eyes filled with confusion and a sadness that was painful to see. "Charlie, not Mickey?"

"That's right," Annalise said. Her heart ached as Max seemed to age before her eyes. His big shoulders slumped forward, and the illumination in his eyes was doused. "Not Mickey," he muttered as he turned away from them.

"That was weird," Charlie said once Max was gone and they entered the doll shop.

"Max is one of the homeless who live in the area. I sometimes give him food," she explained.

"Poor guy," he said with genuine compassion. "I wonder who Mickey is."

"Who knows?"

As they climbed the stairs Annalise tried not to think about her last conversation with Max. *The devil is after you, Annalise*—the crazy ramblings of a mentally ill alcoholic.

The rest of the evening passed quickly as they watched the movie Charlie had brought, then indulged in a crazy pillow fight that made her feel as if she were a young teenager.

By ten thirty Charlie's eyelids drooped and he confessed that he was pooped. Annalise made up his bed on the sofa. He gave her a hug, kissed her on the cheek and within minutes of lying down was sound asleep.

She sat in a chair at the table and watched him sleep. The boy enchanted her with his energy and his sensitivity and his overwhelming love for her. She loved him—loved him like she was afraid to love another human being. From the very beginning Charlie had been determined to get deep into her heart, and as he snored lightly she realized he'd succeeded.

Too restless to go directly to sleep, she decided to sketch for a little while. It was only when she went to search for her sketchbook that she realized she'd left it downstairs in the production area.

Checking on Charlie one last time, she headed for the door to retrieve her book.

He hadn't intended to come inside again. Although he was working frantically to complete the Annalise outfit, it wasn't ready yet. But the allure of being so close to her, the tantalizing aspect of being inside her home, outside her door, made it impossible for him to stay away.

He now lowered himself to the floor behind the boxes on the second floor. As always there was a moment of sweet euphoria that made his pulse race and his breath escape him in ragged pants.

Taking a moment to steady himself, he drew in air through his nose and exhaled through his mouth, calming his racing pulse as he gained a modicum of control.

The moon was less bright tonight, but this was his fourth time inside and he no longer needed the aid of light to maneuver his way to the stairs. He'd memorized where to step, what to avoid to keep moving soundlessly.

He skirted around the boxes, then stood perfectly still for a long moment, breathing in the essence of her. In his imagination he could smell the floral scent of her, could see her blue eyes, wide and empty like the Annalise doll's.

He pressed a hand against the front of his pants where he'd grown hard. Another day, two at the most, and he'd be ready for her.

The lavender dress with its lacy frills was almost done, and he could see in his mind's eye how to do her makeup. It would be light with a little bit of coral blush and just a touch of blue shadow to emphasize the blue of her eyes.

It was growing increasingly difficult to see her during the day and not show his need for her. Sometimes when he talked to her his insides shivered so much he had difficulty concentrating on the conversation.

He'd just touched the staircase railing when he heard the door open upstairs. Her loft door.

She was coming out!

And if she was coming out of the loft there was only one place she could be going ... down the stairs.

He backed away from the stairs, his heart crashing as he tried to think. Think! He crouched behind a couple of cartons and blinked as the light over the stairs came on.

Peeking out, he watched as first her legs appeared, then her torso and finally all of her. Annalise. So close he could reach out and run his hand up her leg or grab her by the ankle.

Not ready, his brain screamed, but he wasn't listening. He could take her now. So easily. He could knock her unconscious and carry her away. Surely he could have her clothes ready before she began to go bad.

By the time he processed all of these thoughts she'd gone down the second staircase to the bottom floor.

He followed her.

Chapter 16

When Annalise reached the back production area she turned on the small lamp over her desk and spied her sketchbook just where she thought it would be. She flipped it open and stared critically at the drawings she'd made for the three outfits the new doll would wear.

"This is not the time to second-guess yourself," she muttered aloud. She closed the sketchbook and grabbed it off the desk, but before she could turn to go back up the stairs, something crashed down on the back of her head.

Her knees and palms smacked the floor as she fell. She cried out in pain, wondering what in the hell might have fallen from overhead. She started to rise; then she heard it—a grunt from someplace behind her that let her know she wasn't alone.

A shove pushed her headfirst into the desk. She hit the lamp with her arm, and it crashed to the floor and plunged the room into darkness.

What was happening? Panic swam inside her as she tried once again to get to her feet. Strong arms grabbed her from behind. She screamed, but her scream was cut off as hands wrapped around her neck, squeezing the air from her lungs.

She couldn't breathe. Instead of trying to get him away from her, she scrabbled her fingers against his hands at her throat, trying to ease the pressure, needing to draw a breath. Tears sprang to her eyes as her vision began to blur. She needed air.

Using one leg she tried to kick backward and connect with his body. She tried to step on his foot, do anything she could to break the grip he had on her. But he was strong, and the pressure around her neck was relentless.

"Annalise?" Charlie's voice called down the stairs.

Oh, God, the last thing she wanted was for Charlie to venture downstairs and get hurt. She increased her struggling.

"Annalise, are you all right?"

Her attacker grunted, released her and shoved her forward, where she once again smashed into the desk, then tumbled to the floor. As she inhaled a ragged breath, she heard the whoosh of the back door opening and knew he was gone.

She was still on the floor next to the desk gulping in air when Charlie found her. "Annalise! What happened? Are you okay?" He crouched down next to her, looking very much like a frightened young boy.

"Call nine-one-one," she managed to gasp out.

As Charlie raced to the phone to make the call, she managed to get into a sitting position, although she was still weak and her throat burned.

Within seconds Charlie was back at her side, his

eyes wide as he hunkered down next to her. "Are you sure you're all right?" he asked.

She nodded. "Just help me up, okay?"

He stood and helped her to her feet, then into the chair in front of the desk. "What happened?" he asked.

She swallowed a couple of times. "I came down to get my sketch pad. Somebody was in here and they attacked me."

Charlie grabbed her hand and squeezed. "I shouldn't have gone to sleep," he said mournfully. "I should have been down here to protect you."

"Nonsense," she replied. "You saved my life." She rubbed her throat. "If you hadn't called my name I don't know what would have happened." She thought she might be in a mild state of shock. She felt out of her body, as if what had just happened had happened to somebody else. But her sore throat and her pounding head let her know otherwise.

Charlie held her hand until they heard a siren approaching in the distance. Only when she told him to let the officers in the front door did he finally release his grip on her.

She struggled to her feet as two uniformed cops came through the shop and into the back room. They both had guns drawn and looked ready for trouble. "I'm Officer McBlaine and this is Officer Calladay. Are you all right, ma'am?"

"I'm okay, mostly just shaken up."

"Dispatch said you had an intruder?" This time it was Calladay who spoke. "Is the intruder still in the building?"

"He ran out the back door," she replied.

"Somebody attacked her," Charlie exclaimed, his voice pitched higher than usual. "I was upstairs sleeping, and I woke up when I heard her scream, and when I got down here she was on the floor."

"Whoa." Officer McBlaine held up a hand. "Slow down, son. Let's start at the very beginning."

The policemen took her name and Charlie's; then she explained about Charlie falling asleep and her coming downstairs to find her sketchbook.

While the officers went outside to look around, she insisted Charlie call Frank to pick him up. Charlie didn't argue with her, and she was grateful for that. Her head pounded where she'd been struck, and as the initial burst of adrenaline fled she was left with aches and pains in every part of her body.

Frank arrived while the officers were still there. He entered the shop, his eyes frantic as he gazed at Annalise. "Are you all right?" He pulled her into his arms for a rare hug. "Thank God," he murmured into her hair. "Thank God you're okay."

Normally she would allow the gesture for only a second, then would step away. But this time she remained standing in his embrace, needing the physical connection with him as she never had before.

"I'm fine," she finally said, and only then did Frank drop his arms from around her. "I just thought it would be a good idea for you to take Charlie home. The police are still here, and I'm not sure how long all this is going to take."

Frank frowned. "I hate to leave you here all alone. I could stay, or you could come back home with me."

"I'm fine, really. I think maybe I just disturbed a

robbery or something." She gave him a reassuring forced smile.

Before Frank could say anything else, Tyler came flying into the shop. "Annalise. Thank God you're all right."

She found herself wrapped in another hug, and this time she hugged back as tears unexpectedly sprang to her eyes. "What are you doing here?" she asked when he finally released her.

"I was grabbing a late burger, and when I got back to the station my partner told me there had been an emergency call from here."

"Tyler, this is my father, Frank Blakely. Dad, this is Tyler King. He's a homicide cop with the police department and a friend of mine."

The two men shook hands; then Tyler walked over to Officer McBlaine, and Annalise walked her father and Charlie to the door. "I'll be fine, Dad. Tyler is here now." She smiled at Charlie. "Sorry to cut the weekend short."

Charlie's eyes misted a bit. "That's no big deal. I just want to make sure you're okay."

Annalise gave him a quick hug. "Everything is fine, Charlie. Go home and get a good night's sleep and call me tomorrow, okay?"

He nodded; then he and Frank left. Annalise walked back to where Tyler was talking to the two officers. "Ms. Blakely, you said you went out to dinner with your brother, then returned home. Was your door locked when you came back from eating?" Officer McBlaine asked.

She frowned thoughtfully and tried to ignore the painful pounding in her head. "I thought so. We got to the door, but before we came in Max talked to us." Her frown deepened as she realized she couldn't remember if she'd actually unlocked the door or not.

Had she forgotten to lock it when they had left to eat? Was that how the intruder had gotten inside? But that didn't make sense, that he would come in while they were eating and would still be in the building hours later. "When we got home we watched a movie, and if the intruder came in while we were at dinner, then he would have been down here for a couple of hours."

"Did you relock the door when you came back?" Tyler asked.

She fought the impulse to reach up and grab the back of her throbbing head. Trying to think was nearly impossible. "I thought so, but now I'm not sure," she admitted.

"Who is Max?" Officer Calladay asked.

"He's a homeless man who lives in the area," she replied. "But Max wouldn't have done this," she hurriedly added. "He'd never hurt me, and besides, if it had been him I would have smelled him." She smiled ruefully. "Living on the streets has given him a distinctive odor."

Calladay eyed her skeptically. "We'd still like to talk to this Max. Any idea where his crib is?"

"I think he sleeps in the alley next to Joey's restaurant, although most nights around this time you can find him under an oak tree in the park," she replied.

"There's really nothing more we can do here," Officer McBlaine said. "We'll file a report. My gut instinct is that it's probable that you interrupted somebody who intended to rob you. I definitely rec-

ommend you be more careful about making sure
your doors are locked."

When the two officers had left, Tyler once again
pulled her into his arms. "Are you really okay?"

She rested her head against his broad chest. "To
be honest my head is pounding and my knees and
hips ache, and I think in the morning I'm going to
feel like I got run over by a truck."

He rubbed a hand up and down her back, the caress relaxing muscles that had been taut with tension. "What you need is a hot soak in a bath, a
couple of aspirins and bed. Come on, I'll tuck you
in."

He started to lead her toward the elevator "I
walk up," she said. She smiled wearily. "I don't like
elevators. It's one of those character defects I don't
tell a man at the beginning of a relationship."

"Then we'll take the stairs," he replied with an
answering smile. "No wonder you stay in shape,"
he said as they reached the top floor. "You probably
climb these stairs a bunch of times each day."

"More times than I want to think about," she
replied as she led him into the loft.

He stopped in the doorway, and his gaze swept
the entire area with interest. "Great place," he said,
and walked with her over to the sofa, where she
sank down amid the blankets she'd laid out for
Charlie.

"It's home," she said as he sat next to her.

"Tell me again what happened down there," he
said gently.

She closed her eyes for a moment, reliving those
frantic moments of panic. "I was leaning over the

desk, looking at some sketches, when something struck me in the back of the head."

This time she didn't fight her impulse and raised a hand to touch the tender spot. She opened her eyes and looked at him. "For a minute I thought maybe one of the doll parts had fallen from its hook in the ceiling and hit me. But then I heard a grunt and I was pushed. I crashed into the desk, and when I got to my feet somebody grabbed me around the neck from behind."

His eyes darkened as he gazed at her throat while she continued. "Charlie called down the stairs to me, and whoever had me let go and ran out the back door."

"So you never saw who it was?"

"Not a glimpse."

"Did you get any impressions? Was he tall or short? Thin or heavy? Did you notice any particular smells coming off him?" He shot the questions at her like the cop he was.

She closed her eyes, trying to summon up any impression she might have unconsciously gotten about her attacker. She stared at him once again in frustration. "I don't know. It all happened so fast. All I can tell you is that he was strong, really strong. Maybe it was some junkie thinking he'd get some ready cash in the register. I probably would have been safe if I'd stayed upstairs and gone to bed instead of deciding to go downstairs."

He nodded and reached out to take her hand in his. "Wrong time, wrong place. Why don't you go take a nice hot bath, and I'll fix you a cup of tea and bring it to you with a couple of aspirins?"

She sighed. "That sounds like a wonderful idea."

She reluctantly released his hand and pulled herself off the sofa. "Tea bags are in the little holder on the counter, and cups are in the cabinet left of the sink."

"I'm sure I can manage," he replied.

She stumbled toward the bathroom, hoping that the steamy bath would relax the muscles that screamed from points all over her body.

It didn't take long to fill the tub with bath oil and hot water; then she stripped and sank down, grateful that at least for the moment she wasn't there all alone.

After she'd disappeared into the bathroom, Tyler looked around the loft with interest. He found the colors soothing and the whole thing chic without being pretentious. There was a homeyness here. Unlike his place it was easy to make guesses about the person who lived here by the items she chose to display.

The wall unit of shelves held no television, indicating that watching the boob tube wasn't an important part of her life. A variety of books filled one shelf, some romances mixed in with fashion design tomes. A collection of elephants were displayed on two of the shelves, elephants of all sizes and shapes and textures.

He'd heard someplace that elephants with their trunks raised in the air brought good luck. He noticed that all of hers had their trunks up in the air. Unfortunately they hadn't brought her good luck tonight.

The teakettle was on the stovetop, and he filled it with water and turned on the burner. As he readied a cup and the tea bag, he thought of that moment when Jennifer had told him that an emergency phone call had come from the Dollhouse.

Maybe it was the murders he'd been investigating that had seared such panic inside him, but panic was what he'd felt as he'd driven here at warp speed.

Or maybe it was because, despite the short time they'd been seeing each other, he'd come to care about her a great deal.

In a million years Tyler would never have considered himself a romantic, but the moment he'd seen Annalise he'd felt a sense of rightness. Spending time with her had only enhanced the feeling.

It had been difficult for him not to talk about the cases he was working, not to share the murder puzzle that never completely went out of his mind. It wasn't that he wanted her to know the gruesome details of those women's deaths; he just wanted to share with her little bits and pieces of his world.

If the relationship managed to survive this case and she didn't get tired of the hours and leave, then he'd know it was something special, something to hang on to.

He fixed the tea, then carried it to the bathroom and knocked on the door. She told him to come in, and he entered. The sight of her in the deep raised tub made him stop short in the doorway.

Her hair was fastened carelessly on top of her head, and sweet-smelling bubbles surrounded her. A dim light shone down on the tub, gleaming on her bare shoulders and allowing the starlit night sky out the window to be visible.

Desire punched him in the gut, and he reminded himself that she had just been the victim of a crime and that the last thing she needed was a panting, horny man jumping into those bubbles with her. Still, his blood heated as he stepped closer to the tub.

He'd love to be in that bubbly water with her. He wanted to smooth his hands down her slick skin, taste her as the water swirled around them.

"Here you are," he said as he set the teacup on the wide porcelain that surrounded the tub. "I'll just let you finish up," he said, and started to leave.

"Wait. Don't go. Stay and talk to me, Tyler."

She had no idea what she was asking of him, had no idea how the thought of her sweet-smelling, naked skin so close to him affected him.

"I'll sit and talk to you, but I don't want to look at you too much," he said. "You look so damned sexy at the moment, if I look at you I'll find it hard to concentrate on anything you're saying."

She gave him a half smile. "It's nice to know I can look sexy when I feel like hell."

Sympathy swept through him as he sat on the edge of the tub. "Head still hurt?"

"I feel like the drum section of a band has taken up residence in my brain."

"Let me check it out." He leaned forward and ran his hand lightly over the back of her head. "Ah, there's a nice goose egg back here, but it doesn't feel like the skin was broken." He ran his hands from her head down to her shoulders and massaged them softly. Her skin was slick with scent and water, and beneath the surface he could see her breasts.

She mewed her pleasure, and he felt himself getting hard. He drew his hands away. "Hmm, don't stop," she said.

"I really think I should," he replied. "I'm a bastard, Annalise, a sick, insensitive creep. You've just been attacked and I'm trying to help you relax, but I am so turned on right now it's embarrassing."

She laughed, obviously delighted by his confession. "Trust me, Tyler, you aren't an insensitive creep. You're just a typical male."

"Still, I think it would be best if I wait for you out in the living room."

She nodded and picked up a sponge as he got up and left.

Once back in the living room he paced the floor, willing the blood to leave the lower part of his body and return to his brain. He walked back into the kitchen area and opened the fridge, looking for something to drink.

He grabbed a bottle of water, then sat at the table and eyed with interest the three boxes that were on it. They were doll boxes, with BLAKELY DOLLS stamped all over them in vivid pink.

He hadn't paid any attention to the doll stuff when he'd come in through the shop. His entire focus had been on Annalise. He'd needed to assure himself that she was all right.

Now he found himself curious as to what kind of dolls she made. He pulled the lid off the first box to reveal a bride doll. Instantly visions of Kerry Albright crashed through his head. For a moment he felt as if he were viewing her body laid to rest in a cardboard casket.

He slammed his eyelids shut in an effort to banish Kerry's face from his mind. When he opened his eyes and looked once again, it was just a doll.

Every dollmaker in the world must make a doll

wearing bridal fashions, he thought. His mother had a bride doll that she'd received from her parents on her tenth birthday. Every morning when she made her bed she placed the doll there, a frothy white centerpiece in the middle of the rose-colored bedspread.

He put the lid back on the box, then removed the lid to the second one. A roar resounded in his ears as he stared at the smiling, dark-haired doll in flapper attire.

What the hell? A bride doll . . . a roaring twenties flapper . . . weird coincidence? He didn't believe in coincidences like that.

His mind raced. Business was bad; profits were down—that was what she'd told him. She was desperate to put the business back on solid ground. Arranging the murders of young women and dressing them like her dolls would certainly garner a new burst of interest and increase sales. He hated the path his mind took. He was thinking like a cop, chasing motive, hunting madness.

Was there madness in Annalise? He stared at the third box with dread. It had to be some kind of crazy coincidence. Annalise wasn't capable of such horror. Surely he would have known if the woman he'd been seeing—the woman he'd made love to— was evil.

Now he was thinking like a man. As a cop he knew better than anyone that the face of evil could hide behind guileless eyes and a beautiful countenance. Evil could wear the mask of many things, including the woman he'd been perilously close to falling in love with.

He got up from the table, his gaze still focused on

the unopened third box before him. There were few things that frightened Tyler King, but the unopened box scared the hell out of him.

He was vaguely aware of the sound of water draining from the bathroom. Still he stared at the box with dreadful intent. Open it, his brain commanded. His fingers touched the lid. Let it be a ballerina in a pink tutu. Let it be a mermaid with a shiny tail.

He drew a deep breath, pulled off the lid and gasped as he saw the geisha doll inside.

Three dolls.

Three bodies.

Three dolls.

Three bodies. The roar in his head was deafening.

Annalise. Jesus Christ, it had been Annalise. Had she been getting her rocks off dating the man in charge of solving the very crimes she had to be responsible for?

A searing rage grabbed hold of him at the same time she stepped out of the bathroom clad in a short bright blue silk robe.

"I'm not sure if it was the tea, the bath or your company, but I'm definitely feeling better," she said with a smile.

"Good, I'm glad," he said, his voice ominously soft as he approached where she stood.

Someplace in the back of his mind he registered the fact that he'd never seen her looking as pretty as she did at the moment. Her face was scrubbed clean, her cheeks flushed with a rosy hue. The color of her robe made her eyes look impossibly blue, and the scent of sweet flowers clung to her.

His mind protested the evidence he'd just seen.

He didn't want to believe it, but he couldn't suppress the cop's rage that nearly consumed him.

"Get dressed, Annalise."

She eyed him in confusion. "What?"

"I said get dressed. I'm taking you down to the station."

"Why? I already made a report of everything with those other two officers." She stared into his eyes and must have seen something there that frightened her, for she took a step back from him. "Tyler, what's wrong?"

"What's wrong?" He advanced toward her. "What's wrong?" he repeated, his volume increasing with each word. "You didn't expect me to show up here tonight, did you? What were you doing before I got here, sitting at the table and gloating over those dead women?"

She gasped. "What are you talking about?"

He grabbed her by the arm and pulled her to the table, where the three dolls stared up out of their boxes. "Tell me, Annalise. Tell me what these are."

Her eyes were wide. "Tyler, you're hurting me," she said, and tried to tug her arm from his grasp. He refused to relinquish his hold on her.

"Is your business more important than three young lives?" he asked. Anger mingled with pain as he stared at her, trying to see a flash of the evil she had to possess inside her.

"For God's sake, I don't know what you're talking about," she half screamed.

"I'm talking about the fact that I have three dead women, women who were dressed exactly like those." He pointed to the dolls and finally released her.

If she were guilty, she was the best actress he'd ever seen. Tears welled up in her eyes, and her lower lip began to tremble uncontrollably. "What do you mean, they were dressed like this?" Her voice was a mere whisper.

"I mean I've got three dead girls, one dressed like a bride, another a flapper and the latest one a geisha girl. They are nearly identical to those dolls. Now, you need to give me one good reason why I shouldn't arrest you right now and haul your ass down to the station."

Chapter 17

"Those dolls were delivered anonymously here over the past couple of weeks. Belinda the Bride showed up first." Annalise's voice trembled. She felt as if she'd been thrust into an alternate reality.

Tyler's features were hard, unyielding as he continued to stare at her. As she tried to process what he'd just told her, all she wanted to do was run back to the bathroom and throw up.

Dead girls dressed like her dolls? The thought made her stomach ill and her headache return full force. She sank down into a chair at the table, afraid her shaking legs would no longer hold her up.

"What do you mean, they were delivered anonymously?" Tyler asked.

"The bride doll showed up in the shop one day on the counter. I just assumed it was a disgruntled customer returning it. But it was odd—and then there was the note."

"Note?"

She nodded and dug in the tissue paper and pulled out a folded piece of paper. She watched as

Tyler opened the note and read it, a muscle throbbing in his lower jaw. "And what about the next one?"

"Fanny the Flapper. The box was left just outside the front door of the shop. Same with Kimono Kim. I found her this morning."

God, had it been only this morning? It seemed like years ago that she and Charlie had worked in the shop, then enjoyed a leisurely dinner at Joey's. "There were notes with them as well." She pulled out the notes and handed them to him. It was only then that he joined her at the table.

A combination half sob, half burst of laughter escaped her. "I thought it was a new dollmaker in town throwing down some sort of silly challenge."

When he looked at her some of the hardness had left his eyes. "I need to call my partner. We need to go over all of this, and it doesn't look good if I take the report alone, given the personal nature of our relationship."

"Personal nature? Two seconds ago you thought I was some kind of serial killer." She bit her bottom lip to keep it from trembling.

His expression softened even more. "I can't apologize for responding like a cop with the evidence that was before me," he said gently.

She nodded and watched as he pulled his cell phone from his pocket. "Jennifer," he said when he'd made his connection. "I need you to come to the Dollhouse in the Riverfront area, and bring the files. We just got a major break in the Costume Killer case."

"Costume Killer?" Annalise said when he'd hung up.

"That's what we were calling him. We thought maybe the perp was into some sort of weird costume fetish." He looked down at the notes and grimaced, the knot in his jaw once again pulsing with energy. "And now we know he calls himself the Dollmaker. You might want to put on a pot of coffee and get dressed. It's going to be a long night."

Annalise got up, grateful for something to do. Her head reeled with the events of the last ten minutes. The idea that somebody was killing women and dressing them like her dolls was absolutely horrifying.

Who could be responsible? Who on earth would do such a thing? Why dress them like her dolls? Surely Tyler had to be mistaken. But she knew he wasn't. She'd seen the certainty shining hard from his eyes.

After she got the coffee going she went into her bedroom and pulled out a pair of yoga pants and a T-shirt, then went into the bathroom to change.

As she took off her robe and nightclothes, she tried not to think about what was happening in her life. For the last several weeks she'd felt the sensation of impending doom, the dread of something awful happening. She'd thought it was just her imagination, but now she knew better, and she had the terrifying feeling that things were going to get worse before they got better.

When she came out of the bathroom Tyler was still seated at the table, the three notes in front of him. He looked up as she returned and offered her a tight smile.

"I was just sitting here thinking about the joke fate has played on us. For the last couple of weeks

I've been pulling my hair out trying to solve two heinous murders, and all the while I was seeing a woman who was a key piece of the puzzle."

She rejoined him at the table. "How can I be a key piece of the puzzle? I don't know anyone who would be capable of something like this."

"But he knows you. These notes and the dolls prove that," he replied.

The very idea shot a shiver up her spine and sent her lower lip to trembling once again.

"You have a catalog or something that shows all the dolls in your collection?" he asked.

She shook her head. "No catalog, but I have a display downstairs in the shop and pictures of them on the Internet."

"I need to see it." He shoved his chair back from the table and stood. "Can you take me downstairs now?"

"Of course." As she stood he reached out to her and drew her into his arms.

"I'm sorry I was mean," he said into her hair. She leaned against him, seeking strength to get through whatever might come. And she knew that whatever it was, it was going to be bad.

"It's okay. I understand." And she did. What else could he have thought when he'd seen those dolls on the table except that she was somehow involved in the murders? He wouldn't have been a good cop if he hadn't considered that conclusion.

"Why didn't you call the police when you started getting the dolls?" he asked, not moving to break the embrace.

"Like I told you, I just thought it was some kind of weirdo throwing down a professional challenge.

There was nothing really ominous about the notes, especially considering I had no idea that dead women were being dressed like my dolls."

"We had managed to keep the costume detail from the press up until yesterday. Unfortunately the latest body was found by a reporter." He explained to her about Reuben and the phone call from the perp.

As he told her everything she burrowed deeper into his arms, needing the warmth of his body to take away the frigid chill inside her.

All too quickly he released her, and together they went down the stairs to the shop. She turned on all the lights, and he gasped as he saw the built-in display of the Blakely dolls that had been created through the years.

"How many are there?" he asked as he stepped closer to the display case.

"Sixty." She moved to stand next to him, taking in the dolls that had been so much a part of her life, whether she wanted them to be or not.

"Two of the three that were sent back to me were older models." She pointed to Belinda and to Fanny. "I thought it was odd at the time that these particular dolls would be returned, because they're collectibles and worth quite a bit of money now. Kimono Kim was the first doll I did after my mother's death."

Tyler's jaw had gone tense again. "Sixty," he said more to himself than to her. "That means we have the potential for fifty-seven more victims."

"That's a horrifying thought," she said, her voice a mere whisper.

A knock on the front door drew their attention. A

tall woman with broad features and short, dark hair peered in at them. "That's my partner," Tyler said, and strode to the front door to let her in. "Annalise, this is my partner, Jennifer Tompkins. Jennifer, this is Annalise Blakely, the woman I've been dating and a key element to the murders we've been investigating."

Jennifer nodded toward Annalise. "So, tell me what's going on."

As Tyler quickly filled her in about the dolls and the notes that Annalise had received, Jennifer eyed Annalise with more than a touch of wary suspicion.

When he'd finished explaining everything Jennifer puffed a sigh. "Well, if this isn't a cluster fuck," she exclaimed. "We have the lead detective dating a potential suspect in a serial-killer case that just went public with this evening's edition of the newspaper."

Tyler narrowed his eyes. "What are you talking about?"

"That little shit Reuben spilled the beans." Jennifer patted the black briefcase she carried. "I've got evidence bags, the case files and a copy of the evening newspaper in my magic tote." She looked at them both expectantly.

"Let's go upstairs. We'll collect the dolls and get down to business," Tyler said tersely.

Jennifer opted to ride up in the elevator, and Tyler and Annalise walked back up the two flights of stairs.

Annalise felt as if she'd been thrust into an awful nightmare with no hope of waking up anytime soon. Tyler was silent as they climbed, and she knew that he was in full cop mode and that the hours ahead promised to be difficult ones.

Jennifer awaited them at the door, her gaze on Annalise still holding something vaguely hostile. When they got inside Jennifer opened the briefcase and withdrew the evidence bags. The dolls each went into a bag, box and all; then the notes went into smaller, separate bags and labeled as to which note came with which doll.

When the table was cleared Annalise poured them all coffee and they sat, several thick manila folders in front of Tyler.

"Kerry Albright. Margie Francis. Sulee Hwang. Those names mean anything to you?" Tyler asked.

Annalise shook her head. "I've never heard of them before. Those are the names of the victims?" Hearing those names made it all so much more real. They had been real people, real women with hopes and dreams.

"Yeah. I need you to look at some photographs and see if you recognize the women."

Annalise steeled herself as he pulled out several sheets of paper and passed them to her. She was relieved to see that the papers held color photocopies of driver's licenses. She stared at the faces, but none of them looked the slightest bit familiar.

"No, I'm pretty sure I've never seen them before." She shoved them back across the table. "They don't even look like my dolls." She knew she was grasping at straws, but she needed something, anything to distance the horror.

"They did when the killer got through with them," Jennifer said brusquely.

Tyler hesitated a moment, then pulled out another photo and pushed it in front of her. A gasp escaped Annalise as she stared at the new photo of Kerry Albright. She'd been transformed into the bride doll. It wasn't just the dress that was remarkably similar, but the hairstyle was an exact replica, as was the makeup used to enhance her doll-like appearance.

Before the complete emotional impact had struck, another photo appeared before her. In Margie's driver's license photo her hair had been shoulder length and straight. In the new photo she was dressed like Fanny and Margie's hair had been cut and curled to mirror the doll's appearance.

Tyler started to push yet another picture in front of her, but she raised a hand, tears blurring her vision. "Please, no more." The idea that these women had somehow died because of her dolls swept an agonizing grief through her.

She was grateful that Tyler paused, giving her a moment to pull herself together.

"Okay, let's start at the beginning," he said as he pulled a pad from the briefcase. "When exactly did you receive the first doll?"

For the next few minutes she talked about the date and approximate time she'd gotten each of the dolls. Tyler took notes, and Jennifer continued to gaze at her with cool, hooded eyes. It was crazy; Annalise knew she wasn't guilty of anything and yet something in Jennifer's demeanor made her feel as if she were.

"We're going to need a list of everyone who works for you," Tyler now said.

"Surely you don't think one of my staff members could be responsible for this," she protested.

"At this point everyone is a suspect," Jennifer said. She got up to help herself to another cup of coffee. "You keep a list of people who have bought your dolls?"

"I have a mailing list, but it's in no way a complete list of buyers," she said. "My mother didn't start it when the business first began. A couple of years before her death she started taking names and addresses of customers. Everyone who came into the store, whether they bought or not, was given the option of being placed on the list. There're over six thousand names."

Jennifer released a low whistle. "Any way of tracking who might have bought these specific dolls?"

Annalise shook her head. "Not with every sale, but my database has information about the customers who wanted to be on the mailing list."

"But not all of the customers are in your database," Tyler said.

"Exactly. Almost everyone who ever wrote a check for a purchase is in the system, but cash and credit card purchases wouldn't necessarily be in there. Some of those people wanted to be in the system, and others didn't want to be."

And so the night went, with question after question about her staff, about her customers and about anyone who might have a place in her life.

She fired up her computer and printed off employee records, the customer database and the list of transactions for the past ten years. She explained to them that anything before ten years ago was not on the computer but would be in boxes on the second floor.

By two thirty Annalise felt as if she couldn't answer another question. Her headache had returned in full force, but the weariness that plagued her wasn't a physical exhaustion as much as it was a soul sickness.

It was Jennifer who called a halt to things. "There's nothing else we can accomplish here tonight," she said as she stood. "We might as well all get some sleep and start fresh tomorrow."

"I'll walk her out," Tyler said to Annalise. As he and Jennifer left, Annalise turned off the living room light and walked over to the window to peer outside.

Hot, exhausted tears burned her eyes. Someplace out there was a madman perverting her life's work, her mother's life's work.

Who would do such a thing? And why? What was the point? She struggled to try to make sense of things, but realized there was no way to make sense of something like this.

She still stood at the window when Tyler returned. He came up behind her and wrapped his arms around her. She leaned back against him and closed her eyes, for a moment just wallowing in the feel of him so close against her.

"I'm sorry. I know I was hard on you," he said into her hair.

She turned to face him. "It had to be done. It's just so scary." Once again she fought against the press of tears. "Tyler, why is this happening? Who is doing this?"

His features took on the same hardness they had while he had been questioning her. "I don't know, but we'll find him. You're the break we needed. And now what you need is bed."

While sleep definitely sounded wonderful, the thought of being here and crawling into bed alone filled her with an unusual apprehension. "What are you going to do?" she asked tentatively.

He looked at her for a long moment. "What do you want me to do?"

"Stay with me. Stay the night."

He leaned forward and kissed her on the forehead. "You got it," he replied. "Go get ready for bed. I'm going to grab my gym bag from the car. I'll be right back up."

It took her only minutes to change into her nightgown and get ready for bed. She got a new toothbrush out for Tyler and set it on the sink. When she left the bathroom she saw Tyler standing at the window and staring out as she had done only moments before.

He turned to look at her, and his eyes were as dark as the night outside. "I was just thinking how ironic it was that in most of my past relationships I talked about my work; I shared some of the details of the cases. And every time I did that eventually the woman I was seeing couldn't handle it and left."

Annalise sat on the side of the bed and remained silent as he continued. "So, I decided not to share anything about my work with you." He joined her on the bed. "I didn't want to taint you with all the ugliness, and all along you were the one I should have been talking to."

"And now I'm part of the ugliness." As she thought of those poor women her vision misted with tears once again. "I somehow feel responsible for those women, for their deaths."

"You know better than that," he chided, and placed an arm around her shoulders. "This probably has nothing to do with you personally. Some nut has found your dolls a vehicle for his madness. I told you, Annalise, we'll find him—and hopefully before he kills again."

"I hope so," she said fervently.

"And now it's time to get some shut-eye. Tomorrow is going to be another long day."

She slid beneath the sheet, and he stepped into the bathroom after placing his gun and cell phone on the nightstand. When he came out he had on a clean pair of gym shorts, and after turning out the lights he got into bed with her.

He gathered her against him and she cuddled close, needing the warmth of him, the security of his nearness. "Thanks for staying, Tyler. You're just what I need after such an awful night." She rested her hand on his chest and he pulled her close to his side. "You make me feel safe in spite of everything that happened tonight."

Tyler's response wasn't immediate. She could feel a tenseness to his body, an uneven rhythm to his breathing. She moved her leg against his, and he stiffened ever so slightly, then turned toward her.

"There's safe, and then there's safe. It's been a rough night for both of us, but something about the way you're curled around my body has me thinking of other things now," he said softly.

"I wasn't aware I was starting anything."

His eyes gleamed in the pale moonlight that filtered in through the window. "Every time you touch me you start something."

"Well, in that case . . ." She slid her hand along his chest and caressed down the flat of his abdomen.

It was like unleashing a tiger. With a groan he pulled her on top of him, and their lips met in a fiery kiss. He stroked his hands up beneath her nightgown, cupping her bare ass as their tongues danced together in hunger.

She ground her hips against his, wanting . . . needing conscious thought to be swept away by mindless desire, by hot physical sensation.

A quiet desperation marked their short foreplay. The past several hours they'd been mired in death. Now they frantically sought life in each other.

The few clothes they wore were ripped off, and he took her hard and fast, as if he knew that was exactly what she wanted. And she wanted it—God, how she wanted it. She clung to him as he drilled into her. She met each of his thrusts with a frantic driving need of her own and cried out with pleasure as her orgasm shattered through her.

Afterward they lay in each other's arms, waiting for bodies to cool, for pants to become breaths and heartbeats to slow.

"I didn't hurt you, did I?" he asked after a few minutes.

"Not at all." She curled up next to him. "But if you approach your cases with as much intensity as you do your lovemaking, you must be one hell of a cop."

He raised himself up on one elbow and smiled down at her. The gentleness of the smile, the soft way he gently moved a strand of hair from her face created a need in her that had nothing to do with sex. And it frightened her how easily this man could slip into her heart if she allowed him in. The idea of falling in love with him scared the hell out of her.

"We'll get through this," he said. "Now go to sleep." He kissed her softly on the forehead and placed an arm around her; then, almost before she could blink, he was asleep.

She closed her eyes, once again desperate to fall asleep. Now that the thrill of their lovemaking had passed, she was left with the vision of dead girls.

Why her dolls? It had to mean something, the fact that the victims were replicating the Blakely dolls. Was it a form of perverted emulation? Was the killer trying to get her attention?

Sleep had just about taken her when she was struck with a new thought and her eyes flew open. She realized there was something important she hadn't told Tyler.

She hadn't told him that there was an Annalise doll.

Chapter 18

"**D**amned stubborn. You should have warned me that was one of your character traits," Tyler exclaimed the next day as the two of them faced off outside the police station. They were arguing about where she should stay.

"I told you before that I make it a habit not to discuss my negative traits in the early stages of a relationship," Annalise replied.

It was just after three, and it had already been an excruciatingly long day. They had arrived at the police station just after seven that morning, where she was once again questioned by Tyler and Jennifer and the rest of the officers working the Costume Killer case.

They had pored over her printouts of the database, trying to make sense, trying to spot anything that might point a finger at the guilty.

She was brought a hamburger and french fries for lunch, although she wasn't a bit hungry. Then the questions began again. The most frustrating part was that she knew she didn't have the answers the officers sought.

She had no idea who might be responsible, couldn't imagine that it was anyone she knew or had contact with on a regular basis. This kind of horror was out of her realm of reality, and she couldn't wrap her mind around the fact that the murders might have been committed by somebody she knew.

She was grilled about her employees, her friends and her family. In the midst of it all her father had called her on her cell phone and told her they needed to talk. She took the call in the hallway outside the interrogation room, then returned to more questions.

Functioning on too little sleep and with aches where she didn't know she had body, she just wanted to go back home and pull the covers up over her head.

She nearly wept with relief when the men broke up the meeting and went in different directions and Tyler indicated that he'd take her home. She hadn't known until this minute that he'd meant his home, not hers.

"I think we're a little past the early stages of this relationship," he now said in obvious frustration. "Have you forgotten that you were attacked last night and that we're hunting a killer who has a thing for your dolls?"

"Of course I haven't forgotten," she replied. How could she forget? Her aching body reminded her of the attack every time she moved. "But the more I think about it, the more convinced I am that I forgot to lock up after Charlie and I got back from dinner, and I interrupted a robbery when I came back down the stairs."

"And you're sure about that?" One of his dark brows lifted.

She flushed. "What I'm sure about is that I'm not going to be chased away from my home, from my business. Besides, I've already made arrangements to meet my father there at six."

"Then why can't I pick you up after your meeting with your dad and take you to my place?" He stepped closer to her. "Annalise, I need to know you're safe." His eyes radiated a depth of emotion she didn't want to see. "Stay at my place until we catch this guy."

"Tyler, I'm in the middle of finalizing plans for the newest doll. I have a shop to run and people who depend on me for their livelihood. I can't just run and hide. Besides, we have no idea how long it will take you to catch this person."

She took a step toward his car. "Now, please just take me home, or if it's more convenient I can call a cab." She wasn't sure why, but she somehow felt that if she moved in with Tyler, the madman won. Besides, she couldn't move in with him and stay forever, not under these circumstances.

He shook his head and took her by the elbow. "Stubborn. Damned stubborn. I'll take you home. I don't like it, but I'll take you home."

"Thank you," she replied.

"Okay, so now I know you're incredibly stubborn," he said as they got into the car. "What else do I have to look forward to?"

"You haven't seen it yet, but I can get very cranky," she replied.

"That's funny—my partner tells me I have a tendency to be a little cranky at times. So, what kinds of things make you cranky?"

She knew what he was doing. He was starting a ridiculous conversation about a ridiculous topic to get her mind off the horror that had entered her life.

"Tardiness makes me cranky," she said, deciding to play along. "I hate people who seem to think that their time is more valuable than mine."

"What else?"

She frowned thoughtfully. "Too little sleep, too much caffeine. What about you?"

He flashed her one of his charming grins. "Too much sleep and too little caffeine."

She laughed despite her weariness. The moment of absurdity lasted all too briefly as reality slammed back to her. "From what I gathered listening to all of you this morning, the man you're looking for isn't a professional seamster."

"Our experts said the sewing is elementary and a bit shoddy."

"Then you can mark Sammy Winfield off your list of suspects," she said. He looked at her blankly. "That's my head seamster. Sammy is a perfectionist and would never do shoddy work."

"The only way anyone is coming off my list of suspects is if they have an airtight alibi for all the times of the murders." Tyler pulled to the curb in front of her building and killed the engine. "I'm coming in with you. I want to make sure there aren't any monsters hiding in closets."

She didn't argue with him.

It took him almost thirty minutes to go through the three-story building and check to make sure they were really alone.

Annalise was shocked when he discovered a window not closed completely on the second floor. "The officers who responded to your intruder call should have found this," he said as he closed and locked it.

"You think that's the way he got in?" she asked.

He frowned. "Hard to tell. I suppose it's possible he could have used the fire escape to get in that way." His frown deepened as he placed his hands gently on her shoulders. "I could put you into protective custody."

"And I just walk away from my life?" She shook her head. "I'm not willing to do that."

"What scares me is the idea of some maniac out there sewing a lavender dress to put you in," he said. She'd shown him the official Annalise doll that morning before they'd left for the station.

"That scares me, too," she admitted. "But there are fifty-seven dolls in the display case downstairs that he could intend to be his next victim. Besides, I'd say at the moment I'm the safest of the dolls. If he kills me, then who is he going to taunt? Who is he going to send the notes and dolls to?"

"You have a point, but I still wish you'd stay at my place." He pulled her against him and wrapped her in a tight embrace. "I just don't want anything happening to you."

"Nothing is going to happen." She laid her head against his chest. His arms had begun to feel like home, and that was exactly why she didn't want to stay with him. Somehow in all the craziness he had gotten in deeper than any man before him. She needed some distance.

"Now that I know what's going on, I'll just have

to be extracareful," she said. "I'll be vigilant about making sure my doors and windows are locked."

She left his arms as his cell phone rang. He listened to the caller, murmured an okay, then hung up. "I've got to get back to the station."

"I'll walk you out."

When they reached the front door she forced a reassuring smile. "I'll be fine, Tyler. I promise."

"Call me when your dad leaves? And call me if you change your mind about staying here. You'd be safe at my place."

"I'll be fine here," she replied firmly.

He eyed her for a moment with grudging respect. "You're either very brave or very stupid."

She smiled. "Maybe a little of both."

It wasn't until she watched his car pull away from the curb that she had a crazy impulse to run after him, to tell him she'd changed her mind about remaining here.

The momentary panic subsided, and after double-checking the door to make sure it was locked, she went upstairs to her loft.

A glance at the clock let her know she had an hour and a half before her father was due to arrive. She didn't even want to speculate about what he might want to discuss with her, but she assumed it had something to do with Charlie.

Sinking down on the sofa, she leaned her head back against the cushions. The events of the past eighteen hours or so still held a kind of dreamlike quality.

She'd sat at the police station and had made a list of staff, friends and acquaintances, and as she'd written each name she'd thought of how impossible it was to imagine that particular person as a cold-blooded killer.

She'd like to think that she didn't personally know the killer. The thought of sitting next to, having lunch with or chatting with the person responsible for the deaths created a cold chill that didn't sweep through her, but rather set up residence deep inside.

What she hated more than anything was that now she had to view each of those people with an edge of suspicion. Ben had been upset lately about the flagging sales and the new direction she'd intended to go with the next product. Mike was more than a little bit in love with her and knew she was worried about the declining sales.

Had either of them resorted to this in an effort to garner publicity? The very idea was sickening, but couldn't be dismissed completely.

George Cole, her insurance salesman, had said that his mother was a collector of Blakely Dolls. Did his mild manner, his gentle nature, hide a soul of twisted evil? And John Malcolm—he'd been in the store just the other day to buy the newest, the Birthday Bonnie doll. Had he wanted it in order to pattern his own sick version?

And then there was Joey, who had been mysteriously absent from his restaurant lately. How many times had she visited with him, talking about her dolls and sharing details of her life?

She pulled herself off the sofa, disturbed by these thoughts of friends and coworkers and neighbors. She didn't want to think that any of them were responsible. These were people she'd considered friends. She'd shared meals with them, sat in the park with them, worked with them.

She focused instead on the loft and looked around the place to see if anything needed to be done before her father arrived.

He'd never been up here. Whenever they met it was always in a neutral place, a restaurant, the park or some other public place. She walked over to her collection of elephants lined up on the wooden shelf.

She'd loved elephants and him, and definitely not in that order. For a long time when she'd been young she'd wondered what was wrong with her, what she'd done to make him leave her. As she'd gotten older she'd recognized that the problem had been his, not hers.

"Old issues," she murmured. So why couldn't she get past it? Why was there still a little piece of her heart that desperately longed to be Daddy's girl?

She knew Tyler was falling in love with her. She could see it in his gaze when he looked at her, feel it in his every touch. It wouldn't be long before he'd want something more from her, an emotional commitment to their relationship.

There was a part of her that desperately wanted to give in to the emotions he stirred in her. Although she'd always told herself a husband and family didn't really matter to her, if she looked deep inside herself she'd see that she did want that.

But she was afraid.

It was so much easier to keep relationships light and casual, so much easier to keep your heart intact that way. She suspected it was already too late for

her to remain unscathed by Tyler. When he left—
and he would leave—she'd feel his absence, just like
she'd felt her father's so long ago.

By quarter till six Annalise had a pot of coffee
brewed and had set out a plate of cookies she'd
found in her pantry. She didn't know how fond her
father was of Oreos, but she ate four while she
waited for him to show up.

At exactly six o'clock the buzzer rang to let her
know he'd arrived. As she hurried down the stairs
to let him in she marveled at the fact that a visit with
her father made her feel almost as tense as knowing
there was a killer somewhere in the periphery of her
life.

"Hi, honey." He leaned forward to press his lips
to her forehead after she'd let him in and relocked
the door behind him. "You doing okay? I've been
worried about you all day. Did they catch the creep
who broke in here last night? Charlie has been worried sick about you."

It wasn't in Frank's nature to ramble, but that
was exactly what he seemed to be doing. "I'm fine,
Dad. Come on upstairs; I put a pot of coffee on a few
minutes ago."

"Did they catch the guy?" Frank repeated as they
climbed the stairs to the loft.

"No, but it was probably just a robbery attempt.
Tyler found a window open on the second floor, and
that's probably how they got in. The window is now
safely locked."

"Charlie told me there was a homeless guy outside your building when you got back from dinner."

"That's Max," she replied. "And I already know
he wasn't the one who broke in. I found out this

morning that the officers who responded to my call found Max asleep in the park last night. They said he was too drunk to stand, let alone come inside and attack me. But I knew he'd never do anything to hurt me. We're friends."

Frank was silent until they got into the loft; then he looked around with interest. "It's a beautiful place, Annalise," he said as he sat at the table and she poured them each a cup of coffee. "But I worry about you living here. Despite all the renovation and development, this isn't a residential area. Who else is around after dark when the businesses close up for the night? It's dangerous."

She joined him at the table, unable to disagree with his assessment. The area still boasted too many empty buildings that were favorite places for drug deals and parties. While Max was a fairly benign presence, some of the other homeless were downright aggressive with their panhandling, and twice two of them had been arrested for breaking and entering.

"It's home," she replied.

He wrapped his hands around the earthen mug and raised it to his lips. She was surprised to see that his hand trembled slightly. Was he ill? Oh, God, was that what he'd come to tell her, that he had some terrible disease?

"Dad, what are you doing here?" she asked.

He lowered his cup. "Doesn't it strike you as odd that you even have to ask me why I'm here to visit you?"

"We haven't exactly had a drop-in-on-each-other kind of relationship," she said drily.

"No, we haven't, and that's what I want to talk

about. Last night when I got the call from Charlie that you had been attacked, I realized how short life is and that at any moment something could happen to you or to me and you'd never really know how much I love you."

"So, now I know," she said with a lightness that caused him to frown.

"Do you really?" He leaned forward, an intensity in his gaze she'd never seen before. "Annalise, you've been angry with me for a very long time, and we're way past due for a real talk."

She fought the impulse to get up from the table, the need to escape from her own emotions. "I don't know what you're talking about," she finally said. "Everything is fine between us." To her horror a hot splash of tears filled her eyes. She angrily swiped at them before they could trek down her cheeks.

"That doesn't look fine to me," he said softly.

The fact that he was so clueless as to why she might be angry made her even angrier. "Okay, you want to talk; we'll really talk." This time she didn't fight her impulse to get up, but rather jumped up from the table. "Why don't we talk about all those times you were going to pick me up to spend the day with you? I'd get all dressed up, and I'd be so excited it would hurt, and I'd sit on the porch stoop and wait . . . and wait . . . and wait, but you'd never come."

She began to pace in front of the table, not looking at him but rather looking back in time, back to those years of need, of want. The bitter pain that she'd always tried to keep suppressed boiled to the surface.

"Let's talk about how important you were to me,

and how unimportant I was to you in your new life." She finally looked at him. "I needed you, Dad, and you gave me elephants."

He leaned back in his chair and rubbed a hand across his forehead, and when he looked at her again there was a wealth of emotion in his eyes. "When I left your mother, she asked me to give you a couple of weeks to adjust. She promised me that after that we would set up liberal visitation for you with me. The first mistake I made was marrying her. The second mistake I made was believing her."

Annalise stopped pacing and looked at him in surprise. In all the years since their divorce she'd never heard him utter a bad word against her mother.

He looked older, smaller, as he stared off at some point just over her shoulder. "I gave it a couple of weeks, thinking it was the best thing to do for you; then I called and tried to set something up. I've never been one to talk ill of the dead, but your mother was a hard woman, Annalise."

He drew a deep sigh. "I walked away from her with nothing. Everything we had was tied up in her business. I could have taken half of it, but I knew that would destroy her. For six months after I left I slept on a friend's sofa because I had no place to go. Your mother convinced me no judge would ever give me custody, that I had nothing to offer you. The reason I left her was because she didn't want to share her life with me. She didn't want to share her dreams, her work or anything else in her life. And it wasn't until I left that I realized she had no intention of sharing you."

He got up from the table but made no move to

approach her. "I didn't know how to fight her, and she had the ultimate weapon—you. She told me you hated me and that I would only be a disruption in your life. She made me believe that it was best for you to stay with her, that a girl needed her mother, but that you had no need of me. When I'd talk to you on the phone, or on the rare occasions I got to see you, you acted like you wanted to be anywhere else but with me."

Annalise clung to her anger, afraid of what might be left if she let it go. "I was a kid, Dad. You should have done something. You should have tried harder." The anger was like a beast inside her, gaining strength as she indulged it. All those years of pain now exploded inside her as she stalked to the bookcase and grabbed one of the porcelain elephants.

"You want to know what I think of your elephants, Dad?" She threw the elephant against the wall, where it shattered into pieces. Someplace in the back of her mind she knew she was out of control. "That's what I think of your elephants."

Tears stung her eyes as a sob wrenched up from someplace deep within her. She grabbed another elephant and threw it into the wall as well.

The shattering reflected the way she'd felt each time she'd thought he was coming for her, each time he'd disappointed her.

She was about to throw the third elephant when he grabbed her and pulled her into a tight embrace. "Let me go," she screamed, and slammed her fists into his chest.

"No." He tightened his grip around her waist. She hit him again, sobs ripping from her throat. She hit him over and over, and still he held her tight, not flinching, not even attempting to avoid her attack.

When she'd exhausted herself she finally stilled, tears spilling silently down her cheeks. Frank pulled her closer, forcing her head to his chest.

She squeezed her eyes closed and allowed herself to grow calm. She could smell the scent of him, the scent she remembered from when she'd been little: a touch of shaving cream and his familiar cologne and his breath, a combination of coffee and a peppermint he must have eaten earlier.

But it was his heartbeat against her ear that surprised her. Strong and steady, it beat in a well-known cadence. A flash of a memory filled her head, a memory of getting up in the morning, getting dressed and going into the kitchen, where her father would be seated at the table drinking coffee and reading the morning paper.

As she entered the room he'd drop his paper, scoot his chair back and motion her into his lap. She'd curl up there with her head against his chest and listen to his heartbeat.

She hiccuped another sob, and his arms tightened around her. "From the moment you were born you've been the first thing I think about in the morning and the last thing I pray about at night," Frank said softly.

He finally released her, but grabbed her hand and led her to the sofa, where they sat side by side. He put an arm around her shoulder and drew her close to him.

"I made mistakes where you're concerned, Annalise. I let your mother tell me what was best for you when you were little; then as you got older and were so mad at me, I let you tell me what was best for you. But I will tell you this: Never did I make plans with your mother to pick you up then not show up. That just didn't happen."

She raised her head to look at him. "I remember at least five times when Mom told me to get dressed up, to brush my hair and look pretty because you were going to come and take me out to dinner or to a movie."

"If I'd arranged to do that, nothing could have kept me away."

She leaned her head back against him. "She was always so sympathetic when you didn't come. She'd fix me a bowl of ice cream, and we'd sit at the table and she'd tell me that you probably had many more important things to do than to see me."

As she thought of the manipulation by her mother, new tears filled her eyes. Her mother didn't like to share. And Annalise had been nothing more than a possession to keep to herself, no matter the consequences.

She'd been nothing more than an heir to carry on her mother's dream. It was a thought that had always been locked deep inside her, and now with the truth staring her in the face, that painful chamber had unlocked and the reality filtered through her.

"I made myself believe that I was important to Mom, that she loved me. Without that fantasy I have nothing," she murmured.

"That's not true. You have me. You've always had me, Annalise. And now you have Charlie. He absolutely adores you. And you have Sherri, if you want her."

Once again Annalise sat up and this time disengaged from her father's arms. "She seems nice."

Frank smiled. "Sherri is the most loving, giving person I've ever known."

"And she shares things with you?"

He laughed. "Sherri shares every thought that enters her head with me." He sobered. "Even though she's a strong, independent woman, she makes me feel like she needs me, that her life wouldn't be as good if I weren't around."

"And Mom didn't."

He sighed. "Your mother was strong and independent, but she always made me feel like I was in her way, that I was an unnecessary burden in her life."

Annalise didn't say anything, but she'd often felt the same way. She'd always suspected that if she hadn't learned how to sew, if she hadn't been involved with the dolls, her mother wouldn't have even pretended to love her. It had always been about the dolls. The damned dolls.

"Annalise, we can't get back those years," Frank said softly. "All I can tell you is how sorry I am that I wasn't there for you. If I could go back and fix things I would, but I can't."

"I know that."

"But hopefully we have a lot of time left, and we can make things different between us from now on." There was a faint touch of apprehension in his voice, as if he feared her reply.

She knew she had two choices. She could hang on to her anger, her pain, and remain in this same place in her life, or she could forgive and move on and welcome in a loving new relationship with her father. There was really only one choice.

She leaned over and kissed him on his cheek. "Yes, we can make things different between us from now on," she said. "You just told me what I told Charlie yesterday. He said he wished it hadn't taken so long for us to meet, and I told him we still have lots of time left to build good memories."

"I want that with you, honey. I want to be a part of your life. An integral part."

"I'd like that."

They talked for another hour—about Lillian, about their lives and what they hoped the future would bring. Annalise talked some more about the pain she'd experienced as a child and felt a cathartic release with each word.

It was funny; all she'd really needed from him was an acknowledgment of her pain and an apology. That was the elixir that began the healing process.

She didn't tell him about the latest development in the murder case. She didn't want to worry him, and hoped that Tyler and his team could catch the killer before Frank knew it had anything to do with her.

It was just after eight when they walked back down the stairs. They hugged at the door. "I'm sorry about my temper fit earlier," she said, thinking of the elephants she'd broken.

"I'm not." He smiled at her, a smile that held the father's love she'd hungered for. "You needed to vent all that. It had to come out to make room for all the positive things the future holds." He leaned forward and kissed her on the forehead. "Lock up after me."

She nodded. "Good night, Dad."

Once she was back upstairs in her loft, she played and replayed their conversation in her head. For years she'd clung to a fantasy about her mother. Danika had certainly seen the truth where Lillian Blakely was concerned. Annalise had been an investment in the future, a handy public relations tool to pull out at will, but Lillian had never seen the value of Annalise as a person, as her daughter.

And for the first time in her life Annalise questioned why she was so determined to preserve the dream of a woman who had never cared a bit about Annalise's dreams.

Maybe it was time for her to rethink the direction of her life. Although she had no intention of doing anything rash or making life-altering decisions at the moment, the thought of a new path was in the back of her head.

The silence of the loft pressed in on her as she curled up on the sofa. But as she listened she heard the familiar sound of the hum of the refrigerator, the tick of the wall clock and the faint whir of the air conditioner blowing from the vents. Comforting sounds, the noises of home.

She yawned as she grabbed her cordless phone. The last twenty-four hours felt as if they'd lasted months. Hopefully she would sleep long and dreamlessly tonight.

She punched in Tyler's cell phone number. He answered on the first ring. "I promised I'd call when Dad left," she said.

"Everything okay?"

"Better than it's been for a long time. We had a long talk. It was just what we needed—what I needed."

"I'm glad. And you locked up tight behind him?"

"I did." His question brought her back to her grim situation. "Tyler, I still think that last night's break-in had nothing to do with these murders. I can't imagine that I'd be a victim, because now it's obvious from the notes he's sent me that he needs to boast to me."

"I hope you're right, but we can't take anything for granted."

"Have you come up with anything from the information I gave you?"

"Nothing concrete yet, except we've managed to take your restaurant friend, Joey, off the list of suspects. He's been in Arizona visiting a relative who has terminal cancer. I'm afraid it's going to take days to try to make sense of everything else. We're planning on working through the night."

"I can't imagine that. I'm totally wiped out, and I'm just looking forward to a good night's sleep."

"And dreams of me?" His voice was low and sexy. "Annalise, did you know that I'm falling in love with you?"

For a moment his words created that old sense of panic in her, but it passed almost as quickly as it had come. "I think I'm falling in love with you," she admitted softly.

"You think? When will you be certain?"

She smiled into the receiver. "I'll let you know."

Max wanted to see the boy again. Mickey . . . no, Charlie. Ever since he'd seen Charlie, Max's head had been full of fragments of memories: Mickey smiling that easy smile of his, his eyes lit with humor, and Sam, slower to smile, but when he did it was like a gift from the gods.

He hungered for them, the smell of them, the sound of their voices. Sometimes it felt as if he'd lost them only yesterday, and his grief was deep and new and stabbed through him with pain too hard to bear. Other times his grief was softer, just a whisper in the back of his head that gnawed at him. But the grief never went completely away.

Tonight the sorrow was fresh, and as he climbed out of his crate tears blurred his vision. He knew that long before the fire had destroyed their bodies, their spirits had flown to heaven. He also had no doubt that eventually, when it was time, he'd join them there.

He'd hold his sons once again in his arms, and their laughter would fill his heart, heal his wounded soul. He told himself he just had to be patient, that when the time was right God would take him and they'd all be reunited again.

Chapter 19

"How in the hell did he get this information?" Tyler asked as he stared at the morning paper. The morning headline read: LOCAL DOLLMAKER LINKED TO MURDERS.

It was a few minutes after five thirty in the morning, and Jennifer had just brought in doughnuts and the local paper, hot off the presses.

They'd all worked through the night, poring over Annalise's database and trying to find the name of a killer. They had made charts, studied reports and, to Tyler's dismay, made little progress.

He now scanned the newspaper article written by none other than Reuben Sandford. It was all there. Somehow Reuben had figured out the connection between the dead girls and the Blakely dolls.

He'd not only listed the specific dolls involved, but also the year they'd been released and the history of the Blakely Dolls business. Apparently Tyler and his team weren't the only ones who had spent the night working.

With the press involved the political heat would

get hotter and their jobs would be more difficult. Even Tyler knew it was inevitable that the press would eventually learn of Annalise's involvement, but he'd hoped to have a little more time before that happened.

"Dammit, I'd like to know where he got his information so fast." Tyler tossed the paper aside. He'd been cranky already at the lack of progress they'd made, and the newspaper article sent his crankiness through the roof.

"I need to get to Annalise's place," he said as he stood from the table. "I need to warn her that she's going to be fodder for every reporter in town." He looked at Jennifer. "Why don't you plan on meeting me there around ten? We'll start taking statements from her staff." Jennifer nodded. He gave the rest of the team their instructions and arranged for all of them to meet back at the station at four that afternoon.

Minutes later, as he drove to Annalise's, his mind whirled with all the data it had received during the overnight hours.

The first task had been to try to identify the buyers of each of the three dolls. Annalise had told them that only five hundred of each had been made, and two of his detectives were now attempting to locate each of those sales in the database.

The computer printouts she'd given them didn't detail sales of two of the dolls, and their next job would be to retrieve the paperwork that she'd indicated was stored in boxes on the second floor of her building.

He stifled a yawn as he parked at the curb in front of a convenience store. He knew Annalise well enough by now to know that the first thing she wanted in the morning was a cup of coffee. He grabbed a couple of fresh doughnuts and the morning paper before leaving the store.

Dawn was still a mere promise in the eastern sky, and the shutting of his car door echoed in the silence of predawn.

It wouldn't take long before this scene would change. Within hours, he had a feeling, the peace of this area would be shattered by reporters hungry to get an interview, with news crews and camerapeople all vying for a story. He knew Annalise had hoped to continue business as usual, but there was no way she was going to accomplish that now.

He rang the bell, knowing he was probably waking her up but also knowing there was nothing to do about it. He waited several seconds, then rang the bell again.

As he waited for her to answer, a deep weariness threatened to consume him. It wasn't just a response to his long hours. It was more a profound exhaustion, a culmination of too many cases, too many victims.

He was flirting with burnout. The last time off he'd taken had been three years ago. He'd taken a week off to attend a four-day seminar on criminal profiling in St. Louis. Not exactly a real vacation.

When this case was over he was going to take a real vacation. Maybe he and Annalise could go someplace together. For a brief moment his mind filled with visions of a sandy beach, a fruity alcoholic drink and Annalise in a bikini. The idea of spending time alone with Annalise with nothing on their agenda more pressing than what to order for dinner sounded like heaven.

The interior shop light flipped on, and Annalise approached the door. Her hair was sleep-tousled, and a pillow crease showed faintly against her cheek. Her eyes held the glaze of somebody not quite fully awake. She belted her short robe, then unlocked the door, a worried expression on her face.

"Tyler? What's wrong? Has something happened? Why are you here in the middle of the night?"

He leaned over and kissed her forehead. "It's not the middle of the night. It's almost morning, and yes, something has happened. You made the morning paper."

"Wha-what do you mean?" She locked the door, then turned back to face him, some of the sleepiness leaving her eyes. "Never mind. Don't tell me until we're upstairs and I'm drinking some of that coffee I see you brought."

"I brought doughnuts, too."

"Then I'll forgive you for waking me up before the crack of dawn," she replied.

They didn't speak again until they were upstairs and seated on the sofa, the coffee and doughnuts in front of them.

"You look exhausted," she said.

"I didn't realize how tired I was until I got into my car to drive here," he admitted.

He'd barely slept the night before last, and realized as her sofa cushions seemed to embrace him that he was running on empty.

She pushed his coffee cup in front of him. "Okay, now tell me how I made the paper."

"A reporter somehow managed to make the connection between your dolls and our murder victims." He handed her the paper and watched as she opened it and read the headline.

She scanned the story, then stared at him in dismay, and he continued. "Your life is about to get considerably more complicated. You're bright and you're beautiful and you've now been identified as a central figure in a heinous serial-killer case. Every reporter in the four-state area is going to want a piece of you."

She rubbed the center of her forehead, as if easing the pressure of a headache. "So, what do I do?"

"First and foremost, don't talk to any of them There are two words that are going to be your best friend in the next couple of days, and those words are, 'No comment.' I also recommend you don't open the shop today. If you do, you'll probably be overrun with reporters."

"What about the people who work for me? Should I call them and tell them not to come in?"

"No. I want them here. I've arranged for Jennifer to meet me here at ten, and we're going to interview everyone. We also need those boxes of your mother's records that you mentioned you had here."

"My paperwork wasn't helpful?" she asked.

"It's too early to tell." A yawn appeared from nowhere, and he hid it with the back of his hand, then grinned apologetically. "Sorry." It took him a moment to regain his train of thought. "I'm hoping your mother's records will be more helpful in revealing who bought the bride and flapper dolls."

"You said Jennifer will be here at ten?" she asked.

He nodded. "And what is your plan for what to do between now and then?"

"I didn't think that far ahead," he replied. "I just knew when I saw the paper that I needed to get over here and warn you about the firestorm to come."

She smiled at him and laid a hand on his cheek. "Then why don't you get into my bed and get a couple of hours of sleep before she gets here?"

He raised a brow. "If I get into your bed I'm afraid the last thing that will be on my mind is sleep."

She laughed, that low, sexy laughter that always fired desire inside him. "I prefer not to make love to men who look like they're about to drop dead from exhaustion." She sobered, her gaze as gentle as he'd ever seen. "Tyler, you're beyond exhausted. Get some rest while you can." She stood and held out her hand to him.

He took her hand and stood and allowed her to lead him to the bed. He undressed, then climbed into the bed and pulled the sheet up over himself. The mattress seemed to enfold his tired body, and he realized he was surrounded with the scent of her.

She got into the bed next to him, and he pulled her against him, spoon fashion. Her body warmth seeped into him, and the adrenaline that had driven him through the night slowly eased away as sleep reached out for him.

The dream began peacefully. He was walking a beach, the white sand soft and warm beneath his bare feet. The sunshine sparkled on the water as it rolled to the shore. The sky was the kind of blue that only happened in paintings, and the breeze was fragrant with the scent of sweet flowers.

As a seagull cried overhead he sat on the sand and breathed a deep sigh of contentment. All he needed was Annalise, and he knew that if he waited here patiently she'd join him on the warm sand.

This was just what he'd needed. The peace. The calm. He closed his eyes, the rhythm of the breaking waves as soothing as a lullaby.

The clap of thunder startled him. He opened his eyes to see tumultuous black storm clouds racing across the sky at warp speed. The sun disappeared and the water began to foam, whitecaps frothing as they leaped upward.

He jumped to his feet as the wind whipped around him, punishing him with the coarse sand that buffeted his body. The smell was now of rotten fish and death, and the sea churned with an intensity he'd never seen before.

He watched in horror as Kerry Albright, in full bridal regalia, rose up out of the water and began to walk toward him, her arms outstretched beseechingly, her dead eyes holding a plea.

To the left of Kerry Margie Francis appeared, her flapper dress dripping with seaweed and her cries rising up in the air. Sulee Hwang joined them, her pale makeup running down her face as thunder exploded and lightning flashed overhead.

Tyler backed up as they approached. "I'm trying," he yelled, his voice swept away by the wind. "I swear I'll find him. I promise you."

The sea swelled and a fourth figure appeared— too far away for him to see her features. Still, the vision filled him with a dread he'd never known before.

Closer . . . closer she came, and as the lightning

flashed he recognized her features. "No!" he screamed in horror as Annalise walked through the water toward him, a perfect doll in her lavender dress.

His eyes snapped open, and he realized the phone was ringing. Annalise lay next to him, holding his gaze as the answering machine picked up the call.

"Ms. Blakely, this is Thomas Brewman with KABC radio. I was wondering if we could set up a meeting. I'd like to get your thoughts about the current situation." He left his contact information, then the line went dead.

Tyler reached out and touched her cheek, the horror of his dream still coursing through him. Her skin was wonderfully warm, and she smiled at his light caress. But the mood was broken as the phone rang once again.

"Annalise, hi. This is Sam Watters from WDAF television. I'd love to get your comments on the connection between your dolls and the murders. My number is 555-0734. That's a direct line. I hope to hear from you soon." He hung up.

"And so it begins," Tyler said softly.

She closed her eyes as if to hide from the storm to come.

Chapter 20

"This is a publicity wet dream!" Danika exclaimed as she flew in the back door of the shop.

It was the first time in her life that Annalise was utterly disgusted by her best friend. Jennifer looked as if she wanted to slap Danika, and even Tyler sighed in obvious repugnance.

"Excuse us," Annalise said, and grabbed Danika by the arm. She steered her to the front of the shop.

"You won't believe the calls I'm getting," Danika said. "Talk shows and news programs." She seemed unaware of Annalise's mood as she continued, pacing with frenetic energy in front of the display cases. "This is great. They all want you on their shows. You'll be able to promote the hell out of your dolls, both the old ones and the new."

"Are you insane?" Annalise stared at her in stunned shock. "There are three dead young women dressed like my dolls."

Danika grimaced and stopped her pacing. "I know, and that's horrible. But, Annalise, we can't do anything about them now. But you can do something about your crappy sales by taking advantage of the situation."

"I'm not taking advantage of any situation. In fact, I'm shutting down until some of this craziness passes." She pointed out the front window. "Do you see all those trucks out there? The reporters and cameras? I can't go with business as usual when it's anything but usual. And I won't dishonor those dead women by exploiting their deaths."

Danika shrugged and cast her a crooked grin. "I knew you'd take the high road. I was just testing you." She walked closer to the front window and peered outside. "It is a zoo out there, isn't it?" She turned back to face Annalise. "How are you holding up?"

"It's not even noon yet and I'm completely mentally exhausted," she confessed. "My phone started ringing just after eight, and it hasn't stopped since."

"Have you talked to your dad? He must be worried sick by all of this." Danika moved away from the window.

"I called him earlier to prepare him for the morning headlines."

Danika moved closer to Annalise, all trace of brashness gone from her expression. "It's creepy, isn't it?" She looked at the doll display case, then back at Annalise. "Do the police have any suspects yet?"

"Tyler would tell you that everyone is a suspect. They're fairly sure the killer is a male, but that's about all they know at the moment. Tyler and his partner, Jennifer, have been interrogating the staff this morning."

"You don't really think Ben or Sammy or any of

the other guys could have anything to do with this, do you?"

Annalise hesitated before replying. "I just don't know what to think," she finally said. "What I really hate is the fact that now I'm playing and replaying every conversation I've ever had with any of them. I keep wondering if I've missed something, if one of them hates me so much they could do this."

"That's crazy," Danika exclaimed. "You know they all adore you."

Annalise sighed. "Then I start wondering if maybe somebody cares too much. Oh, not about me, but about the business. You know how sales have fallen off over the last couple of years. I keep wondering if maybe somebody decided to get our dolls into the headlines."

Danika released a small whistle. "You know me—I'd do just about anything for a client. But what you're talking about isn't just cold. It's downright evil."

"I know. What do you think of Mike?"

"Mike Kidwell? Your lawyer?" She frowned. "I've always thought he was a stand-up kind of guy. A little too traditional for me, but nice enough. Why?"

"I don't know. Last time we had dinner together he said something that under the circumstances bothers me a little."

"What did he say?"

"First he told me that he wanted a more personal relationship with me; then later he said something about it wouldn't be long and Blakely Dolls would be in the news again."

Danika stared at her, openmouthed. "Did you tell Tyler about it?"

Annalise nodded. "This morning. I told him it probably meant nothing, but that's what I'm talking about. Suddenly I'm seeing the most innocent of conversations in a new light, and everything seems sinister."

Danika reached out and gave her a hug. "You'll get through this. Tyler will find the bad guy and life will go on."

At that moment Tyler stepped into the shop area. "Annalise, I need to talk to you and Danika; don't run off. My partner needs to interview you."

"Why? I didn't do anything. I don't know anything." Danika looked at him with panic.

He smiled. "Chill, Danika. We just want to ask you a few questions. Go on; she's waiting for you." When she'd left the shop to return to the back room, Tyler turned back to face Annalise. "You mentioned yesterday that you have some records stored here from when your mother was keeping the books. We're going to need them."

She nodded. "I can get them now. They're in a couple of boxes on the second floor."

"I'll go with you."

Within moments they stood on the second floor amid the boxes and furniture. "I hope you have an idea what they're packed in," he said with a touch of dismay as he viewed the number of boxes.

"Everything is pretty well labeled," she assured him. Even so it took them nearly half an hour to locate the two boxes that held Lillian's records.

Tyler took the lid off the first one and sat on the floor next to it. Annalise joined him on the floor. "Did you find out anything from my people?" she asked.

"We got their alibis. They'll all be checked out."
He frowned as he pulled out several sheets of old
advertising.

"I hate the idea of any of them having anything
to do with this."

"It's entirely possible none of them is responsible," he replied as if to ease her mind. But her mind
wouldn't be eased until the perpetrator was caught.

He stopped pulling papers out of the box and
looked at her. "Annalise, there's no way you can
conduct business as usual with all the reporters outside. The minute you open your shop door to the
public, we won't be able to keep them out."

"I know; I've already thought about that. Does
the offer to stay at your place still stand?"

"You know it does," he replied.

"I was thinking that maybe if I just close up the
retail area and stay with you for a couple of days,
then surely some of this attention will go away."

"You're probably right. Another big story will
break, they'll all get tired of watching an empty
building and they'll go away."

"Then I'll just go on upstairs and pack a bag."

She was ambivalent about staying at Tyler's. The
work ethic her mother had honed in her was strong,
and she couldn't imagine taking off for three or four
days. More than that—she was afraid that being
with Tyler in his house, sharing their personal living
space, would build a new intimacy between them.

As she packed her clothes and toiletries into a
suitcase, her mind worked out the details of taking
a couple of days off. She would tell the staff they
could still come into the back and continue to work
on the Anniversary Annalise dolls. If they came and

went through the back door then maybe the reporters wouldn't hassle them too much.

When she had packed all the items she thought she might need, on impulse she added in several of her sketch pads and her pencils, knowing she was going to have far too much time on her hands at Tyler's.

She carried her suitcase back down to the second floor. Tyler and the boxes were gone, so she went on downstairs.

The interviews were finished, and Jennifer told her Tyler was loading the boxes into the back of his car. Annalise's coworkers all looked at her expectantly, and briefly she told them that they were to continue their work, but that the retail shop would be closed and she wouldn't be coming in for a few days.

"I'll be in contact with each of you by phone, and in the meantime I would appreciate it if none of you would talk to the reporters," she told them.

"Screw 'em," Sammy exclaimed. "Let them have to work for their story."

Annalise smiled at him gratefully. "I had hoped that the new doll would put Blakely Dolls back in the news. I certainly didn't want to make the news this way."

By that time Tyler had returned and the group began to prepare to leave. Tyler reiterated what she had said, that he highly recommended that nobody speak to the reporters outside.

It took only minutes to clear the place; then Tyler picked up her suitcase and together they went outside to get into his car.

Like a frenzy of hungry sharks the reporters

surged forward, shouting questions to both of them. Tyler threw an arm around her shoulders as if to shield her from the pack. He led her to her car, where she slid behind the steering wheel and locked her door, half-afraid that one of the more aggressive reporters might try to get in on her lap.

She didn't wait for Tyler to get to his car, but instead started her engine and took off from the curb. She didn't need him to lead the way to his house, and she just wanted to get away from the crowd.

As she drove, she tried not to think about what she was leaving behind. Her home. Her life. Her work. No, not her work, but rather, the continuation of her mother's work.

At odd moments during the morning she had found herself replaying the conversation with her father. Although she had forgiven him for everything he hadn't done, everything he couldn't do, she was having more difficulty forgiving her mother.

She recognized now that her mother had adored Annalise the doll, but she hadn't much cared for Annalise the little girl. That knowledge hurt, but she was also wise enough to know that it had been her mother who had been lacking, not her.

She knew she had two choices: She could either allow her painful childhood experiences to forever shape her future, to keep her from seeking the happiness she knew she deserved, or she could embrace the love she felt for Tyler, the love she knew he had for her.

She could choose happiness or bitterness.

Tyler arrived at his house only minutes after she

had pulled in. He opened the garage door and told her to park her car in the garage.

"I can't believe you're willing to put up with my terrible-colored kitchen for the next few days," he said as they walked inside the front door.

She smiled at him. "What makes you think I intend to do any cooking?"

"Touché," he replied. "You realize I won't be here much."

"I know. I'll be fine. At least no reporters will find me here, and maybe if I get really bored I'll paint your kitchen for you."

"Be still, my heart." He carried her suitcase to the master bedroom. "This okay with you?"

"Perfect," she replied. "You know I have no intention of being a prisoner here in your house. I'll stay away from the loft for the next couple of days, but that doesn't mean I'm not going to go to the grocery store or anywhere else."

"I understand. I'll just feel better knowing you're sleeping in my bed, staying in my home until some of the heat is off you." He frowned. "I've got to get back to the station. I want to get started going through those records of your mother's."

She walked with him to the front door, where he gave her a copy of his house key, kissed her on the cheek and told her not to wait up for him.

"Oh, and, Annalise," he said just before he stepped out the door, "I love you."

The words shimmered in the air for a long moment, holding the sweet promise of happiness. She knew all she had to do was reach out and grab it. That ancient fear rose up inside her, holding her mute for too long.

He smiled with just a touch of disappointment. "I know—you'll let me know."

With that he was gone.

She was gone.

He sat in a chair and rocked back and forth, despair consuming him. He'd seen her go. She'd had a suitcase and she'd left the building. It had been easy for him to get lost in the throng of people outside of her business.

He'd hoped she'd come out and face the crowd, talk about how she felt about seeing his work. But she'd left without saying a word.

Dammit. Dammit. If he hadn't bungled it all she'd be his. She'd be sitting right here in the chair where he now sat, getting her makeup done, having her hair combed and curled. Instead he was here alone and she was gone.

Stop sniveling, you baby. His mother's voice thundered in his ears. *It's your own fault. You can never do anything right.*

"How did I know she had a kid brother? How did I know he was going to be there?" he asked the empty room.

You're nothing but a loser, boy. Always have been, always will be.

"I'm not a loser. I made the morning headline. You never did anything like that, you fat bitch," he said. He thought that would shut her up, but it didn't. She kept talking, on and on. Noise. Such noise.

He slammed his fist into the front of his forehead, hoping to dislodge her hateful voice from his head. He hit himself again . . . and again . . . and again until the pain made it impossible for him to strike himself any more.

He stood and began to pace, agitated to a point he'd never been before. He was going to explode. That was what it felt like. He felt like a bubbling volcano ready to spew.

The lavender dress was ready. It hung on a hanger in the corner, freshly pressed and awaiting her body. He needed her! He drew a deep breath as his gaze lit on his bulletin board.

The three photos there calmed him. His dolls. Everyone was talking about his dolls. He walked to the board and touched first Belinda's, then Fanny's, and finally Kim's pictures. His dolls.

As the calm descended, his mind began to work, this time without interference from the ghost of his mother, but rather independently, brilliantly.

She was gone for now, but she wouldn't be gone forever. The suitcase she'd carried out had been small, and she had a business to run. Eventually the reporters would go away and she'd be back.

And he'd be waiting for her.

Chapter 21

Annalise rolled the buttercup yellow paint across the puke green wall, then stepped back and eyed it critically. Perfect. When she'd insisted she'd paint the walls, Tyler had told her to buy whatever color she thought would look okay, and the yellow looked beautiful. He'd even taken an hour the night before and patched the holes.

She'd been here three days, and she didn't even want to think about how comfortable she'd become. Tyler flew in and out at odd hours of the day and night, and despite the craziness of his hours they had fallen into a kind of comfortable routine.

She wasn't sure what time Tyler came to bed each night, but she awakened each morning with a vague memory of him getting into bed and pulling her tight against him. His arms around her, his body so warm and close to hers felt right. And in those sleepy moments of togetherness she knew she was where she belonged.

He had already been gone when she'd awakened that morning, his side of the bed cold. She'd showered and dressed, then hunted down the nearest hardware store for paint supplies.

She needed to stay busy. She hoped the physical activity would keep her mind from dwelling on the horror of the murders and the terrible knowledge that somebody was turning living human beings into her dolls.

Rolling another coat of paint on the wall, she thought of how cheerful the kitchen would look with the yellow color. White curtains would be nice at the windows, and a bouquet of daisies in the center of the table.

She didn't know how long she'd been working, totally absorbed with the job, when a knock sounded on the back door. She looked out to see a dark-haired older woman standing just outside, a large box in her arms.

In a matter of seconds several thoughts whisked through Annalise's brain. The woman didn't look threatening; rather, she looked a lot like Tyler. She had the same dark hair, lean face and gray eyes.

Annalise unlocked the door and opened it with a tentative smile.

"You must be Annalise. Hi, I'm Nancy King, Tyler's mother." She swept past Annalise and set the box on the table, then looked at the work Annalise had accomplished and smiled. "Ah, thank goodness you're getting rid of those god-awful colors. I've been itching to pick up a paintbrush ever since what's-her-name moved out."

Annalise smiled. "It's nice to meet you."

Nancy nodded. "Tyler called me this morning and said he had an important, beautiful woman staying with him, and asked if I'd mind bringing over some of his favorite chicken salad." She began to unload dishes from the box as Annalise set down the roller and washed her hands.

"Actually, I think he couldn't care less about the chicken salad, but he was more worried about you," Nancy said.

"Worried about me? I'm fine." Annalise dried her hands, then stood awkwardly next to the table.

"I think maybe he thought you were lonely here and that lunch with another woman might be a nice idea." Nancy looked at her with interest. "I heard something in his voice when he spoke your name, something I've never heard before." She smiled. "I couldn't wait to get over here and meet you."

A few minutes later the two sat at the table sharing chicken-salad sandwiches, cole slaw and conversation.

"Tyler always knew what he wanted to do with his life," Nancy said. "From the moment he found that poor man's body in the lot next to our backyard, he knew exactly what he'd commit his life to doing. He's good at what he does, but I worry about him. What about you? Did you always want to make dolls?"

"I never really felt like I had a choice. I always knew that's what I would do. It was just a given as I was growing up."

"And you're happy doing it?" One of Nancy's eyebrows rose in exactly the same way Annalise had seen her son's do.

It took a long time for Annalise to answer. "I thought I was, up until lately. Even before I knew about the murders I'd begun to question whether I was doing what really made me happy."

"It's not too late, you know. You're young enough to do whatever you want to do." Nancy picked up her sandwich, took a bite and chewed with a thoughtful expression. "Tyler will never do anything other than what he's doing now. Being a homicide cop isn't just what he does; it's who he is. The best I can hope for is that he'll find some balance in his life. He's never had anyone as important to him as his work." She smiled at Annalise. "I think you just might be the person he's been waiting for."

"I care for him very much," Annalise replied. She wasn't ready yet to speak of the depth of her feelings for Tyler. She'd hardly acknowledged it to herself.

Nancy studied her for a long moment, then nodded. The rest of the meal was spent with entertaining tales of Tyler as a child.

"He was a precocious thing, always asking questions, always wanting to know why people did what they did. If he hadn't been a cop he probably would have become a therapist," Nancy said.

By the time they'd finished eating Annalise felt as if she had a new friend. Nancy was warm and funny, and it was easy to see where Tyler got much of his charm.

"You sure you don't want help with the painting?" Nancy asked as she got ready to leave.

"Thanks, but I can handle it. I need something to do while I'm here."

As they reached the back door Nancy gave her a quick hug. "I know you're going through a bad time right now, but it will pass. Tyler is smart, and he and his team will eventually get the man responsible for those murders."

"I know. I have total confidence in your son."

Nancy held her gaze for a long moment. "Don't break his heart, Annalise," she said softly. She didn't wait for a reply, but instead turned and left.

Annalise locked the door after her, then sat in one of the kitchen chairs and stared out the window. *Don't break his heart.* That was the last thing she wanted to do. She was in love with Tyler, and yet something held her back from telling him, from giving in to the emotion that burned bright in her heart.

The murders. Everything was so unsettled at the moment. Was it any wonder that she wasn't ready to get on with her personal life? She didn't want to make a decision now, not with so many other things going on. She was afraid to reach out for love when so much death surrounded her.

She worked the rest of the afternoon on the painting, and at four o'clock knocked off to put a smothered steak in the oven. As usual she had no idea when to expect Tyler, but he'd called earlier and said he was going to try to make it home by seven.

She showered and put on clean clothes, and was sitting at the table sketching when Tyler came in. "Hmm, something smells wonderful," he said as he entered the kitchen.

"Smothered steak," she replied. "And I hope it tastes as good as it smells."

"I thought you couldn't cook." He came to stand behind her and placed his hands on her shoulders.

"Pouring a can of tomatoes and some seasoning on a steak, then wrapping it in foil and shoving it into the oven doesn't exactly take any great culinary skill."

"What's all that? New clothes for new dolls?" He

peered over her shoulder at the sketches she'd been working on.

"No, it's just something I dabble with whenever I have a little free time." She started to close the sketch pad, but he stopped her by placing a hand on it.

"So what is it?" He pulled a chair up next to hers and sat.

"It's part of a dream I once entertained when I was young." A touch of embarrassment swept through her. "There was a while when I was a teenager that I dreamed of having a line of clothing. Upscale fashions at affordable prices."

"Why didn't you pursue it?"

"Because it was a stupid idea. Too risky, too silly. The world had enough fashion designers, but there was only one Blakely Dolls business."

Tyler's eyes were dark as he gazed at her. "I'm sorry." He reached out and tucked a stray strand of hair behind her ear. "I'm sorry that you didn't have anyone to support and nurture your dreams."

Oh, this man touched her, and in that gentle statement he'd stirred a need inside her. "How hungry are you?" Her voice sounded low and sexy to her own ears.

His gaze focused on her mouth. "Ravenous," he replied. They both knew that neither of them was talking about food.

It was an hour later before they once again sat at the table to eat the steak and salad she'd prepared. "Anything new?" she asked him as she cut into the tender steak.

"Tons of new stuff, but still nothing that really makes sense," he replied. "We've got the names of sixteen people who bought all three dolls over the years. Now we're trying to locate all those people."

"What about the alibis of the people who work for me? I'm assuming they checked out."

"All except your friendly lawyer. Apparently Mike Kidwell spends most of his nights alone. He has yet to provide us with anything that would take him off our list of potential suspects."

"I just can't imagine Mike having anything to do with this," she said. "He's a lawyer, for crying out loud."

"And that makes him what? A paragon of virtue?" Tyler laughed. "You haven't met some of the lawyers I have." He sobered immediately. "It isn't just his lack of alibi that has caught our attention; it's also that he fits the profile."

"The profile?"

"There's always a profile." He frowned and set his fork down. "Are you sure you want to talk about this?"

"Tyler, unlike the women you've dated in your past, I want to share everything with you, and that includes your work."

"It can get ugly," he warned.

"I know that. Life is sometimes ugly." She reached across the table and took his hand in hers. "But it's less ugly if you have somebody to share it with."

He squeezed her hand tightly, then released it. "Okay, the usual serial-killer profile is of a Caucasian male between the ages of twenty-five and forty. He's intelligent, organized and high-functioning. He either owns his own business or works at a job where he doesn't have to account to anyone for his time. His neighbors probably see him as a quiet but pleasant man. He has no close relationships with women and most likely has never been married."

"Sammy's divorced and Ben is gay. Surely neither of them fits the profile."

"True, but the worst thing we could do right now is to be wed to the profile. Still, Sammy and Ben have been cleared because each of them had alibis that were confirmed."

"What about the others? Glen and Robert and Joshua?" She mentioned the part-timers who worked putting the dolls together.

"Glen and Robert both had solid alibis. Joshua is still up in the air."

She picked at her steak with the fork, discouraged by the fact that there seemed to be no front-runner as the guilty party.

"Annalise, it's been less than a week since we realized your dolls were a part of this." He leaned back in his chair and rubbed the center of his forehead. "Most people don't realize how many hours, how much tedious work it takes to catch a killer who doesn't want to be caught, especially one as smart as the one we're chasing."

"Has he called Reuben's phone any more?" she asked. Tyler had told her about the killer calling the reporter to lead him to the last victim, then calling again and getting Tyler on the line.

"No. We've got Reuben's number forwarded to a phone in the station and an officer manning it twenty-four hours a day, but so far no call from the killer." He sighed and dropped his hand from his forehead. "It's been almost a week since we found Sulee."

She knew what he was thinking: The murders had all been committed approximately a week apart from one another. If they didn't catch him in the next day or two, the odds were good that there would be a fourth victim.

Chapter 22

The ringing phone awoke Annalise from a sound sleep. For a moment she didn't move to answer. She and Tyler had agreed that it was best to let his machine talk to anyone who called when he wasn't home.

When the phone rang again she realized it wasn't Tyler's but her cell phone. She fumbled in the darkness of the bedroom for the switch on the bedside lamp. When she'd managed to turn it on she grabbed her cell phone at the same time she glanced at the clock.

Eleven. She'd been asleep for only about a half an hour, although she must have been in a deep sleep. The caller ID let her know the call was coming from her father's house.

"Charlie, you shouldn't be calling me this late," she said as she answered, assuming it would be her brother.

"It's not Charlie."

"Dad! What's wrong? Why are you calling me at this hour?" She sat up and shook her head to dispel the last of her drowsiness.

"Probably nothing is wrong, and I really hate to bother you with everything that's been going on."

"What is it, Dad?" She pressed the phone closer to her ear, hearing the underlying concern in her father's voice.

"Charlie's gone. Apparently he's run away or something. He came home late from a friend's house this evening and we had a go-around. I told him he was grounded for the next three days, and he stomped off to his room. Sherri went to check on him a few minutes ago and he's gone. He and his backpack are missing. The little shit crawled out his bedroom window. I just thought maybe he might be there with you."

"Dad, I'm not at the loft." She swung her legs over the side of the bed and stood.

"Oh, sorry. I didn't realize that. Then he's probably at a friend's house. I'll just make some more phone calls. I'm sure he'll turn up somewhere."

"Dad, wait. I gave Charlie a key." Her mind raced as the last of her grogginess fell away. "It's possible he has gone to the loft even though I'm not home. Look, I'll drive over there and check it out."

"And I'll meet you there."

"No, you and Sherrie stay there in case he comes home. If that happens you can call me on my cell and let me know."

"Are you sure you don't mind?"

"It's not a problem," she replied as she grabbed her clothes off the chair where she had laid them before getting into bed.

"I swear, that boy isn't going to see daylight again until he's at least twenty-one years old," Frank exclaimed.

Annalise laughed. "Don't be too hard on him. He's just a kid. I'll call you when I get to the loft."

She dressed, grabbed her purse and car keys, then called Tyler on his cell phone. The call was routed directly to his voice mail. "Tyler, it's me. Charlie has gone missing, and I'm heading over to the loft to see if he's there. It's eleven fifteen right now. I'll probably be back home and asleep by the time you get there."

Minutes later she was in her car heading toward the loft. There had been several times in the last couple of days when she'd called Tyler and had gotten his voice mail. It usually meant he was in the middle of a meeting, or something bad had happened.

God, she hoped there hadn't been another victim. Everyone seemed to be holding their breath, waiting for a new "doll" to be found, and hoping desperately that it didn't happen. But she knew that was one of the few things that would force Tyler to have his phone turned to voice mail.

She rolled down her window and allowed in the humid night air. It was a beautiful night. The sky was clear, and the stars hung so low she felt she could reach out the window and grab one.

I'm sorry you didn't have anyone to support and nurture your dreams. She tightened her grip on the steering wheel as she thought of Tyler's words.

No, she hadn't had anyone to nurture her dreams, to encourage her to find her own path. She'd allowed Lillian to control every part of her life, plot every path she might choose to take. Even in death Lillian's hold had been strong.

When Lillian had passed away Annalise could have sold the business, gotten out from beneath it.

But it never entered her mind because she knew her mother would never have forgiven her.

Now she considered what her life might be without the doll business, and to her surprise it wasn't a scary thought at all. Rather it filled her with excitement, the kind of excitement she had never felt for the business.

Maybe it was Tyler's support that had made her realize it was time to let it go. The business her mother had loved more than anything else in the world was nothing but a noose around Annalise's neck, slowly suffocating her to death.

She'd go ahead and finish this last doll and give her staff plenty of time to find other jobs. She'd offer them each attractive severance packages. She'd sell the business and take the money and run.

She'd take some classes in fashion design, focus on building a portfolio and developing the line of clothing she'd always dreamed about. It was time to grab for her own dream. "I'm taking back my life, Mother," she said aloud.

"I told you she'd be mine, Mother," he breathed in a quiet whisper as he watched the boy unlock the front door of the shop, then disappear inside.

A frown creased his brow as he saw a shadow near the side of the building. Max. The homeless old fool didn't worry him. Before long he'd be stretched out beneath his tree, slobbering drunk and dead to the world. And if he did talk to anyone, nobody would believe him; nobody would even listen to the rantings and ravings of a drunk with delusions.

A shiver of excitement coursed through him. He'd been waiting for her for the past three days.

The reporters and newspeople had left on the second day, and since then nobody had gone in or out of the building.

He'd broken the window above the fire escape. With nobody home it had been easy to break it enough to unlock it and secure a way in once again.

Now the boy was here, and he would bring her back. And when she got there he'd be waiting. Tonight she would be his.

Chapter 23

Tyler stood outside the apartment building where Eleanor Stanko had met her death at the hands of her husband. The husband was still holed up inside with a gun and his two young children.

The Stankos had a history of domestic abuse, and tonight it had ended in tragedy. Now the goal of the team was to make sure the kids got out of there safely and the tragedy didn't get any worse.

Tyler used his cell phone and punched in the number to ring the phone in the Stanko apartment. It rang ten times. "He's not answering," Tyler told his chief, who crouched beside him next to their car.

"Keep trying. Nick Barnes should be here any minute, and then he can take over, but we need to get some communication going as soon as possible," the chief said. Nick Barnes was the best the department had when it came to addressing a hostage situation.

Tyler punched in the number again and listened to it ringing over and over again. He glanced at his watch. It was just after eleven thirty. He looked up at the third-floor apartment where two children's lives hung in the balance. It was going to be a very long night.

Annalise pulled up in front of the loft, grateful that the street was deserted. No reporters, no cameramen, nobody to see her as she parked her car out front.

As she got out of the car she looked up to the third floor, where a light was visible from the street. "Ah, kid, you're in big trouble," she muttered as she walked to the door.

She unlocked it and stepped inside. A small security light shone, playing on the faces of the dolls in the display cabinet. They looked eerie in the faint illumination, their eyes unnaturally bright. "I'm done with you all," she whispered.

The rightness of the decision she'd made on the drive here flooded through her. She had never loved the dolls the way her mother had. In fact, if she looked deep in her heart, she'd hated them.

She thought of the nightmare that had plagued her for much of her life: dolls all strangling her, suffocating her. She should have known it was her subconscious telling her to let them go.

She turned away from the dolls and headed for the stairs. "Charlie, if you're up there you're totally busted, kid," she called as she climbed.

There was no reply, but she knew that if he was in the loft with the door closed he probably couldn't hear her. She smiled and shook her head as she reached the second floor. If she knew Charlie he'd probably packed his bag with half a dozen movies to get him through his snit.

The one thing she needed to make clear to him

was that he couldn't use her place as an escape from consequences at home. While she wanted to support him, she needed him to understand that she wouldn't condone his running away when he got into trouble.

"Charlie? Are you here?" she called as she climbed the second set of stairs.

The loft door was closed, but the elevator stood with its door open on that level. "Charlie, you're in big trouble," she said as she opened the door and stepped into the loft.

Charlie sat on the sofa, his face as pale as milk, and next to him sat John Malcolm. She stared at the maintenance supervisor in surprise. "John, what are you doing here?" she asked.

"Waiting for you. I saw this kid sneaking in here and thought he might be up to mischief." John made no move to leave Charlie's side.

"It's okay. He's my brother." Uneasiness slithered through her. Charlie said nothing, but his eyes screamed a silent plea.

An alarm buzzed in her head. "Thanks, John. I appreciate your being a good neighbor, but everything is fine now. You can go on home."

He smiled, much as he did each time they met in the park. "I'm not ready to go home yet. We have business, Annalise. You and me, we have doll business."

It was at that moment that she spied the knife he held to Charlie's side. As his words sank in a deep, shuddering horror filled her.

Doll business. He was the Dollmaker. John was the murderer. Every muscle in her body tensed.

"Now, don't go doing anything stupid, Annalise.

This boy here, he doesn't mean nothing to me. I'd just as soon stab him as look at him. It's you I want. It's you I need."

"I'll do whatever you want me to do. I'll go wherever you want me to. Just let him go." She'd worry about her own safety later. At the moment her sole concern was for the boy she loved, the boy who had crawled so deep into her heart.

"I won't go," Charlie cried as tears filled his eyes. He raised his chin with a touch of defiance. "I won't leave you, Annalise."

She ignored him and kept her gaze focused on John. "You made the dolls. I saw them, you know. I saw the pictures of them that the police had."

"They were works of art." It was John's turn to raise his chin, wild pride gleaming from his eyes. "They were better than your dolls. Better than *her* dolls." He spat the last sentence as if the words tasted bad in his mouth.

Her dolls? Who was the *her*? "Charlie is too young to understand all of this," she said, trying desperately to keep the terror from her voice. "Let him go and we'll talk about your dolls."

"I'm afraid I can't do that," he replied easily. "He'll tell."

"He doesn't know who you are or where you live. He won't tell," she protested. "Let him go and you and I can have a serious discussion about your dolls."

Charlie stared at her intently, terror in his tear-filled eyes. Frustration overrode her fear. She needed to get John away from Charlie. She needed to save Charlie, to make sure that he got out of here without harm.

"There's nothing to talk about," John replied.

"That's not true. You must want to talk to me about them. You wrote me those notes. We can lock Charlie in my bathroom. He won't be able to tell anyone from in there; then you and I can really talk or whatever."

She searched John's face, looking for a glint of evil shining from his eyes, seeking malevolence somewhere on his features. But there was none. He just looked like an ordinary man, except for the knife he had pressed against Charlie's side.

He stood and pulled Charlie to his feet, and a ray of hope shone inside her. If she could just get Charlie someplace safe, then she could worry about getting herself out of this mess.

"Just run, Annalise. Get away," Charlie cried, tears now streaming down his face.

"Shut up, Charlie," she said coldly. "I want to talk to John about his dolls." She took several steps closer to the two. The only weapon she had was her purse, inadequate against his knife.

"The police said they found your work shoddy, that the sewing was sloppy," she continued. A flash of something dark shone from John's eyes. "But I told them I thought it was the work of a genius. I can't believe your attention to detail."

"What do the police know? They're a bunch of fools who wouldn't understand the artistic talent it took to take a real person and turn her into a doll." As he spoke the knife lowered and she saw her chance.

If she screwed up then Charlie could be hurt or worse, but she knew that if she didn't do anything they both were dead. Muscles bunched and adrenaline flushed through her. Without warning she charged, slamming into John. He toppled backward and fell on his back on the floor.

She grabbed Charlie's hand. "Run, Charlie," she cried, and the two of them raced out of the loft as John bellowed from someplace behind them.

Knowing they could never get down the stairs fast enough, she pulled Charlie into the elevator and pushed the CLOSE button. As the doors began to slide shut John ran out of the loft, his face twisted with rage.

She screamed, then nearly sobbed with relief as the doors closed before he could reach them. The elevator began to move, but her mind spun. By the time the elevator hit the bottom floor John would be waiting for them. She hit the EMERGENCY STOP button and the elevator groaned to a halt.

A thick silence resulted. Charlie moved closer to her, and she pulled him into her arms. He trembled in her embrace, and she closed her eyes and drew a deep breath to still the frantic trembling that threatened to consume her.

"What happens now?" Charlie asked in a whisper.

"We wait. I think we're between floors."

"What if he hits the elevator button?"

"It won't override the emergency stop. He'd need to have a key to do that or do it from here on the control panel. We're safe, Charlie. We just need to wait for somebody to find us."

Already she felt it—the slow, sickening feeling of suffocation as she stood in the tiny boxlike structure. Her heartbeat, rather than slowing, was increasing, and a scream rose up in the back of her throat, a scream she swallowed again and again.

Stay calm. You have to stay calm. For Charlie's sake. For your own sake, she thought. Still, the walls of the small enclosure seemed to press in, and the air felt too thin to breathe.

"His name is John Malcolm. He lives in the apartment building across the street," she whispered. "He works as a maintenance supervisor, and he's the Costume Killer." She knew she was telling this to Charlie in case something bad happened, in case somehow he got out of this and she didn't.

Charlie remained in her arms, holding her tightly as he continued to shake.

"It's going to be all right, Charlie. We're going to be just fine." She wanted to calm him even as the panic rose higher in her.

She couldn't breathe. The elevator was too small, the air too thin. She wasn't sure now who was trembling more, Charlie or her. Her lungs felt as if they were about to burst, and she tried to breathe through her nose in an effort not to start hyperventilating.

"It's okay, Annalise," Charlie said from beside her. He patted her arm, as if knowing her fear wasn't just of the man who had chased them, but also of this tiny place.

She nodded. Where was John now? Had he left the building? She didn't think so. He couldn't leave now. He couldn't leave them alive. They knew his secret, and there was no way he could allow them to survive this night.

Thank God she'd left a message on Tyler's cell phone before she'd left. Both Tyler and her father knew she was coming here. Sooner or later, when they didn't hear from her, they'd come looking for her.

"This is all my fault," Charlie said, his shoulders shaking as sobs ripped through him. "I should never have come here. This would never have happened if I hadn't been so stupid." He stepped out of her embrace and looked at her, his eyes pools of tortured pain. "You should have run when you had the chance. You should have forgotten about me and saved yourself."

"How could I do that? You're my favorite brother. I love you, Charlie. I wasn't about to leave you behind." He returned to her embrace, and at that moment a loud boom sounded on top of the elevator.

Max sat beneath his tree, his gaze focused on Annalise's building. He'd seen the boy again, and his heart sang with the vision. Mickey. He wasn't sure what he was doing inside, but Max intended to wait here until he came out. There were so many things Max had to tell his son, and he needed to find out where Sammy was. Why wasn't he with Mickey?

Maybe Sammy had been inside all along. Maybe Mickey had come here to meet his brother. Yes, yes, that must be it. And when they came out Max would be waiting.

Would they remember him? Anxiety fluttered Max's heart. It had been a long time since his sons had seen him. Would they recognize him?

Of course they would, he consoled himself. After all, they had been the Three Musketeers, united in love until that night . . . that awful night.

Max could still remember exactly what he'd been

doing when the police officers had appeared on his doorstep. He'd been putting together a puzzle on a card table in the middle of the living room. It was a puzzle they had all worked on whenever they got time. It was a puzzle of angels. Dozens of them in white gowns and golden halos.

Max had joked when he brought it home from the store that since he could never get the boys up on Sunday mornings to go to church, then he'd bring angels into the house.

That night the boys had gone to a football game, and Max had sat home by himself, working on the puzzle and watching sitcoms.

The officers had knocked, and when he'd seen their expressions he'd known something bad had happened. A drunk driver. A wreck. Boys trapped in the car, and a fire. Dead. His babies. His sons. Both dead in the resulting fire.

Max now choked back a sob, the need to drink— to escape, to forget—so strong it clawed at his insides. But he wasn't giving in. He wanted to be sober when they came out of the building. He didn't want the stench of booze on him when he held them in his arms once again.

He'd always known they'd be together eventually. And now it was just a matter of time.

And so he waited.

Tyler stared at the body of Eleanor Stanko. She'd been shot in the stomach and had died a slow, painful death. Half an hour ago Nick Barnes had managed to talk Elliot Stanko into giving himself up.

The children had been whisked away by their

grieving maternal grandparents, and the homicide team had moved in as Elliot had been placed in handcuffs.

An empty bottle of Scotch sat on the kitchen table, along with the remnants of a couple lines of cocaine. Anger fueled by drugs and alcohol had written a story without a happy ending. He saw it over and over again, and wondered when people would get a clue that this kind of violence never solved anything.

"At least this one isn't a mystery," Jennifer said as she came into the kitchen.

"It's always a mystery to me," he replied.

"And that's what keeps you going—the mystery, the puzzle that each murder contains. I know that's what keeps me going." She cast a disgusted gaze toward the table. "I don't get drugs. I figure I've got enough problems keeping my mind straight without mixing in chemical additives."

Tyler nodded. "We should be able to wrap this up pretty quickly." He grabbed his phone and saw that he'd missed a call. He punched in his number to retrieve his voice mail.

"Tyler, it's me." Annalise's voice filled the line. "Charlie has gone missing, and I'm heading over to the loft to see if he's there. It's eleven fifteen right now. I'll probably be back home and asleep by the time you get there."

He disconnected and looked at his watch. It was almost twelve thirty. She should be home by now. Probably once again sound asleep.

He hesitated a moment, then called her cell phone. It rang six times, then went to voice mail. Surely she was just so sound asleep she hadn't heard the phone, he told himself. But a flutter of apprehension shifted through him. He called again. Six more rings, then voice mail.

"Can you wrap things up here?" he asked Jennifer.

"Sure. Why, is there a problem?"

"I need to get home and check on Annalise. I don't know; I've got a bad feeling."

Jennifer eyed him worriedly. Over their time together as partners she'd come to respect his instincts and fear his "bad feelings." "You want me to come along?"

"Nah, it's probably nothing. I'll check in with you later." He turned and left the apartment.

Chapter 24

The thump on the top of the elevator was followed by the sound of something being pried. Annalise looked up, terror shooting through her as she saw the small trapdoor in the roof of the elevator.

He was there . . . trying to get in . . . and if he managed to succeed they would be trapped like animals in a cage. They had to get out. They had to get out now.

She punched the OVERRIDE button, then hit the DOWN button, and the elevator began to move once again. It had just hit the bottom floor and the doors had begun to open when the trapdoor in the ceiling opened and John dropped into the elevator.

Sobbing, she grabbed Charlie and pulled him through the half-open elevator doors. "Run!" she screamed, leading him toward the front of the shop and the outside door.

They were halfway to the door when Charlie tripped over a trash can and sprawled to the floor. Annalise turned back to help him and screamed as

John jumped on him and the knife plunged into him.

"No!" Deep, wrenching anguish momentarily held her still. "Charlie!"

Before she could move John was up and running toward her. She whirled to run, but something hard crashed into the back of her head. She fell to her knees, then to the floor, the world spinning in a crazy whirl.

Somewhere in the back of her mind a voice screamed for her to get up, to run, but her body couldn't obey the command. Spots of darkness shot before her eyes even as she desperately tried to cling to consciousness.

Where was he? Where was John? She saw Charlie lying on the floor and a sob ripped through her. He was so still. Was he dead? Oh, God, the thought was too unbearable.

But where was John? She couldn't see him, and the darkness was growing, becoming deeper. Get up and fight! the voice screamed in her head. Too late.

What? What was that she smelled? Gasoline. She could hear it now, the splash of liquid. The unmistakable smell of the gas.

There was a moment of silence, then a loud *whoosh*, and she knew he'd lit the gasoline. Almost immediately the crackle of the flames was audible, and a wave of heat rushed through the air to her.

Then John was there beside her. Without a word he picked her up in his arms and carried her toward the front door. No, her mind cried. No, please. Don't leave Charlie behind.

As John carried her out the door and into the

darkness of the night, all she could think about was that Charlie was back there in the burning building and he was afraid of fire.

Tyler decided to head for the loft instead of going home first. He couldn't ignore the faint alarm that sounded in the back of his brain, an alarm that told him Annalise wasn't home sleeping peacefully in bed.

He tried not to focus on the unsteady beat of his heart and told himself he was probably overreacting. Maybe it was just the residual adrenaline of the Stanko scene that made him feel so uneasy.

But as he drove down the quiet streets, the vision of his nightmare kept playing and replaying in his head. The dead girls rising out of the ocean. Three of them begging for him to get them justice. And that fourth figure springing forth like Venus from the frothy waves . . . Annalise.

He tightened his grip on the steering wheel. For the first time in his life he'd found the woman he wanted to spend the rest of his life with, the woman whom he wanted to be the mother of his children.

He couldn't lose her now, not when he'd only just begun to realize the life he could have with her. Don't panic, he told himself. Don't jump to conclusions. He'd probably get to the loft and find nobody there. He'd drive back home and find her warm and sleeping and snuggled deep within the covers.

His grip on the steering wheel eased as he imagined crawling into bed next to her, pulling her, soft and yielding, into his arms. Even though she had yet to say the words out loud, to tell him she loved him, he knew she did. He tasted her love for him each time they kissed; he felt it in her every caress.

He didn't need the words, although someday he'd like to hear them. He hoped like hell he got the chance to hear them. She had to be all right. She just had to be.

He stepped on the gas, the sense of alarm inside him growing louder. As he rounded the corner that brought Annalise's building into view, he gasped and yanked his car to a halt at the curb. He was out of the car before the engine had completely quit running.

A nightmare. That was what he saw in front of him. Smoke boiled out the windows, and dancing flames were visible within the building. He grabbed his cell phone and punched in 911, screaming that he needed fire and ambulance at the location.

As he hung up from the call a figure appeared in the doorway. Backlit by flames and seeming to float on the black smoke, the tall man carried something . . . someone out of the building. Tyler drew his gun, his heart in his throat.

As the figure drew closer he realized that it was Max, the homeless man Annalise had told him about, and that the old man was carrying Charlie in his arms. As he rushed to meet them, Max bent down and gently placed Charlie on the ground.

"He's okay. I saved him. Mickey's okay." The old man looked at Tyler and his eyes shone with joy. He gently touched Charlie's face. "It's okay now, Mickey. Daddy is here."

Charlie's eyelids flickered open. Tyler knelt down beside him, noting the bloody pool on the front of his shirt. "Charlie, where's Annalise? Is she inside?" he asked urgently.

"No, he got her." Charlie's voice was reed thin, and his eyes fell closed again.

"Charlie! You need to stay awake. You need to tell me what happened to Annalise." Frantic fear welled inside Tyler as he gently slapped the boy's paper white cheek. Charlie's eyes drifted open once again. "Where's Annalise?" Tyler repeated.

"John . . . John Malcolm." Charlie raised a hand and pointed to the building across the street.

Tyler grabbed the boy's hand and squeezed. "Hang on, Charlie. Help is on its way." As if to prove his point sirens sounded in the distance.

"I gotta go," Max said. "Mickey is okay, but I gotta get Sammy. Sammy is waiting for me." He started toward the burning building.

Tyler stood. "Max . . . wait. There's nobody in there."

Max turned and smiled. "I can save them. This time I can save them. It's going to be just fine."

Before Tyler could respond, Max turned and raced back inside and disappeared into the flames. "Max!" Tyler ran after him, but the heat at the doorway drove him back. "Max, get out of there."

"Daddy's here, Sammy boy." Max's voice drifted out from someplace inside.

"Max!" Tyler screamed at the top of his lungs, the scream swept away beneath the blare of the approaching fire engine.

"There's one inside," he yelled to the first fireman on the scene. "And one there that needs immediate medical attention." He pointed to Charlie.

There was nothing more that could be done here,

and now his only thought was for Annalise. He drew his gun as he ran toward the apartment building Charlie had indicated. He had no idea which apartment she might be in, but he'd break down every door in the whole damn place to find her.

Consciousness came in bits and pieces. Her first thought was that her head had somehow exploded and she'd managed to live through the ordeal. The pain was so intense that she didn't want to move, didn't want to even open her eyes.

It wasn't until she tried to lick her lips that full consciousness slammed into her. Her mouth was taped closed. Her eyes sprang open. She was in a chair, upper arms and wrists tied down. Her legs were also tied, making escape impossible.

"Ah, you're awake." John stood in front of her, a bemused expression on his face. "I've never worked on one of you while you were alive. I thought it might be fun." He pulled a bottle of fingernail polish from his pocket and began to shake it. "We'll start with your nails. It took me a while to find the perfect color. Lush Lavender . . . it will make your nails look just like the Annalise doll nails." He pulled up a stool in front of her.

Her eyes darted from side to side, trying to figure out where she was. By the board-covered windows up high on the walls she guessed they were in a basement somewhere.

The small room had been transformed into a work area. A sewing machine sat in one corner, along with a tub of material and trim. And in another corner a familiar life-sized lavender dress hung on a hanger. The sight of it filled her with a numbing horror.

Sirens. She heard sirens. Was it somebody looking for her? I'm here, her mind screamed. Please, somebody help me. Please find me!

"You hear that?" John clucked his tongue as he gave the polish a final shake. "Tragedy. Your building is burning to the ground."

Charlie! Grief the likes of which she'd never known stabbed through her. Charlie. Oh, God, Charlie. Tears began to trek down her cheeks and she tried desperately to stanch them, knowing that if she began to cry her nose would stuff up and the tape across her mouth would make suffocation easy.

She couldn't think about Charlie right now. Her grief would have to wait. Instead she tried to figure out some way out of this, some way to save her life. She tried to talk against the tape. If she could get him to remove it then maybe she could scream.

The sharp pain in the back of her head, combined with the fear and grief, all brought a dizzying nausea perilously close, but she knew that to give in to it would mean certain death.

John uncapped the bottle of polish and looked at her unadorned nails. She wanted to pull her hand back, keep him from touching her, but the ties around her wrists kept her from moving.

"Cooperate, Annalise. It's the easiest thing to do," he said, as if he could read her thoughts. "Just relax and let me do what needs to be done."

Once again she tried to talk to him as he began to apply the polish on the index finger of her left hand. "I think you're going to be my finest creation," he said as he worked. "And best of all, after tonight there will be no more Blakely Dolls. The Dollhouse will be gone, burned down to the ground, and you'll be gone. No more Blakely Dolls to ruin little boys' lives."

Annalise stilled as he continued with her next finger. He seemed lost in a haze of memories where she couldn't follow.

"Dolls shouldn't be more important than little boys." He stopped, his hand poised in the air as he stared at Annalise. "That bitch and your dolls made my life miserable. That's all she cared about was your dolls."

His hand shook as he began to paint another of her nails. "Shut up, you bitch," he muttered beneath his breath. "You shut up, Mother. I'm not a loser. I'm the greatest dollmaker in the world."

As he continued to mutter it was obvious he was growing more agitated. Annalise had been in danger before, but as his mood deteriorated and sanity seemed to slip away, she knew the danger was now at peak level.

He suddenly threw the bottle of nail polish across the room and jumped up off the stool. He covered his ears with his hands, and his entire body shook.

He was insane. The insanity had been hidden deep inside him, but something about her dolls had brought it to the surface, caused it to explode into something unmanageable.

She knew then that she was going to die. She stopped trying to talk around the tape that covered her mouth. There was no way she was going to reason with him. He was beyond reason.

She could only guess that his mother had been a bigger monster than he, that she'd been a collector of the Blakely dolls and had abused him when he was young.

Hysterical laughter bubbled up inside her. She'd never get a chance to tell him that she was a victim of the dolls as well. She'd never get an opportunity to tell him that she hated them as much as he did. They were alike in that, and the thought both amused and appalled her.

He drew several deep, long breaths through his nose, then calmed down. When he approached her again he shook his head sadly. "I'm sorry, Annalise. I just can't create my magic with you alive. You have to be dead so I can transform you." He pinched her nose closed and immediately a new panic clawed up inside her.

Frantically she moved her head from side to side, dislodging his fingers as she sucked in air. "Don't make this hard, Annalise," he said, then tried to grab her nose again.

Back and forth she whipped her head, wanting to believe the irrational thought that if he didn't get hold of her nose, then she wouldn't die.

Instead he wrapped his hands around her neck and began to squeeze. No way to evade, no way to escape.

As his hands crushed the air from her, images flashed in front of her eyes. Her father holding her in his arms, his familiar scent filling her heart. Charlie, with his wide smile and zest for life. And Tyler, his love embracing her both body and soul.

And she'd never told him she loved him. And that was the real and true tragedy of all, that love had reached out to her from so many places and fear had kept her from reaching back.

It was the last thought she had before the darkness descended.

Tyler burst into John Malcolm's third-floor one-bedroom apartment, Jennifer at his heels. She'd arrived moments before with the apartment number where Malcolm lived.

A sickness gripped his soul as he stepped into the tidy living room. He kept his gun drawn as Jennifer moved forward to clear the other rooms. But he knew the apartment was empty. There was a lack of life in the air, a stillness that told him he and Jennifer were alone.

"All clear," Jennifer said as she came out of the bedroom.

Tyler's heart sank as a ball of emotion formed in his chest. "Where is she?" His voice was low, hoarse. "Charlie said it was Malcolm and that they'd come here." He couldn't breathe. Jesus, he didn't want to find her dressed in that lavender gown, her eyes blank and her chest still.

"Where else could he have taken her?" Jennifer asked.

Think, Tyler. Think, he commanded himself. Malcolm was the maintenance man. Surely he'd have an office or a workroom in the building somewhere. "The basement," he said, and flew out the door and down the hall. He didn't wait for the elevator, but took the stairs.

Too late. You're too late, a little voice whispered inside him. No. He would not be too late. She would not be the fourth victim.

He was vaguely aware of Jennifer at his heels. When they reached the basement he held a hand to his lips to make sure that Jennifer didn't say anything. Now was the time for stealth.

The basement area they had entered held locked cages that tenants used as storage. As they crept past each one, Tyler glanced inside to make sure nobody was hiding there.

At the end of the long corridor of cages was a closed door. He paused before he reached it, and Jennifer moved close to his side.

"How do you want to handle this?" Her voice was a low whisper.

"I'll show you." He drew a deep breath, then threw himself at the door, crashing it off its hinges as he barreled through.

He bellowed in rage as he saw John Malcolm with his hands around Annalise's neck. "Get away from her. Get your damned hands off her or else I'll shoot. I swear to God I'll shoot you now."

He wanted to. He wanted to pull the trigger and watch his bullet go through the man's forehead and blow out the back of his head. He wanted to see his brains splattered on the wall.

"Okay! Okay!" Malcolm raised his hands and backed away from Annalise. Annalise who didn't move.

"I got him," Jennifer yelled, her voice penetrating the red haze that had descended in Tyler's head. As he saw Jennifer handcuffing Malcolm, he ran to Annalise.

"Don't be dead. Don't be dead. Oh, sweet Jesus." Sobs ripped from him as he tore the tape off her mouth. "Annalise . . . baby." He needed to get her out of the chair and on her back so he could perform

CPR. He tore at the tape that held her wrists, his sobs ripping through him.

With a deep gasp she drew a breath and opened her eyes. "Oh, God. Thank you. Thank you." Tyler fell to his knees in front of her as she reached for his hand.

"She would have been my greatest," Malcolm said.

Jennifer slammed the butt of her gun into his mouth. "Resisting arrest," she said. "I'll just get him out of here." With a shove she escorted him from the room.

"Tyler." Annalise's voice was a hoarse whisper, and as he saw the bruises already beginning to show on her throat he wished he had pulled the trigger.

"I'm right here, baby. You're going to be all right." He untied her, then helped her up out of the chair. When she was standing he pulled her into his arms, tears once again trailing down his cheeks.

"Tyler," she said again.

"You don't have to talk. It's all right now." He released her and framed her face with his hands.

She shook her head. "I'm letting you know." She coughed, and he looked at her questioningly.

"What? What are you letting me know?"

She coughed, then smiled. "I'm letting you know that I love you."

His heart exploded in his chest and joy rushed through him. He scooped her up in his arms. "Let's get you out of here."

When they exited the building it was like walking into a war zone where a bomb had just exploded. Firemen were fighting a losing battle to save the building, but as he and Annalise stood in the park and watched, the roof collapsed in on itself.

Annalise leaned into him and cried.

"You can rebuild, Annalise," Tyler tried to console her.

She raised her face to look at him, her eyes tortured pools of pain. "He killed Charlie."

"No, no, he didn't. Max ran in and got Charlie out. The last time I saw Charlie he was conscious and on his way to the hospital."

The darkness in her eyes lightened as she held his gaze. "Really? Then I'll have to make sure Max never goes hungry again."

Tyler nodded.

"Please take me to the hospital. I need to see my brother and to thank Max."

It was morning before she got to see her brother. The knife wound Charlie had suffered had required surgery to remove his spleen.

In the hours that they waited for him to get out of surgery she sat between her father and Sherri, holding their hands as they awaited word from the doctor.

It was only when the doctor came out to tell them that the surgery had gone fine and Charlie was resting comfortably that Annalise allowed herself to be taken into another room to be questioned by police officers.

It was Jennifer who told them that Max hadn't made it out of the fire. During the hours that they'd waited for Charlie to get out of surgery, Jennifer had done a little investigative work.

"His name was Max Leonard," she told Tyler and

Annalise. "I managed to locate a cousin of his, and he told me about Max. Ten years ago he lost his two sons in a car accident. The two boys were driving home from a football game and a drunk driver hit them. According to the reports the boys died instantly, but before the authorities could get them out of the car it caught fire. The cousin said that Max went crazy with grief. The morning after the funeral he got out of bed and took off walking, just disappeared. His sons were named—"

"Mickey and Sammy," Annalise said softly. Tyler squeezed her hand as she wept silent tears. "He thought Charlie was Mickey. He got him out of the fire because he thought he was saving Mickey's life."

"And he went back in for Sammy," Tyler said.

Annalise leaned against Tyler, her heart aching for the man who had saved her brother. "He's in heaven now with his boys." She swiped the tears from her cheeks, the certainty of her statement ringing inside her. "He's finally at peace."

The dawn light crept in through the windows as an hour later Annalise stepped into Charlie's room. He appeared to be sleeping, and she crept on tiptoe to his bedside, love expanding in her heart.

He looked so pale, so small in the big hospital bed. He was just a kid, but he'd survived the ordeal of the night like a brave man.

She sat in the chair next to the bed, intending to be there when he opened his eyes. John Malcolm had left his mark on all of them, even the ones who had survived his reign of terror.

He would face the death penalty with four counts

of murder against him. Even if he escaped a date with the needle, he'd spend the rest of his life behind bars.

"Annalise?" Charlie's voice was groggy as he saw her sitting next to his bed. "Are you okay?"

She reached out and took his hand in hers. "I'm better than okay, thanks to you. How are you doing?"

"Okay. I hurt some, but mostly I feel stupid." He turned his head away from her.

"Stupid?"

He nodded, still not looking at her. "If I hadn't gone to the loft then you wouldn't have had to come there looking for me and he wouldn't have got you."

"Charlie, look at me." He turned, and tears filled his eyes. She squeezed his hand. "If I hadn't come back to the loft for you, I would have come back for a pair of shoes or a different purse. Then he would have taken me and nobody would have known. You saved my life, Charlie. You held on long enough to tell Tyler where I was."

"I just feel like I screwed up," he said miserably. "I should never have run away because I was mad at Mom and Dad."

"Now, that's true," she agreed. "That was a screwup, but let me tell you a little secret, Charlie: We're family, and family supports one another even when they screw up a little bit." She thought of her father. He'd screwed up, but she had to accept responsibility for the years they'd been distant as well.

Charlie smiled at her, his tears dried. "I love you, Annalise."

"Oh, Charlie, I love you."

He smiled and his eyelids fluttered closed, and he slept again.

The sun shone brightly when Tyler and Annalise finally left the hospital. As they reached his car he wrapped her in his arms and held her. "I thought I'd lost you."

She laid her head against his chest. "I thought I'd lost you, too. And the worst thing of all was that I thought I was going to die before I got a chance to tell you how much I love you."

His arms tightened around her. "I spoke to the fire chief a few minutes ago."

She raised her head to look at him. "And?"

His eyes darkened. "You lost everything, Annalise. The building is a total loss." His expression held sympathy and his voice was gentle, as if he feared his words might shatter her.

"Things, Tyler. That's all I lost. Oh, I hate losing my favorite pair of shoes and the elephants my father bought for me over the years. I'll miss my big coffee mug and maybe a few other items. But nothing that can't be replaced."

"What about pictures and things from your past?" he asked.

She frowned thoughtfully. "There's nothing from my past I want to keep. As I was driving over to the loft to see if Charlie was there, I'd already made the decision to sell the doll business, to move my life in a new direction. I want to go back to school, take some classes in fashion design and figure out who I am without the burden of the dolls. Now, instead of taking the money from selling the business to start again, I'll use the insurance money for that. That fire took my past, but now I'm ready for my future."

"Is there room for one intense, slightly obsessive, overworked homicide cop in your future?" He seemed to be holding his breath as he waited for her reply.

"I was hoping you'd ask," she replied with a smile. He kissed her then, a kiss of simmering desire, of gentle promise, and she knew it was the beginning of a wonderful future.

Epilogue

"**A**nnalise! Watch this," Charlie yelled from the end of the dock. When he was certain he had her full attention, he did a backflip off the dock and into the lake water. He surfaced with a grin on his face.

"That was great, Charlie," she yelled back from her position on the porch swing on the back deck of her father's lake house.

"That boy adores you," Sherri said from beside Annalise.

"The feeling is totally mutual," she replied.

"Now show me those bridesmaid dresses again."

Annalise opened the sketch pad to display the page of drawings. Her wedding to Tyler was scheduled for October, and over the past couple of weeks Sherri and Annalise had been working on the preparations.

In a million years Annalise would have never guessed that she'd be close to the woman who had married her father. But in the two months since that terrible night, she and Sherri had become good friends.

"Ladies, dinner will be served in about two minutes," Frank said from the door. "Charlie, get out of the water. It's time to eat."

"Guess we'd better get in there," Sherri said.

As the two women stood from the swing Charlie joined them, a towel draped around his waist. "I hope this is going to be good. I'm starving." He looked at Annalise. "Sometimes Dad tries to get creative and it's totally puke-worthy."

Annalise laughed and ruffled his wet hair. "Whatever it is, I'm sure nobody is going to starve."

As they entered the small living room, the scent of something wonderful filled the air. "Smells good," Annalise said.

Charlie grimaced. "Don't let that fool you."

They all went into the kitchen to see Frank pulling a large pizza from the oven. "Homemade pizza," he announced proudly. "Tyler made the crust."

Annalise laughed and walked over to Tyler. "Tyler *is* the crust," she said as she dusted flour off the front of his shirt.

"Frank made the sauce, so if it stinks it's his fault," Tyler exclaimed.

"We all know the secret of good pizza is in the crust," Frank said with a wink to Annalise.

As they all got settled at the table a wealth of emotion rose up inside Annalise. She was surrounded by family and love, and her heart had finally opened wide to receive that love.

She'd been afraid that once the horror of that night had passed she and Tyler would somehow lose each other. She'd worried that the passion they'd felt for each other, the utter commitment to each other, would all fade as things returned to normal.

But that hadn't happened. They had grown closer with each passing day. Tyler had cut down on his work hours, and their summer project had been redecorating his house . . . their house.

She'd fallen in love with his parents, who had embraced her with warmth and affection. She'd enrolled in school for the fall semester and couldn't wait to begin classes in fashion design to take her one step closer to her dream of her own clothing line.

In the meantime she had a wedding to plan, a man to love and a family to embrace. The Dollmaker was gone, and he'd burned her past to the ground, but she'd risen from the ashes as a woman finally realizing her very own dreams.

Bitterness or happiness. She'd had a choice, and she had chosen happiness.

Read on for a sneak peek at Carla Cassidy's

BROKEN PIECES

Coming from Signet Eclipse in
September 2008

Wasn't this the way it always was? Mariah thought with a touch of irritation. While her light had been on and she'd been trying to read, she'd grown so sleepy the words had blurred together and her eyelids had been too heavy to keep open. The minute she put the book down and turned off her lamp, her sleepiness disappeared.

She lay on her back in the darkness, her mind tumbling thoughts around and around. Janice's unexpected arrival had been a pleasant surprise, and Mariah looked forward to showing her around the town where Mariah had been raised.

And then there was Jack. She felt like a teenager experiencing her first bloom of love and sexual awakening. He might have had a crush on her in high school, but she was developing a crush on him now. She smiled at the thought.

The smile fell and she froze as she thought she heard a noise from downstairs. She remained perfectly still as she listened.

Nothing.

Nothing except an overactive imagination and

her racing heartbeat, she thought. Her heartbeat slowed and she yawned. Then she heard it. The distinctive creak of one of the stairs. She sat up as her heart stopped.

The fourth stair.

Somebody had just stepped on the fourth stair rung. Somebody was inside the house! Terror kept her frozen. She bit the inside of her mouth to keep from screaming, not wanting whoever it was to know she'd heard.

The tangy taste of blood filled her mouth as a second creak sounded. The fifth stair. There was a total of fourteen stairs leading from downstairs to the upstairs hallway. And somebody was on the fifth stair, somebody who didn't belong.

Somebody creeping up the stairs in the darkness of night.

The inertia that had gripped her broke as terror seized her. It was *him*. She knew it was *him*. He'd come back for her. Once hadn't been enough.

Oh God. Oh God.

He'd be in the room within a matter of seconds. She wouldn't survive it again. She couldn't survive *him* again. Without thought, acting only on instinct, on habits honed long ago, she rolled silently from the bed and crept on her hands and knees to the closet.

Help me, she screamed inside her head. Somebody, please help me. She opened the closet door and got inside, pulling the door closed behind her.

Scrambling to hide behind the hanging clothes, in the darkest recesses of the enclosure, she curled into a fetal ball, her heart pounding so loudly she could hear nothing else.

Confusion muddied her thoughts, confusion bred of terror. She was ten years old again and waiting for her father to find her, to punish her. She squeezed her eyes tightly closed. If you can't see the bogeyman, then he can't see you.

She was seventeen and on the ground beneath the trees, a bag over her head as she was brutalized. And now he was looking for her again. Not her father, but her rapist.

Holding her breath, she listened and waited for the closet door to be ripped open and his strong arms to yank her out of her hiding place. Seconds felt like an eternity as she waited for evil to find her for the second time in her life.

From outside she heard the sound of car doors; then the front door of the house opened. "Mom!" Kelsey's voice rang out. "The movie sucked, so we left early."

Any fear Mariah might have felt for herself was superseded by her fear for her daughter. "Kelsey!" she screamed as she burst out of the closet. "Get out of the house."

She expected to encounter somebody in her bedroom, a person on the stairs, as she stumbled down to where Janice and Kelsey stood at the front door, shock on their features.

"Somebody was here!" she exclaimed with a half sob. "I heard them on the stairs. We have to get out. He could still be inside, hiding. We have to call the police."

She grabbed them both by their arms and pulled them out to the front porch, the terror still clawing up her throat, burning in her stomach.

Janice pulled a small revolver from her purse. "No need to bother the police. I'll check it out."

Before Mariah could protest, Janice disappeared back into the house. Because she worked with troubled teens in some of the more dangerous areas of Chicago, Janice not only carried a gun on a regular basis—she also knew how to use it.

Mariah shot glances around the area as she pulled Kelsey closer to her side. Was the person still in the house? Or had he left when he heard the car approach and realized Kelsey and Janice were home?

The darkness around the house was lit up as Janice turned on light after light inside, and with each new glow of illumination, some of Mariah's fear ebbed.

Kelsey remained quiet by Mariah's side, her gaze intent on the front door, as if willing Janice back in the doorway safe and sound.

Finally Janice returned to the porch. "I checked every room, every closet and cabinet big enough to hide somebody No one is there." She looked at Mariah with a hint of worry. "Why don't we all go back inside?"

Kelsey immediately ran upstairs to check on Tiny, whose barking could now be heard behind Kelsey's closed bedroom door. Mariah and Janice sat at the kitchen table.

"The front door was locked when we got home," Janice said. "And when I checked out the house, the back door was locked as well." A worried frown tugged Janice's eyebrows together as she gazed at Mariah.

"I swear I heard somebody coming up the stairs. The fourth and fifth steps creaked, and that's what I heard." Mariah leaned back in the chair and wrapped her arms around herself, feeling an icy chill deep inside her as she thought of those two ominous creaks. "I know I heard it. I know it," she said forcefully.

Janice continued to hold her gaze. "Is it possible you fell asleep, and the noise you thought you heard was part of a dream?"

Mariah rubbed a hand across her forehead, where a fierce headache blossomed. "I wasn't sleeping. I hadn't fallen asleep yet." She frowned. "At least I didn't think I was asleep." God, was she losing her mind? Had coming back here created more internal stress than she'd realized? She dropped her hand from her head and stared down at the table. "I thought it was him," she confessed.

"Him?"

She looked at her friend. "You know, him."

Janice's features all fell in dismay. "Oh, honey, why would you think such a thing? It's been so many years, you don't even know if he's around this area. You don't even know if he's alive."

"I know, I know. Rationally I understand all that." Mariah broke off and sighed in frustration. How could she explain to Janice the feelings of dread that overtook her, the feeling that her attacker wasn't dead or gone, but rather was far too close? How could she make Janice understand the crazy feeling she had that it wasn't done, that it would never be finished?

"When I heard those footsteps, all I could think was to hide. I got into my closet, and for a moment I got confused. I thought it was my father coming upstairs to beat me. Then I was certain it was my attacker returning."

Mariah's stomach was nothing but an icy center, and she wondered if she'd ever be warm again, ever feel sane again.

"Look, maybe the best thing for you to do is get out of here. You've made some nice progress on the house, but leave it for the new owners to complete. Put the for-sale sign in the yard, pack your bags and go home."

Mariah knew it was good advice, but her heart rebelled at the idea. "I don't want to do that. I need to see this through." Once again she raised a hand to her throbbing forehead. "I know it doesn't make sense, but I need to see this place turned into something beautiful. I need to erase all the ugliness that's still in my head. I know it sounds stupid, but I know it's what I need to do."

Janice smiled. "It's not stupid. It's called closure. You had a crappy childhood with even crappier parents. If fixing this place is what you need to do to put it behind you, then I'm all for it." She reached out and took Mariah's hand. "I just don't want you to be drawn back into the terror of that night." She leaned forward and kissed Mariah on the cheek. "Get a good night's sleep and I'll see you in the morning."

The night was long and sleepless as Mariah wondered if she was truly losing her mind. Was she being stalked by some unknown person or by her memories of a traumatic experience?

Certainly she knew all about post-traumatic stress syndrome. Janice had spoken to her at length about it. A scent that brought back the horror of a specific event, a sound that triggered an intense memory—yes, she knew all about it. But was that what was happening to her? Was she suffering some form of mental illness or was somebody after her?